MW00849983

Dana Hammer

The Cannibal's Guide to Fasting

Published by: Cinnabar Moth Publishing LLC
Santa Fe, New Mexico

Cover Design by: Ira Geneve

ISBN-13: 978-1-953971-50-0
Library of Congress Control Number: 2022939337

The Cannibal's Guide to Fasting

DANA HAMMER

Content Notes

The Cannibal's Guide to Fasting addresses a range of topics that may be disturbing or triggering for some readers. As the following list is not necessarily exhaustive for everyone's needs, reader discretion is advised.

- Murder
- Addiction
- Physical violence
- Withdrawal

CHAPTER ONE

Igor is a huge, scary looking man. Standing six feet, six inches tall, encased in bulges of muscle, he attracts attention everywhere he goes. Ropey veins snake beneath his taut, tanned skin. A spider web sprawls across the left side of his face, a tattoo choice that has not endeared him to potential employers or dates, and one that he regrets deeply.

He is not the type of man one can ignore. He is also not the type of man who one confronts about breaking the park's "no picking wildflowers" policy. He carries an old-fashioned woven basket, which is filled with bluebells, daisies, and a few shy violets he managed to find hiding behind a rotten stump. He picks wildflowers regularly. It is zen as fuck.

There was a time, not so long ago, when he would have mocked such a pursuit. There was a time when he turned up his nose at botanists, botany, and plant-based careers in general. He'd thought of them as glorified gardeners, hobbyists puttering away in the dirt. Those days are long gone now.

He gasps and slaps at a mosquito that tastes his neck. He always kills mosquitos if he can. He knows that his virus can't be transmitted via mosquito bite, but the thought makes him panic all the same. Too many rumors and fake news articles have done their damage, and he can no longer be bitten without fear. That's why he has covered himself in a long-sleeved T-shirt and long pants, despite the hot day. He doesn't want to risk it. Infecting another person is his worst nightmare.

It's been six months since he was released from the rehab center that purported to cure him of the urge to eat human flesh. The program itself was lengthy, and long on religion, but since his graduation he has managed to stick to a socially acceptable diet, and so, he supposes, the program was a success. He's stuck with it and kept himself out of trouble. That's more than many of his friends can say.

It's getting too hot. He needs to get his flowers home and get them pressed between the pages of the *Encyclopedia Britannica* he purchased from a garage sale a few weeks ago. After they are pressed, he will categorize them, label them, and add them to his growing collection of pink, glittery scrapbooks. Igor does not understand why all scrapbooks are designed for basic eleven-year-old girls.

He also needs to tend to his vegetable garden; in this heat, the plants will dry out and die, and then where will he be? It's hard to get fresh, good-tasting produce nowadays, so he has to grow it himself. It's either that or give in to temptation and eat the stuff he *really* wants to eat.

A family on a nature hike stares at Igor. He's sure it's not often they see a man like him, especially not out here, especially not with a basket of flowers, but their rudeness irritates him all the same. Igor glares at them.

"You got eye problems?"

The parents put protective hands on their children's shoulders and scoot them away from the dangerous man. Igor rolls his eyes. "Douchebags," he mutters as he walks past them.

He is tired of being stared at, tired of being an outcast.

He is tired of everything.

Igor's home is a single-wide trailer in a "community" that the government has set up for former cannibals. Decent, law-abiding, non-infected folks do not want man-eaters to live in their neighborhoods, but they won't go so far as to demand executions for the infected, and so the forced cannibal community was born.

For a time, the infected were held in prisons and jails, until those became too overcrowded, and the state was forced to find other solutions. Now, the official plan of action is this: identify the cannibals, send them to a treatment center, and then house them in secure, guarded communities with their own kind.

Igor's community is one of the nicer ones. The trailers are small but clean, and the neighborhood is kept tidy and quiet. Each trailer even has a small patch of lawn, for residents to use as they please. Igor uses his for fruit and vegetable gardening. Some other people plant flowers, and some of them plant nothing at all, but fill their yards with furniture or above-ground pools.

Other communities aren't so lucky. Igor is grateful for his home, despite the security guards who occasionally take their jobs a bit too seriously. Despite the constant scrutiny of the inspectors, despite the fact that his ID lists his address as "High Risk Containment Center" and that any time he has to show that ID to anyone, he gets glares or looks of disgust or flat refusals of service. He is grateful, because without it, and without a job, and without anyone willing to take him in, he would likely be homeless.

He enters his trailer and takes a deep breath. He immediately turns on the air conditioning, glad to have it after his hike. His flowers are already wilted; he hopes he got them home in time.

He flops on the couch, needing to cool down before he does anything else.

knock knock

"Shit," he whispers, throwing a forearm over his eyes. Who would be bothering him now? He is not expecting company.

He opens the door and there's Jud, standing there in his trucker hat and baggy jeans, looking squirrely like usual. Jud was in rehab with Igor. In fact, Jud was there long before Igor arrived, and he kind of took the newcomer under his wing and helped him get adjusted.

Igor is grateful for all the help Jud gave him in those days. But now that they're both out in the real world, sometimes Igor finds Jud's company a little bit much. Like, why does the guy always come unannounced? Would it kill him to call first? And he doesn't ever want to do anything fun, he mostly just likes to bitch about the government and how the infected have been royally screwed by it.

He thinks it must be hard to live in Jud's head. Igor gets exhausted just listening to him for an hour.

"Hey Jud. Come on in, man."

Jud strides in quickly, like he's in a big rush.

"Whoa buddy. You ok?"

Jud runs a hand over his trucker hat, patting. "I don't know man. It's been a weird day."

"What do you mean? Sit down, let me get you a beer."

Jud sits down on the couch, leans forward onto his knees. The couch screeches in protest; it's old and the springs are desperate to retire. "You know your brother, Karl?"

"What about him?"

"I think he's feasting again."

Igor hands Jud a beer and sits down on the other end of the couch. It shifts beneath his bulk. "What makes you think that?"

It's true that former cannibals often relapse. In fact, some studies show that upwards of 90% of them are feasting again within five years. But Karl isn't the type. He'd been one of the program mentors when he was in rehab, helping out the new guys, teaching them how to control themselves around human flesh, all that.

"It's these guys he's hanging out with, dude. I saw him in town yesterday, at the grocery store, and he was with these guys...they were buying Clamato."

Well, that doesn't sound good. Everyone knows that human meat tastes best with Clamato. Nobody knows why, but it does.

"That...doesn't necessarily mean anything. Maybe his friends genuinely like Clamato."

"Nobody likes Clamato, Igor."

Igor shrugs. "I don't know, dude. I don't think it's time to panic, not over that. Did you talk to him? How did he seem?"

"He seemed like he was feasting, that's what I'm telling you. He was all happy and glowing and like, dizzy. So were the guys who were with him."

Igor sits back and closes his eyes. He remembers that part all too well. The lovely, thrumming buzz you got when you ate some human. How good it felt, like you'd just defeated all your enemies and fucked the most gorgeous girl on the planet.

Igor has never killed anybody. He isn't one of those guys. But... there are other ways to feast. Ways he doesn't like to think about too much.

"So what are you gonna do? You gonna talk to him?"

Jud shakes his head, looking down at his feet. "I don't think I can, man. Those guys, if they're feasting — and I think they are — I can't be around that shit anymore. If they've got any on them, or if they happen to mention where they get it...it could really fuck up my abstinence."

Igor presses his lips into a tight line. Now he sees where Jud's going with this.

"You want me to talk to him."

"Aw, man, would you? It would mean the world to me, dude. You know I'd do it myself if I could, but..."

"Say no more, Jud. I'm happy to help."

Igor is not happy to help. He and his brother aren't close, mostly because being around him brings up bad memories. Also, the idea of being around guys who might be feasting makes him clammy and sick. After all, he's not superhuman. He has the same fucking urges Jud does, for Christ's sake.

But he owes Jud. Jud's been there for him lots of times, and it's not as if Igor is overwhelmed with friends at the moment. And how bad can it be, anyway? He just has to find Karl and check up on him, make sure he's still abstinent, then report back to Jud, make him feel better. And if Karl is using again, well...he'll cross that bridge when he comes to it.

"Where's he staying? Can you get there ok?"

"He was assigned to Containment Center C, out by the river."

Igor has been out there before, but it's been a while. "Alright. I'll go check up on him."

"Thanks, buddy!" Jud pats Igor on the back, friendly and thankful. He stands up.

"You leaving already?" Igor is amused. Jud isn't even pretending he didn't come only to ask for a favor.

"Yeah, I gotta get down to my sister's. She thinks she might have a job hookup for me, so that'd be awesome."

Igor is impressed. It's almost impossible for a cannibal, even a reformed cannibal, to get a legal job. Nobody wants to hire an employee who might snap and literally bite their heads off. Igor understands. Really, he does. Still, it sucks for guys like him.

"Is that a basket of flowers?"

Igor, startled, glances to where Jud is looking, where he'd abandoned his flower basket on the floor.

"Yeah. So?"

Jud chuckles, nervous. Like most people, he is slightly afraid of Igor, even though Igor has never given him any real cause for fear. Usually, this frightened response annoys him, but Igor doesn't want to hear any shit about his hobby. Collecting wildflowers is zen as fuck, and it helps keep him sane. He is glad that Jud is uncomfortable.

"No, no reason. Anyway, thanks for checking up on Karl, man. I'll call you, alright?"

"Alright."

After Jud leaves, Igor presses his flowers, smoothing them patiently between the pages of an encyclopedia. He likes to use an M word, something in the middle of the alphabet. Today he chooses "masticate."

Igor would like to head to Containment Center C right away, to get it over with, but the CanCare inspector is scheduled to stop by today, and if he isn't around when she shows up, she'll be in a pissy mood when she comes by next time.

CanCare is a lot like Medicare, except it's for those infected with the virus, rather than old people. Since most of the afflicted are unemployable, and cannot afford medical insurance, the government provides them with taxpayer funded healthcare. In theory, this is a humane and sensible program designed to take care of the less fortunate, to make sure they are taking care of their health. In reality, the CanCare inspectors are meddling, annoying, and often downright abusive. When you get an inspector who hates the infected, it can be a real pain in the ass.

Igor's inspector is a woman named Helen. She doesn't exactly hate cannibals, but they clearly make her uneasy, and she would obviously rather be doing anything rather than hanging out in Containment Center trailer parks trying to make sure the inhabitants are maintaining their abstinence.

Helen is afraid of Igor, and her evident fear makes him intensely uncomfortable. Once, he tried to cover up his spider tattoo with an old girlfriend's face makeup, to try to make Helen less skittish, and not only had he looked goddamn ridiculous, she hadn't been reassured in the least.

He goes through his refrigerator and cupboards, looking for offending items. According to the "guidelines" issued by CanCare, those infected with the virus should keep a meat-free home. The idea is that consuming animal meat is a slippery slope, and it could tempt the infected into flesh eating. Once Igor had a can of tuna fish in his cupboard, and Helen found it. He will not make that mistake again.

In addition, rehabilitated cannibals are encouraged to avoid alcohol, nicotine, and "other stimulants" that can alter the brain chemistry and create an "excitable state" wherein they might go crazy and murder their neighbors for their rump roasts. Igor removes his beer from the fridge and hides it in a particularly lush tomato bush. Helen never bothers checking outside his home. She's not that great at her job. He prefers her to the last inspector he had, a grumpy, angry man who liked to preach about how the virus was a punishment for Igor's sins. He used his position as an excuse to make Igor take off his shirt and ogle him, ostensibly to give him a "medical exam" but really just because he was a dirty, sexually repressed old man.

Igor was not sad when the inspector got bitten by one of his clients and was forced to retire.

He flips on his little TV and goes through his TiVo, deleting any recordings that might be construed as "too violent" for his tender, barely rehabilitated psyche. He wonders if he should record a few episodes of Wheel of Fortune or The Bachelor or some simple shit like that, but decides against it. It's one thing to pretend to follow the rules, it's another thing to pretend to be a pansy.

By the time she arrives, Igor's home is tidy, meat- and alcohol-free, and ready for inspection. She looks around his place with her usual worried, tired face.

Igor looks at her and clenches his fists. She's such a tiny, pretty thing. He hates that she sees him in this ugly little trailer. He hates that she sees him as a threat. He hates that she sees him as part of a job that she despises.

"Come in, sit down," he says, trying on his best manners. "Can I get you anything to eat? I've got some great blueberries, fresh from the garden."

If she finds his gardening abilities impressive, she doesn't say so. She's looking at his *Encyclopedia Britannica*, the books stacked up in a tall tower next to the TV stand.

"What are you doing with these?" For the first time, her face doesn't look scared or upset. In fact...she looks sort of amused.

Igor isn't sure what to say. He could tell her about the wildflowers. It's not against the rules. But he doesn't want her to think he's a pussy. It would be too much, on top of what she already must think of him.

He decides to stick with a partial truth. "I got them from a garage sale a few weeks ago."

"I haven't seen a set of these in years. We always had one in the house when I was growing up, but we got rid of them once we got the internet. God, that makes me sound old, doesn't it?"

Startled, he smiles at her. "Not at all. Hell, I'm the one who still has a set, right?"

She laughs a little, a sound that makes him light up inside. How long has it been since he made a pretty woman laugh? He wishes she'd known him before, back when he was somebody.

She walks into his bedroom, which he was careful to clean and deodorize before she came. She sees his mat and free weights. "Still doing the weightlifting I see?"

She frowns. CanCare doesn't like it when its patients participate in sports, body building, or anything that could be construed as aggressive. They would rather everybody do yoga or Pilates or synchronized swimming. And that's all fine, but not for Igor. Igor would be lost without his weights. It's all he's really good at anymore.

He nods, curtly. He doesn't want to have this discussion again.

She takes out a little notebook from her jacket and writes something down. Igor scowls. Was he just thinking she was pretty? Had he really cleaned his room up for her? He wishes he hadn't. He wishes he'd left his stinky, sweaty socks on the floor, so she'd have to pinch her dainty little nose against the smell.

Irritated, he turns around. "I'll be in the living room if you need anything."

"You know, I used to lift," she says, suddenly.

He whips back around. He was not expecting that. "Really?"

She smiles and nods. The smile changes her whole face, and the effect is breathtaking. "Back in college. I gained the freshman twenty five, and so a friend of mine took me to her trainer, to help me lose the weight. I was pretty into it for a while. I still do it a little. Just for fun, not competitively or anything."

He cocks his head and looks at her, appraising. She can't be more than five foot two. He can't see much of her underneath her big, boxy, professional getup, but he guesses she might have some good tone under there. He wonders about that and starts to get a little stiffy.

He changes the subject.

"So you need to take a look at my cupboards? No tuna this time." His weak joke doesn't land. She looks sort of put out, and he can't tell why.

"It's alright. I think I'll just go."

"Alright. I'll show you out."

He holds the door open for her as she leaves. He watches her go, eyes lingering on her shapely, elegant calves, smiling a little at her clumsy, old-grandma shoes. He wonders why she wears such clunky shoes on such lovely legs. Maybe she needs orthopedic shoes, because of a foot injury. Maybe it's hard on her feet, walking around all these trailer parks all day. Maybe she just likes ugly shoes. It can't be a money-saving thing. CanCare inspectors make excellent money; it's why most of them get into it.

He wishes he could ask her. He wishes he could take those shoes off her poor feet and set them in his lap, and rub them while she tells him all about her day.

He shuts the door. He has to get ready to go to Containment Center C.

CHAPTER TWO

Containment Center C is a tight-knit community, where everyone knows each other and shares vegetarian recipes and minds your business for you. Which makes Karl's disappearance from the place all the more surprising and suspicious. Friendship and belonging are hard to come by if you're a reformed cannibal. You don't just turn your back on that for no good reason.

A neighbor stands outside his trailer, tinkering under the hood of a red pickup truck, smoking a cigarette. Igor raises an eyebrow. Plenty of folks in his community smoke, but not out in the open like this. What if an inspector came by? Clearly, this is a man who plays by his own rules.

Igor comes closer and says hello.

The man turns and looks at Igor, his mouth dropping open slightly, his eyes widening. Igor tries not to roll his eyes, but he is impatient with the man. Does everybody have to react to his appearance this way?

He keeps his voice quiet and soft, knowing it will ease the man's panic.

"Hello, there. I'm looking for my brother, a guy named Karl.

Used to live next door. You know where he might have gone?"

When Igor had knocked on Karl's door, it had flown open, not locked or even shut in any serious way. The inside had been completely cleaned out. No furniture, no food, no sign of anybody living there at all. It was damn weird. This neighbor must have seen Karl moving all his stuff out. He had to know something.

The mechanic sticks out a grease-blackened hand to Igor. "Lenny. What do you want with Karl?"

Igor shakes Lenny's hand, resisting the urge to wipe it on his jeans. He doesn't want to be rude. "My friend is worried about him. Thinks he might have got himself into trouble or something. He wanted me to come check on him."

Lenny stamps his cigarette under a worn-out hiking boot. "Well, I don't know about that. He always seemed alright to me. But he moved outta here a couple weeks ago. Said he wanted to live off the land or some shit. Went with those buddies of his."

"Buddies? What buddies?" Those must be the guys Jud was worried about. The ones who were feasting. Igor's stomach sank. Maybe Jud was right, and Karl was back on the flesh.

Lenny waves a hand. "Them guys who hang out down at Moonlight Run. There's a bunch of 'em."

"You been down there with them?"

"Naw, that's not my scene. I'm too old for that crap."

"What crap?"

Lenny looked at Igor and lit another cigarette. "Look, it's not my place to talk shit about people I don't know. But they don't seem like entirely good news, those guys." He shrugs. "But that's all I'll say about that."

Igor nods. He understands the man's reluctance to snitch. He's got a pretty good thing going here. Nice neighbors, a clean house, a truck to tinker with. He's not trying to piss anybody off, or cause drama. He just wants to be left alone, in peace and quiet. Igor doesn't blame him.

He turns to leave.

"Hey, fella?"

Igor turns back to Lenny.

"I don't wanna tell you how to do your business, but if you're thinking of going out that way, looking for Karl, you might wanna bring a few buddies with you."

Igor raises an eyebrow, shocked. He can't remember the last time someone worried about his physical safety.

Lenny, seeing his reaction, chuckles. "I know, you're a big boy and you can probably take care of yourself. But there's a lot of them, and only one of you. That's all I'm saying."

"You think they're dangerous?"

Lenny exhales a long stream of smoke and looks skyward. "I'm not saying that. But I'm saying it doesn't hurt to be careful, does it?"

"I'll keep that in mind."

Moonlight Run is a fast, narrow river that snakes around through the woods, cutting a wet smirk into the county. The ground around it is rocky and inhospitable, and the fishing isn't great, so it's never caught on as a recreational spot, at least not for your mainstream outdoorspeople. Mostly, it's used by kids who want a place to fuck, by drunks who want a place to drink, and by gun enthusiasts who want a place to shoot at tin cans and assorted garbage. Piles of discarded shotgun shells, condom wrappers, and empty bottles attest to the good times had by all of the above.

Igor parks his motorcycle where the road peters out and walks the rest of the way toward the spit. He can already hear the sounds of people talking and smell smoke from a fire. As he gets closer to the site, he smells something else, something intoxicating that makes him salivate and pant like an old-fashioned cartoon dog. His eyes dilate and he has trouble controlling himself.

Human meat. Roasting over a charcoal fire.

It turns out, Jud wasn't being paranoid after all.

Igor reaches into his jacket pocket and pulls out a stick of beef jerky. He needs something to sustain him, to keep him from snatching the meat and feasting. Beef jerky is not a great substitute, but it's better than nothing.

He walks through the bushes and emerges onto the spit. He is surprised by what he sees. Not the usual tents and trucks and folding chairs he associates with camping at a river, but strange structures that look like teepees.

He is spotted by a short man with a pudgy middle. The man walks toward Igor. He does not look friendly.

Igor extends his hand, showing that he means no harm, hoping he'll shake it and let him in. The smell of human meat clouds his brain though, and he can't remember the polite words he's supposed to say. He scans around, looking for the source of the smell. There are a few fires burning along the water's edge.

"What are you doing here?" Short Man asks.

Igor brings his attention back to the man in front of him. "My name's Igor. I'm here looking for a guy named Karl. You think you can help me find him?"

The man's eyes widen, surprised. "What you want with Karl?"

Igor shrugs, trying to look innocent. "He's my brother. Haven't heard from him in a while. Just wanted to check up on him."

Short man extends a finger and pushes Igor's chest. "Karl doesn't need nobody checking up on him, and neither do we. This party is invite only. That means you're not welcome here."

Igor looks down at the short man. This is the problem with being a huge ox of a man. The world is full of tiny little fellas who are insecure about their size, and they insist on picking fights with men who could crush them with one fist. It's a win-win situation for the small man. If he wins, he's a tough guy who felled a giant. If he loses, it's ok, because he was outsized, and he sure was brave to try.

Igor ignores the jabbing finger and keeps his fists at his side. The meat smells so good. "I'm not looking for any trouble. I just want to find my friend, and then I'll get outta here."

Short Man reaches into his pants and retrieves a knife. He unsheathes it and points it at Igor's belly. "You got hearing problems? I said get the fuck outta here, now. Or there's gonna be trouble."

Igor and Short Man have caught the attention of some of the other campers, and some of them are drifting closer, to see what's going on.

Igor is a patient man, but he can't allow this little pecker to point a knife at him for no good reason. Enough is enough.

He extends his forearm and brings it down on Short Man's forearm, hard, causing him to drop the knife. He reaches around with his left arm and grabs the little guy's jacket, forcing him into a headlock. With a quick, heavy fist, he punches the man's soft, flabby paunch and drops him to the rocks below.

Igor looks up at the worried looking crowd now assembled around him. He hates this part of getting in fights. When they're over, it's never fun victory dances and joy, like in the movies. It's always embarrassment and sickness and sometimes criminal charges. He will be happy if he never has to hit anyone again.

"It's alright folks. We've got this all worked out. But I'm looking for a guy named Karl. Can anyone help me out with that?"

The assembled people are all sort of raggedy and worn out looking. Their clothes are stained, and their faces are gaunt. Nobody seems excited to talk to him.

He rubs a tired hand over his face. "Alright then."

Short Man writhes and groans on the ground, and Igor reaches a hand down and pulls him up with one strong jerk. "Sorry about that, little fella. But you can't go around pointing knives at people. That shit's not polite."

"Fuck you," the guy grunts, hobbling away, not looking at anybody. Igor shrugs. He tried.

A powerful arm slaps Igor's shoulder and he spins around, expecting another attack, maybe one of short man's friends. Instead, he sees Karl's face, shining and smiling at him.

"Karl! It's good to see you, man."

A flash, as Igor sees Karl as a small boy, hiding in the closet.

"Good to see you too, Igor."

Karl pulls him into a hug, and Igor allows it.

Finally, he pulls back and looks closely at Karl. He takes in his matted, black hair, the vacant look in his eyes, the dreamy expression on his face. He's feasted, Igor realizes. And not long ago.

"What you got going on out here?" Igor gestures to the teepees and the fires and the people. "What is all this?"

"It's a new way of life, man. A better way. Let me tell you all about it."

Karl escorts Igor into camp, passing groups of straggly people doing straggly things, breathing in meaty smoke, rocks crunching underneath their shoes. Tall trees surround the river on both sides, dampening sound, creating a dark, green-scented haven. As they near the river, they take up residence on a fallen log, facing the running water.

"It all started when I met Nevin and Olaf back there. Nevin's the one you gut-punched."

"Yeah...I'm sorry about that. He pulled a knife on me."

Karl waves a distracted hand. "Don't worry about it. He's got a temper on him, and he doesn't know how to stay in his lane. It's not the first time. Won't be the last. Anyway, we started having these meetings, talking about how life was for us, as cannibals. How none of this shit's our fault. How the government uses any excuse it can to lock us up, to monitor us, to take away our freedoms. Sure, some of us have killed, some of us have maimed. But most of us are just regular folks trying to make it through the day. Yet, they've punished all of us as if we're all murderers. That shit's not fair, buddy."

Igor nods. He's heard these arguments before. To an extent, he agrees with them, though he can see the government's point, as well.

"So anyways, we started thinking. Why do we have to live on these goddamn compounds? Just because the man says so? Fuck that shit. So we made our own way."

Igor looks around at all the shelters, the dozens of people living in them. "So that's all it is? You guys formed your own commune or something?"

Karl shrugs. "Kinda. I mean, I guess we all work together to live, so in that respect, it's a commune. But mostly, we're here because we want to live our lives the way we see fit. The virus isn't a sickness, Igor. It's not like all the normals and politicians and preachers have been telling you. It's an alternative lifestyle. One we didn't choose, but one that we won't apologize for. Not anymore."

"So...you're feasting." Igor looks at Karl intently, trying to see what effect this accusation is having on him. He tenses, in case a punch is coming.

Instead, Karl grins. "Yep. But we're doing it our own way. An ethical way. See, each and every one of us has made an agreement. We agree to sacrifice ourselves for the greater good."

Igor isn't sure he understands. "You mean..."

Karl nods encouragingly. "We each take turns sacrificing our own flesh. We've made a whole ceremony out of it." Karl takes off his boot to reveal a missing toe. "An old Apache ceremony, one used to strike fear into the hearts of our enemies." He waggles his eyebrows at Igor. "First, we fast for a day before the feast. Then, the high priest — that's me — washes the flesh, while doing the ceremonial chant. I've got a hat I wear. Then we all paint ourselves with sacred mud. It's not sacred. I just say I blessed it. Then we roast the meat over a similarly sacred fire, and then we each take a bite, passing it around until it's all gone. It's a whole thing."

Igor recoils a little. "But...you're not Apache."

Karl laughs. "Nope. But these guys don't know that. Look at them, they're living in teepees. They eat all that shit up. Look, I know it's kinda messed up, but the ceremony helps everyone feel more comfortable with what we're doing here. And it makes it special, something to be appreciated."

"And you donated a toe?"

"I also gave a little bit of my ass, but I'll spare you the sight for now. Maybe later though, if you're lucky." Karl gives a silly, exaggerated wink.

Igor chuckles along, unsure how he feels. It's true, that the idea of cutting off pieces of your own body is absolutely disgusting, but all the same, he can't help but admire their outside-the-box thinking. It is a neat solution to a terrible problem.

"Wow. So...how did you come up with this?"

"Well, it wasn't our first idea. Actually, at first, we were grave robbers."

Igor shakes his head. He'd heard of infected folks robbing fresh graves for the meat, but he'd never partaken himself. It seemed disrespectful and rude, and also probably dangerous because of the formaldehyde. But he guessed in a pinch, if you were desperate, it would do.

"What changed?" His voice is weirdly croaky.

"The people did, dude. Once folks figured out what we were doing, they stopped burying their dead, started cremating. Turns out, people don't like the thought of cannibals making use of the flesh of their dead loved once. Who knew?" He laughs a grim laugh. "Well, after that, we were thinking we might have to shut down this whole camp, go back to the trailer parks. But then, Oscar — that guy over there — he had a little accident with his Bowie knife. Sliced off the tip of his finger. Well...it was a slippery slope from there, I guess."

Igor forces himself to smile. He hates how the idea of Oscar's amputated finger makes him salivate. He hates the part of himself that wants to join up with these crazies and live the life the virus has chosen for him.

He has to get out of here, before he does something he regrets.

Karl seems to sense Igor's unease. "Hey, why don't you let me show you around a bit? So you can see what it's all about?"

Igor frowns. He's not sure it's a good idea. But he is curious.

Karl has already stood though, and Igor follows him.

There are a few dozen people living in the camp. Igor shows him a large wooden tub with a laundry mangle. A few women are pulling wet clothes out of it and hanging them on a line, like it's Little House on the Prairie or some shit. Several salmon are roasting on sticks over a teepee shaped fire. The smoke is luxuriously fragrant.

Igor can't see the source of the human meat. He is afraid to ask about it, afraid that if he sees it, he won't be able to control himself.

There are buckets of blackberries in the river, wedged in place with rocks, the running water keeping them cool and fresh. A few men are floating down the river on inner tubes, a cooler of beer strung between them. It's a nice day for it. Igor is a little jealous, not just of the activity, but of their easy camaraderie. When was the last time he did something fun with his buddies? Shit, he hardly has any buddies anymore.

There is still a lot of the camp that Igor hasn't seen, and he has many questions. But Karl seems to want to conclude the tour, and he stops walking and pointing at things, and speaks.

"Look, Igor. I know this isn't your kinda thing. But you're my brother. I'm trusting you to keep this place secret. I mean, you can't tell the authorities what we're doing here. Do I have your word?"

Igor understands. He's never been a snitch. And Karl is family. He extends his hand and shakes Karl's. "You have my word, man. It's not the life for me, but I'm not here to mess with how you wanna live."

"Good man," Karl pats Igor's back. "'Cause I didn't wanna have to have you killed."

Karl laughs, and Igor laughs as well, though perhaps a little less enthusiastically. Could Karl have him killed? Would he? It wouldn't be hard to find him. The six-foot-six cannibal with the spider tattoo on his face named Igor. It might ring a few bells for people in town.

Igor is tough, and able to defend himself, but there are a lot of people in this camp. And Igor has to sleep sometimes.

He would like to think Karl would never do that to his own

flesh and blood. After all, Igor wouldn't. But Karl has always been a different sort of person. More ruthless, less inclined to follow the rules. Hence, the cannibal commune.

But in truth, Igor doesn't really find what they're doing to be all that terrible. These are consenting adults. They have a right to do as they please with their bodies, even if Igor—and he's pretty sure most of society—thinks it's fucked up.

He walks back to his motorcycle and heads home. He has to figure out what to say to Jud.

Jud's trailer is on the east end of the city, in a small, dumpy park known for its drug use and unkempt populace. Jud's place does nothing to dispel the stereotype; it smells strongly of weed and cigarettes and has not been dusted or mopped since Jud moved in.

Igor is not a meticulous housekeeper, but he is an adequate one, and Jud's home always makes him feel a little queasy if he stays more than a few minutes.

Jud opens the door and lets Igor in.

"So, I checked up on Karl," he says with no preamble. "He's got a little community down at Moonlight Run."

Jud sits down in his badly stained teal recliner. He pops up the footrest. "Yeah, I figured it must be something like that. He was always the kind of guy people wanted to follow, you know?"

Igor nods. "Yeah."

It is true. It's one of the reasons Karl had been such an effective mentor back when he was in rehab. He'd managed to make the residents feel good about their abstinence, to give them hope that they could reclaim at least some parts of their lives, in spite of the virus. It's what makes his relapse so unsettling.

"Is he back to feasting?"

Here is the tricky part. Igor doesn't want to make Jud panic, but neither does he want to lie.

"Well, yes. But, it's not like how you're thinking."

Jud pushes the footrest back down and pops up out of his chair. He reaches for his phone.

"Hey, wait, wait," Igor reaches out to Jud, trying to calm him down.

"Wait for what? For Karl to start killing people again? It's hard enough for us guys out here, without guys like Karl relapsing and making us all look bad. I know he's your brother, but fuck, man."

Igor stands to his full height and puts a hand on Jud's shoulder. Gently, but firmly, he presses him back into his chair.

"Like I said, it's not like you're thinking. He's not killing anybody."

"Look, Igor. You're real good at math and science and all that shit, but when it comes to people...sometimes, you just don't get it, man. You can be a little naive. Remember that guy in rehab who 'borrowed' that nice watch you had?"

He misses his watch. It had been his grandpa's.

"They aren't killing anybody," he repeats.

Karl chuckles, sarcastic. "No, of course not. He's just chopping off people's fingers and arms and shit. Or breaking into biology labs and chomping on cadavers. No big deal."

That little dig about chomping on cadavers hits Igor hard. He can't believe his friend would bring that up, just to hurt him. No. He probably just wasn't thinking.

The airy sizzle of a Bunsen burner flicks through Igor's consciousness. He sets it aside.

"Karl's community isn't like that. They've all signed an agreement or something. They donate parts of themselves for everybody to eat. It's like a... really fucked up food bank. Kind of."

Jud cocks his head and sits back in his chair. He steeples his hands. "Huh."

"Yeah. That was kinda my reaction, too."

"So... they're just... cutting themselves up and eating it. Like... self-cannibalism or something."

"Yep."

"That's fucked up."

Igor laughs. "Yeah, it is."

Jud leans forward. "No, dude. I don't mean fucked up funny. I mean really, deeply fucked up. How many people are living out there?"

Igor frowns. "I'm not sure. Looked like a couple dozen."

"OK. Let's be generous and say there's fifty of them. How many fingers and toes does one person have? How many feet, ears, butt cheeks? They're gonna run out of body parts before too long, and then what are they gonna do?"

Igor shrugs. "Recruit more people I guess."

"OK, but then what? How many people you think wanna sign up for that kind of life? Not too fucking many, I'm guessing. Eventually, they're gonna run out of fresh bodies, and then they're gonna have to find someplace else to get their people meat. They'll be right back where they started."

Igor hadn't thought of this before—or maybe he hadn't wanted to think of it before—and it gives him pause.

"Breaking your abstinence is serious business, Igor. They can't just play around with it like this. Yeah, it might be all consensual and fine right now, but once you get the taste... you know how hard it is to stop. You remember the Week Two Frenzies! Jesus."

Now Igor feels sick and sweaty. Everything Jud says makes perfect sense, and he feels foolish for not coming to this conclusion himself. This is how it's always been with Karl. Igor can never stop seeing him as the cute but deeply flawed little boy in need of Igor's protection and understanding.

"We need to call the authorities, get them to shut that place down. Those folks out there might think they're doing fine, and not hurting nobody, but they're a danger to all of us, and we can't let it continue. We've gotta go all Julius Caesar on their asses and take over their shit."

Igor knows that Jud is right. He does. But he remembers Karl, and how he'd helped him when he'd been in the center.

It was visiting hours at the center. He'd come out of week two with bruises on his ribs and dark circles under his eyes. He was queasy, tired, and weak. He'd been moody and truculent, reluctant to share anything, glaring at his feet.

Visiting hours were hard for Igor. He had no wife, no kids, and most of his friends had ditched him when they found out he was infected. So Igor would sit by himself at a table, reading, glaring, or some combination of the two.

But on this particular day, Igor had a visitor. Karl. Karl had been out of rehab for months at that point—he was one of the first people sent to the mandatory treatment centers. Karl was shining with good health and good spirits, and looking at him made Igor ashamed and sick.

It took a long time of silent sitting before Igor was able to speak, but when he did, it came out in burbling sobs.

"I've done some terrible shit, Karl. You wouldn't believe what I did."

"That's ok. Let it all out. Sometimes it's good to cry." Karl patted him on the back, like a friendly coach comforting a badly performing little league player.

"There was this girl... Francine. I brought her back to my place, you know..."

"Go on."

The florescent lights and clatter of trays from the cafeteria were at odds with Igor's heart-wrenching confession. He wished to be somewhere else.

"God, she was so sweet. And the way she smelled. I couldn't keep my hands

off her. So we're in bed, and..."

"It's ok, Igor. Whatever you've done, somebody in here's done worse. I'm not here to judge you. I'm just here to listen."

Karl pushed his long black hair behind his ears and leaned forward onto his knees. He really seemed to want to hear Igor's story.

"I... bit her. I bit her right on her hip. And I was so hungry, so out of control, I just kept biting and biting and biting, and she was screaming and... Oh god, it was so fucking awful."

"Did you let her go?"

It was a hard question to answer, because Igor knew that he had not let her go, she had run away, taking advantage of his momentary shock when he realized the horror of what he'd been doing. And the thought of what might have happened if she hadn't freed herself makes him sick.

"She got up and ran out of my place, screaming and bleeding. She just ran naked into the street. Well, then someone called the cops, and now I'm here."

"So you assaulted a woman, because of the virus."

"I... I couldn't help myself Karl. I just... lost control. I feel so goddamn bad, so goddamn sorry. I just, I just—"

Igor lost control of his voice. It cracked and fizzled into a spray of tears. He hadn't cried, really cried, since he was a kid. It was sort of liberating, if a little embarrassing.

"Hey hey hey, man. Come here, bring it in. Look, it's ok. You weren't in control of your actions. You're suffering from an illness, a real, medical problem that makes you behave in ways that you never would if you were in your right mind. The important thing is, you're here now, and you're ready to make a change. And you'll never do anything like that, ever again. Right?"

"Right."

"Exactly. Look, your girl got away. That's more than a lot of guys in here can say. You showed a lot of restraint, not killing her. You certainly could have, if you'd really wanted to, a guy as big as you. You're a good man Igor. You

always have been. You're gonna come out of this stronger and better than ever."

"I... thanks, man. I think I really needed to get that off my chest. And I really needed to hear that."

"Anytime, brother. That's what I'm here for."

Karl is making a mistake. A terrible, misguided mistake. But Igor has made mistakes too. This disease, this virus... it makes animals out of all of them.

Igor will not let anyone hurt his brother. Even if it means pissing Jud off, who has been a good friend to him.

"There has to be another way," he says.

Jud frowns. "What do you mean?"

"I mean, we gotta handle this without involving the law. Do you really wanna see Karl locked up in prison? You know what they do to repeat offenders."

The US government is relatively tolerant of first-time offenses in the newly infected. But anyone committing acts of flesh-eating after completing a rehabilitation program is shown no mercy in any court of law in the country. After rehab, they should know better. They should be cured.

"Shit." Jud crosses his arms over his chest. "I know."

"Give me some time. Let me go to Karl and see if I can talk sense into him. Maybe we can come up with a solution together. If not, well... then we'll see."

"Yeah. We'll see."

CHAPTER THREE

Igor is worn out when he gets home, bone tired and stressed. His little porch needs washing; there are smears of dirt and dust all over it. He reaches into his mailbox, expecting the usual assortment of flyers and junk mail, but this time, there is a neat, small envelope, creamy and smooth, the color of ripe quince. It's addressed to him by hand.

He can't remember the last time he received a piece of handwritten mail. It must have been before his grandma died. She used to send him birthday cards with little notes written in them, a five-dollar bill stuffed into the envelope.

He goes inside, sits down on his couch, and reads.

Igor,

I don't know why you aren't answering my emails. Perhaps you aren't getting them? Maybe an old-fashioned letter is the way to get your attention.

I'm working on a research project, and I need your help. You were the best research assistant I ever had, and that's saying something. The work I'm doing is top-secret, but I don't think I'm exaggerating when I say it's going to be massively important for the whole world, if it's successful.

I was deeply saddened to hear about your infection, and the ensuing unpleasantness. Believe me when I tell you that if I had any say in the matter, you would still be at the university. Unfortunately, I was not consulted on the matter. I hope you haven't been holding your dismissal against me.

I heard that you've been through treatment, and that you're busy doing nothing in a Containment Center. Igor. This is a waste of your talents and brains. You need to rejoin the scientific community. Please write me back, and let me know if you'll be willing to join me. I can't offer you money, but I can offer you a free room , the labors of my culinary adventures, access to my library, and of course, an opportunity to save the world.

Because Igor — I am very close to curing Pestis Manducans.

Sincerely,

Dr. Jesse Tran

89 Adams Street

Park Ridge, IL 60068

For one glorious moment, Igor is transported on a magic carpet of happiness and hope. A cure! A biomedical research job! It would be glorious, a perfect opportunity.

Then, reality intrudes.

Igor sets the letter down next to him, staring straight ahead. Of course, he remembers Dr. Tran, his friend and mentor. The last he'd heard of her, she'd quit her job and started her own laboratory, funded by some eccentric billionaire. She was a classy, elegant woman of late middle age, with stylish glasses and a brilliant mind.

The idea of working for her again, doing what he loved, was a dream come true. But it would have to remain just that—a dream.

Igor remembers the Bunsen burner. He remembers the sizzle

of meat, the fat dripping onto the cool metal, oozing onto the Formica table. He remembers the cadaver lab. He knows that he cannot be trusted in a science lab. He knows what will happen if he ever lets himself return.

He hopes that she's right, and that she's close to a cure for the virus. He would love to be a part of that. But he can't be.

Igor wads the letter up into a ball and tosses it across the room, hitting the wall behind the little card table where he should eat his meals, but where he instead places assorted homeless objects. He will not answer the letter. He'll pretend he never saw it.

Igor's motorcycle is an old, classic one. It's not flashy, not fancy, but it's well-maintained and gets him from place to place. However, like most motorcycles, it's loud, and so he can't take it to Moonlight Run this time. Last time, he was checking up on his brother. This time, he's doing sneaky reconnaissance.

He takes the bike to the sloop a mile out. There's a lookout there where tourists sometimes park to stretch their legs and take pictures of themselves. He stashes his bike in the bushes next to a tree, locks it up, and starts walking.

If it were on an ordinary sidewalk, or a flat surface, the walk would take him less than fifteen minutes. But it's not an ordinary walk, it's a cluttered, branch-laden walk full of thick tree roots and various tripping hazards. In addition, he wants to be as quiet as possible, just in case some of the river people are nearby. He is dressed in army green, hoping it will help him blend in.

He reaches the river and peers out over the rocks. He has a pair of binoculars, which he brings to his eyes now, watching over the people.

The teepees are still there, dotting the shore. There are people standing and sitting around, talking, smoking, not doing much of anything interesting. Igor is not sure why he came. What was he hoping to find? What was he hoping to see? He doesn't know. He just hopes that something will happen, something that will give him some reassurance that these people are basically decent folks who have found a new way to live, and that's all.

He hears a laugh, which would not normally bother him, but this one disturbs him in a deep, fundamental way. It's a child's laugh.

He zooms his binoculars around, trying to find the source of the sound, and he locates it. A tiny little kid, maybe six or seven years old, playing with an older kid, maybe ten years old. They're throwing something around, and the bigger kid is pretending that the thing hit him in the head and made him dizzy. He's stumbling around in a corny, theatrical way that makes the littler kid laugh hysterically.

Igor wants to smile, but instead he has to force down an unexpected wave of vomit. Kids. They've got kids here.

It's one thing for a bunch of adults to agree to chop off their body parts, it's another thing entirely to make kids do it. It doesn't sit right with Igor, at all.

Still, he can't be sure that they're making the kids participate. Hell, maybe the kids don't even know about the agreement. Maybe they just eat their meat and don't ask questions about it. The thought comforts Igor slightly, but he can't dispel the notion that something very sinister is happening here.

There shouldn't be children here. There just shouldn't.

He can't remember the last time he saw kids hanging out with infected adults, just running around outside like this. It's illegal for cannibals to have any contact with children, whether they are infected or not, so when adult cannibals do have contact with kids, they are typically discreet about it.

He pulls out a stick of beef jerky and gnaws on it. The chewy saltiness of it calms him a bit. He needs sustenance. He's going to need to stay here for a while now, until he can be sure that those kids are safe.

He leans back against a tree trunk and extends his long legs out in front of him. He's glad he brought some emergency supplies in his pack. He might need them.

After several hours, Igor's legs are numb and his ass hurts from sitting on such an uncomfortable surface. The heat is killing him, and his sweat draws mosquitos. Panicked as usual, he swats them away, smooshing them whenever he can.

There's a change in the sounds by the shore. Whoops of excitement and loud voices reach him. He peers through his binoculars, to see what's causing the commotion. Everyone is looking in the same direction, toward the path that leads to the camp.

He turns his sights on the path and draws in a sharp breath. Four men are carrying a cage. It looks like a dog crate, or a cage you might use for a pet monkey. The bars are thick and round, and it's obviously heavy, since it requires four strong-looking men to carry it.

Inside the cage is a child.

"Shit," he whispers, blinking hard to make sure he's seeing correctly. Jud was right. Igor had no idea how right he was. He'd wanted to believe the best about Karl, who'd once been so kind to him. But Karl had obviously fed him a line of bullshit, and now Igor feels like an idiot. A terrified, disgusted idiot.

"Shit shit shit."

It's not that he doesn't understand the impulse. After all, Igor has the virus, too, and he's certainly entertained those thoughts. In fact, just thinking of that soft, tender child down there in that cage is enough to make him salivate and hate himself.

But it's wrong. It's so wrong, on every possible level. Igor has to put a stop to it.

He reaches into his pack, retrieving a Bowie knife. There are a lot of people, and the knife's not enough to keep him safe.

A memory occurs to him, and he exhales in sweet relief. The ceremony. They aren't going to eat the child right away. Karl has to do a bunch of priest shit, and then they paint themselves in mud. Don't they fast beforehand, too? He seems to remember something about that.

Maybe he doesn't have to act right away. Maybe he can go back to town, get some help, even call the police.

The whooping and hollering has died down now, and he can hear the child, screaming and begging to be released. It makes him sick to his stomach. Even the little kids he'd seen playing earlier aren't helping her. He doesn't know why that surprises him, but it does. He guesses he tends to assume that kids are nicer than adults, most of the time.

He knows he can't leave the kid there, not even to get help. It would be the smart thing to do, but he's not capable of doing it. He can't leave her here all alone with these hungry hungry cannibals. What if they lose their self-control and eat her right away, without waiting for the ceremony? What if it takes a long time for the police to get out here?

He needs a plan.

It is hard for Igor to sneak around anywhere. In fact, he is certain, based on his own life experiences, that there is no Bigfoot, because it's damn near impossible for a large object to move around undetected. If there were giant hairy bipeds roaming around the woods, many people would have heard one or seen one by now.

Still, he does his best. He waits until it is as dark as can be, and the only light is from the stars, and a faint twinkle from a distant fire. He steps slowly, cautiously, backing off any time he hears a snap or crackle beneath his heel, carefully replacing his foot in a quieter spot. The voices in the camp have settled down; he is sure that most of them are asleep.

Before dark, when the twilight covered the river in its eerie gloaming, Igor had watched with sick fascination as Karl emerged from his teepee wearing a tan colored robe with many fancy tassels and feathers on it. He'd had a red scarf tied on his head, his long black hair swinging around his shoulders. Carrying a stick of some kind, he'd waved it around at the crying child in the cage, shouting something Igor couldn't understand.

A few of the Moonlight Runners had approached the cage and thrown cups of liquid onto the girl. It had been hard to watch.

The crowd chanted and held hands and danced in a circle, until Karl held his stick high above his head and shouted something that clearly meant "STOP."

Everyone had stopped. And then, one by one, they'd filed away, leaving the girl to cry and marinate in whatever liquid had been thrown onto her.

After that, the camp had grown quiet, presumably waiting for some kind of signal that it was time to eat. Igor hopes that they plan to wait until dawn, but he wouldn't bet on it.

He doubts that everyone is asleep. He remembers the weird energy that pulses through your body when you're anticipating a feast, that pulse of electricity that sends jolts through your legs, shooting into your fingertips. It's possible to sleep through the excitement, but it's difficult.

He inches closer. He can't believe how long it's taking him to get to the camp, and part of him wants to speed up his slow progression, to end this prolonged anxiety, for better or for worse. But he doesn't want to hurt anybody, and he doesn't want to fight.

He can see the cage now. The child inside is so small, curled up into a little ball, head buried in her arms, as if protecting her face from seeing the horrors around her. He can see messy, disheveled pigtails; he assumes it is a girl.

The teepees that surround the cage are quiet. The inhabitants are either sleeping or trying to sleep. Either way, they can't see him. He crouches low to the ground, creeping like an animal, trying to make himself as quiet as possible.

Silently, he reaches into his pocket and pulls out a multitool.

Downriver, he can see the outline of a couple people, sitting by a fire. They talk quietly, but he can't make out what they're saying. If he can't hear them, he reasons that they probably can't hear him, and he is grateful for the rush of the river, which covers all manner of tiny sounds.

He is close to the cage now. The girl is still hiding her face, possibly sleeping. He doesn't want to frighten her, he can't have her yelping or screaming and attracting attention. What to do?

He circles the cage, wishing he could see it better. He can't see a lock or a door. How the hell is he going to pull this off?

The girl in the cage makes a little yelp.

"Sssssh, I'm here to help you. I'm here to help." His whisper is frantic and panicked. God, please let the girl listen to him, and keep quiet.

She stays quiet, except for a little sniffle.

"Ok. Good. I'm gonna get you out of here. But I need you to help me."

She stays quiet. She is a good girl.

"Ok. I need to find the lock. Can you help me?"

There is a long pause. Then a soft *clang*.

He follows the sounds, feeling along the cage with his fingertips. He reaches it. A padlock.

Thank god, it's just a regular padlock, an old-fashioned one that won't give him much trouble.

He works quickly, by feel. He hasn't picked a lock in a long time, and he's a bit rusty, and it's much, much harder in the dark.

The little girl is breathing fast, and he can hear that she's close to crying. He needs her to calm down.

"Deep breaths," he counsels in his faintest whisper. "Almost done."

The lock springs free, as if it never wanted to be a lock in the first place. The door swings open with a much-too-loud creak, as the girl eagerly pushes her way out and jumps into Igor's arms.

"HEY! SHUT THE FUCK UP OUT THERE."

The voice is coming from one of the teepees. Both the girl and Igor freeze. They wait.

Nobody comes out.

The poor little kid is shaking and trying hard not to cry. Igor feels a stab of intense, protective sympathy for her. She's trying so hard to be brave and good, and he wants to find the motherfuckers who snatched her, yank them out of their fake-ass teepees, and stab them in the fucking throats.

He does not. Instead he cradles the girl close to his chest and carefully, quietly, sneaks away, back into the forest.

Maybe Bigfoot exists after all.

CHAPTER FOUR

The girl is silent at first. She sits on the front of his motorcycle, and he tucks her into his jacket, snug and warm. She is limp and small against him, a soft warm weight. He is certain that nobody can see her in the dark, hidden under his coat, which is important.

He is mildly panicked. Of course, the cannibals will notice she's gone, if they haven't already. He's not sure if they'll put her disappearance and his recent visit together, but they might, and the idea makes him worried.

Also, there is the problem of what to do with the kid. He'll have to get her home to her parents, of course, but what is the best way to do that? Will she identify him as her rescuer? Her parents might not be the forgiving types. He would like to think that they'd be so grateful to get their child back that they'd be willing to overlook the fact that a cannibal had been alone with their child, but he knows that is naive. Parents can be crazy overprotective when it come to their kids and cannibals. He's seen it before. There was a story in the news just recently about an infected guy whose daughter showed up on his doorstep unannounced. She just wanted to see her dad.

The girl's aunt found out about it and had the dad arrested. He is now serving a seven-year sentence.

The girl hasn't seen him yet, at least not very well. She wouldn't be able to identify him if he dropped her off at home, right now. But he doesn't know where to drop her off and can't find out without waking her. And if he wakes her and talks to her, she will see him. They aren't in the pitch black anymore; they are in town, with all the streetlights and glowing storefronts that that entails.

Could he drop her off at the police station? No, he can't do that. She might be infected. The police are notoriously unkind to infected children, and he will not submit her to that kind of treatment.

Without warning, the girl lets out a high, keening wail and shakes and squirms in his arms. It startles Igor so badly that he nearly loses control of the bike, and the swerve dangerously close to the ditch on the side of the road. This scares the girl more, and her shrieks hurt Igor's ears.

"Shhh! Hey! Hey!" Igor makes vaguely calming words to try to get her to stop. The last thing he needs is a motorcycle accident. The cops will come. They will see him in possession of a little girl. His life will be over.

He pulls over to the side of the road. He needs to get her calm.

"Shh, I got you," he says, soothing and quiet. "You're safe now." He picks her up off the bike and sits her down on the ground beside him. It's gravelly and cold, but it's the best he can do under the circumstances. He can't see her face well, but the headlight makes her mostly visible. She is pale and tired and tear-streaked. Her hair is light brown and matted and snarled.

"Who are you? Where are we?" Her voice is a near wail, and he can tell she's near hysterics, and he doesn't blame her. Still, he needs her to calm the fuck down.

"Shh. Like I said, you're safe. Let's talk."

"Who are you?"

For a moment, he considers answering her, but instead he shakes his head. No names. It's bad enough that his face is so recognizable. Stupid tattoo. He's not sure how well she can see him by the light of the motorcycle, but it's probably well enough.

"First of all, I can't tell you my name. Nobody can know that I'm the one who rescued you, ok?"

"Why?"

"Just because," he snaps. Then he softens his voice, when he sees how scared his snapping made her. "It would be best if you don't tell anyone about me. Is that ok?"

"I guess."

"Good. The plan is, you stay with me tonight, and tomorrow I'll take you back to your parents. Do you know your address?"

She rolls her eyes. "I'm eight, not four. Of course I know my address."

Amused, he suppresses a smile. "Well, good then. I'll take you there tomorrow, alright? In the meantime, try to get some sleep if you can. We're going to get back on the motorcycle, ok?"

The girl just nods.

He sighs an exhausted sigh. He doesn't want to take her home with him. It's risky. He will have another talk with her in the morning, impress on her the importance of keeping his identity a secret. She's old enough to understand about keeping a secret.

It is in no way an ideal situation. His trailer is small and not suited to children. What if his neighbors see her? What if Helen stops by for a surprise inspection? What if the girl tells everyone who will listen about the cannibal who gave her a ride on his motorcycle and took her back to his trailer, alone?

As he nears the compound gate, he tucks the tiny girl closer to him, adjusting his jacket and his body to obscure her. George is the entry guard tonight; that's good. George is one of the less uptight ones, and Igor thinks he won't stop him or examine him too closely. Sure enough, he sails right through the gate, with George barely looking up from his phone.

He holds her close as he pulls into his carport and gets off the bike. The movement and the sudden quiet wake her up a little. He is surprised she actually managed to sleep, but he supposes she must be emotionally exhausted.

He carries her tiny body inside and sets her on the couch. He isn't sure why he's carrying her—it's not like she's an infant who can't walk—but something about it seems right, like he needs to take care of her in this way. She's so goddamned fragile-looking.

He goes into his room and gets an old afghan from the closet. He brings it into the living room and covers her up with it. He realizes that he doesn't have an extra pillow to give her and so he retrieves his own from his bed and throws it to her.

He hesitates. Is he supposed to read her a bedtime story? Or make her brush her teeth? He doesn't have a spare toothbrush, and he won't let her borrow his, for obvious reasons. Is he supposed to get her some pajamas? He does not know the rules of childcare.

"Is there... anything you need?"

She shakes her head. She is lying on the couch, still and quiet, blinking up at the ceiling.

He sighs, relieved. "Good, good. If you need anything, I'll be in there." He gestures to his bedroom.

She nods and stares straight ahead. It's kind of creepy and unsettling.

"Um. Are you ok?"

The girl nods, but now tears are streaking her face, and her little chest is heaving up and collapsing down and, oh god, she's crying, and Igor does not know what to do.

"Uh. There, there," he says. "We'll get you home tomorrow, ok? It's just for tonight. Would it... do you want me to take you home tonight? What am I saying, of course you do. Jesus. Alright, come on."

Igor feels incredibly stupid. What was he thinking, bringing her here for the night? He gestures for her to get up off the couch. But now the girl is wailing even harder, and he is confused.

"What? What is it?"

"I lied. I lied before. I don't know my address. Or like, I don't have one. Those guys, the ones who took me, they—" she breaks off and gasps, trying to calm herself. Igor shifts his weight uncomfortably. "They took me from the place I usually sleep. I can't go back there, because maybe they'll come get me again. Don't take me back there, ok?"

Igor stares at her blankly, taking all this in.

"OK?" She is nearly screaming now, and Igor needs her to quiet down. The walls on these trailers are not thick.

"Ok, ok. No problem. Look, I'll take you wherever you want to go. Just don't cry, ok?"

She cries.

He shifts his weight again.

"So, when you say you don't have an address... so you and your parents are homeless?"

"My parents aren't allowed to have me," she says, and Igor understands.

It's a thing that happens now. Parents get infected, and sometimes there's no place for the kid to go. Technically speaking, these kids are supposed to go into the foster care system, or to other relatives, but in actuality, it's not uncommon for them to slip through the cracks. "Displaced children" is what they're usually called, but typically they're older than this. Teenagers who refuse to stay in foster homes, who prefer to live in tent cities and cars, on their own terms, rather than submit themselves to an uncaring system.

Eight years old is way too young to be on her own, on the streets.

"So, who takes care of you?"

She wipes her eyes and shrugs. "Other kids. They help me with food. Sometimes the lady at the Burger King gives me stuff to eat. This one girl lets me sleep in her car with her at night. That's where those guys got me though, so I probably won't sleep there anymore."

Anger floods Igor like a shot of heroin to the eyeball. Those fucking monsters are targeting homeless kids, kids like this little girl who don't have anyone to protect them.

Well those sons of bitches fucked with the wrong little girl. She might not have had anyone to protect her then, but she sure as hell does now. They're gonna wish they'd never drawn breath.

"What's your name?" His voice is harsh with anger, and the girl looks terrified. In an attempt to ameliorate this effect, he plasters a friendly smile on his face, which doesn't seem to help matters. He returns his face to normal.

"I'm sorry. I'm not mad at you. I'm mad at those guys who took you. Now, I just want you to tell me your name. Is that ok?"

She looks uneasy, but less scared. "Elli," she replies.

"Elli. That's a great name, Elli. My name is Igor."

She giggles.

He raises an eyebrow. "What?"

She giggles some more. "That's a silly name."

He frowns. He does not enjoy being mocked for his name, but

he is damn glad she's not crying anymore. He will let her mock him for whatever she wants, as long as she stops crying.

"Yes. I guess it is. Anyway, Elli, since I'm not taking you back to live in a car, you'll have to stay here until we figure out what to do, ok?"

"OK, Igor," she laughs.

He sighs. "Are you ok now? Do you need anything?"

"Nope, I don't need anything, Igor."

"Alright. Try to get some sleep."

"I will, Igor."

"That's enough, ok. Goodnight, Elli."

"Goodnight, Igor."

He turns and walks into his bedroom and shuts the door, listening to Elli giggle on the couch. He smiles, despite himself.

As he enters his bedroom, he has a quiet panic attack. He is hungry. So damned hungry. There is a little girl in his living room right now, with no family, no friends, no one who would miss her.

He slaps himself in the face, hard. He locks his bedroom door. He gnaws on a piece of beef jerky. He lays in bed, trying to sleep. He fails.

Igor wakes up to the distant sounds of shouting and violence. He jolts up in bed, already out the bedroom door before his eyes are fully open.

Elli is sitting on the floor, cross-legged, watching *Gladiator* at top volume. A bowl of dry cereal is on the floor in front of her, and she drags her hand through it absently, rooting around for the sweet marshmallow pieces. Her eyes are glued to the TV screen.

He sighs and picks up the remote, turning down the volume. She looks over at him, quizzically.

"Why are you doing that?"

"Because it's too loud." He is annoyed that he needs to explain this. "I see you got some cereal. You want some milk with that?"

She shakes her head, eyes back on the TV.

Igor shrugs and heads into the kitchen and heats up some water for coffee. It's gonna be a long day.

He settles into his couch and looks at the back of the girl's head, unsure how to begin.

"So, Elli. Besides you parents, do you have any other family? Maybe a nice grandma? A wacky aunt?"

She doesn't say anything, but her tiny shoulders shrug.

"What about friends? Did your parents have any friends who might be able to help you out?"

Again, she shrugs.

"Ok, the thing is, I can't send you back out onto the streets. So I need to know where to take you. When—" he breaks off, unsure how to phrase this delicately. "When your parents and you got separated... where did you go? Who was supposed to take care of you?"

She stays silent, and Igor is getting frustrated.

"Can you help me out here?"

Silence.

With a flick of the remote, he shuts off the TV.

"Hey!"

"I need to talk to you Elli. It's important. I need to know who is supposed to be taking care of you."

She spins around on her bottom, staying cross-legged. She glares at him, and Igor is taken aback by the adult-like anger he sees in her. "Nobody is supposed to be taking care of me. It's just me. And my friends. That's it."

"But that's not how it works," he protests. Surely, the government wouldn't send an eight-year-old girl out into the streets. They would at the very least place her in a group home somewhere or something.

"I'm not going back there." She's looking at her lap now, and a tear drop drips onto her hand. Oh god. Igor can't handle this again. He absolutely cannot.

"Ok, ok. You don't have to go anywhere. Just don't cry, alright?"

"Please don't take me back there, ok? Promise me."

"I promise. But take you back where? I don't know what you're talking about."

"I don't want to talk about it." She is not focusing on him, and he is glad for that. He is not sure he could handle looking directly at her pain.

"You don't have to talk about anything you don't want to. I'm just trying to help. I want you to be safe, that's all."

Without warning, Elli leaps up from the ground and jumps onto Igor's lap. He is unprepared for the sudden weight of her, and he rocks back for a second. She is sobbing, loud, wet sobs, the kind of heartbreaking crying that you see in the seriously grief-stricken. He supposes that she is grief-stricken. She's lost her parents, her home, her friends, her safety... all of that. And she's so tiny.

Without thinking of the risks involved he wraps his arms around her in a protective hug. He pats her hair and rocks her a little. This seems to calm her down, but it makes Igor tense as fuck. Because, as much as he hates himself for it... the girl's scent is mouth-watering. The oils on her skin are as appealing as a nice, crispy, greasy piece of fried chicken.

He will not bite her. He will not eat this child. He absolutely will not. If he did, it would be a blight on his soul so deep and so dark it could never be erased. It would be the ultimate betrayal of this sweet, sad child. He will not eat her, not a single part of her, not even a fingernail.

She is not sobbing anymore, just sniffling and holding him tight. He carefully extracts himself and sets her down on the couch next to him. It's still too close. Her tender little arm is inches from his own gigantic one. His mouth is a warm pool of saliva. He stands up and walks into the kitchen.

The girl can't stay with him. It's far too dangerous, for him of course, but especially for her. He will not be able to live with himself if he hurts her. It will be the end for him.

But there is nowhere else for her to go.

TV Pundit Everett Fletcher is interviewing Geraldine Hemings, the outspoken Vice President of Mothers Against the Cannibal Takeover.

"We have all seen the wreckage caused by these monsters and their appetites. The fact of the matter is, these so-called rehab centers are just not effective. Bottom line, the cannibals have to want to change, and in my experience, they simply don't."

Everett tilts his head thoughtfully and nods. His heavy load of slicked-back hair doesn't budge an inch. "But Geraldine, what about the many infected people who have successfully completed their programs and have managed to stay out of trouble? Would you make an exception for these people?"

Geraldine smirks. Her trademark frizzy half-ponytail is at odds with the angry angles of her face. "And here is where our critics fail to understand the situation. You call them people, Everett, but they are not people. This disease has hijacked whatever it was in them that made them human, and now they are no more people than the chicken I ate for lunch."

She smiles at the camera, knowing she has her audience's attention. "And to those of you at home who hold out hope that your loved ones might still be in there, somewhere hidden deep under their heinous urges, my heart goes out to you. Truly, it does. I think we've all been affected by this in one way or another. But the man or woman you loved...he or she is gone. And the sooner you accept that, the better off we will be, as a society."

"And how will that make us better?" Everett looks genuinely curious, though he must already know what she's about to say. These are not new talking points for Geraldine, or for MACT in general.

"We need to let go of our attachment to these shells, Everett. The sooner we can do that, the sooner we can put them to a painless, humane death. I know it sounds harsh, but think of it this way. You have a family dog. You love that dog. But if he gets rabies, and he becomes a danger to your child, what do you do? Do you spend huge amounts of money to put the dog up in a hotel for the rest of its life? Do you let the dog live in your kid's room and hope for the best? No, of course not. You put the dog down. It's a kindness, both for your family, who you want to protect, and also for the dog. The dog doesn't want to live with rabies! That dog is suffering."

"But what about the ones who we've interviewed who seem mentally quite normal? How can you argue that we should kill human beings capable of rational thought?"

Geraldine raises an eyebrow. "They eat people. And you say they're mentally normal?"

Igor shuts the TV off and runs a hand through his hair. He hates these TV segments, but is compelled to watch them for sick, masochistic reasons. At least this time they didn't show footage of "out of control" cannibals, more accurately known as "Week Two" videos. Those videos, shaky and amateur, captured by "innocent bystanders" are always terrifying and sobering. They remind Igor of who he could be, if he loses control.

A particularly famous video captures three adult males, dressed in the kind of thuggish clothes one wears to strike fear into the hearts of white suburban housewives everywhere. Eyes full of crazy, the thugs snatch a little blond boy off a swingset and drag him into a nearby stand of trees. The cameraman doesn't intervene, presumably out of fear, but he manages to follow along at a safe distance and record the little boy's screams as he is ripped to literal shreds. Every time an anti-cannibal group proposes a new piece of legislation, they trot out that fucking video.

The guys in that video, and in the other "out of control" videos, had obviously been suffering from the Week Two Frenzies. Normal cannibals don't behave like that, only the detoxing ones do, during the second week of abstinence. If they'd been given proper treatment during their detoxing, the attack never would have happened. Those guys had been stupid, probably, trying to white knuckle it at home, instead of checking into a rehab center. Idiots. And now, the anti-cannibal zealots use Week Two footage all the time, as if it's an accurate portrayal of regular infected folk.

Elli is playing solitaire on the floor, and doesn't seem to notice the sudden quiet. They are running low on groceries, and that's a problem. First of all, Elli needs to eat something besides pickles and cereal. He's no Mary Poppins, but he knows that much about childcare. And second, he is afraid to leave the confines of the Containment Center.

He realizes that it's only a matter of time before the Moonlight Run folks realize he had something to do with snatching Elli. After all, there are only so many people who could have taken her, and as an outsider who has paid them a recent visit, he's bound to come under suspicion, sooner or later. As long as he stays home, he is protected by the guards. He never thought he'd be thankful for the gun-toting fascists who roam the trailer park, but he supposes he is now. If he leaves, though, he won't have any serious protection against anyone who might want to hurt him.

Will Karl stand up for him, when the Moonlight Runners accuse him? Igor would like to think so. But he knows better.

There are no grocery delivery services who will come to Containment Centers. Too risky, apparently. So Igor needs to find a way to get some food, and soon. He checks the cupboards and figures they'll be ok for a few days, supplementing from the garden, of course. Hopefully a solution will present itself shortly.

In addition, he needs to figure out what's to be done about the Moonlight Runners. Sure, he rescued Elli, but that doesn't mean it's all over and they're going to stop their evil murder plans. Hell, for all he knows, they might be feasting on another kidnapped child right now. The thought turns his stomach and makes him salivate at the same time. He will have to do something about them, as soon as possible, but at the moment, he has his hands full with Elli.

He is operating under the assumption that Elli is not infected. If she were, she would be the most self-controlled little cannibal he'd ever heard of. Children are not known for their self-regulation under the best of circumstances. When they have a virus that makes them hungry for human meat, they are generally pretty insane and intractable. In fact, there are children's detention centers specifically for the youngest cannibals, where they aren't allowed contact with anyone but a few well-armored nurses.

He has heard terrible things about those detention centers, and he hopes to never see one.

If Elli is not infected, then he needs to get some utensils and cups that will be for her use only. Yes, washing dishes eliminates the virus, but it's not a risk he is willing to take. The girl must be protected at all costs.

"Elli? You know what I am, right?"

She looks up from her cards. She shrugs. "A guy."

"Right. But you know I'm... like your parents. I'm infected."

She looks back down at her cards. "Yeah, I figured."

"Well... how do you feel about that?"

She shrugs again. "I don't know."

"I mean, does it bother you?"

She shakes her head. "Not really."

"And you're... you're not infected, right?"

She grins up at him. "Why? Are you scared I'll eat you up?"

He smiles back at her. "Just checking."

Well that settles it. He will get some good nutritious food, some silverware and cups, a toothbrush, a pillowcase, all that stuff. He will make a nice, safe home for this sweet, uninfected child. He might not be the best guardian, but he's a better guardian than the streets.

He picks up the phone. He needs to call Jud.

Three hours later, there's a loud, angry knock on the door. Igor jumps up, glad that Jud is here with supplies. He is eager to discuss tactics with someone who is on the same page regarding the Moonlight Runners and cannibal protection in general, and who is not eight years old.

"Igor Fenenko. This is security. Open up."

Igor freezes. He'd been about to open the door, just like that, and he curses himself for relaxing, even for a minute. He turns to Elli, where she's playing some strange card game of her own invention and puts a shushing finger to his mouth. She looks at him, eyes wide.

He points hard at his bedroom and mouths "HIDE."

The girl doesn't need telling twice, and she scurries into his room. Igor tries not to think about the hiding capabilities of an eight-year-old who just got herself kidnapped. Perhaps the kidnapping has taught her a thing or two about caution. Regardless, Igor cannot ignore the knocking any longer.

He opens the door and recognizes one of the security guards, a thick-waisted, flabby-chinned guy named Frank. Frank is holding a brown paper grocery bag out in front of him, glaring at Igor with mean-spirited suspicion.

Out the corner of his eye, he sees movement, and his eyes flicker toward it. It's Jud, and he's in handcuffs, shaking his head frantically at Igor, trying to communicate without hands or words. Igor looks back to Frank.

"Can I help you, Frank?"

Frank glares harder. The security guards don't like it when the infected refer to them by their first names. Familiarity breeds contempt and all that. They prefer the more respectful "Officer Soandso" or, at the very least, "Mr. Soandso."

Igor does not give a fuck about Frank's preferences in this regard.

Frank jerks his head toward Jud. "This guy's your buddy, right?"

"Yes." Igor sees no reason to deny it. All visitors to the Containment Center are required to register at the gate and identify who it is they are visiting and why, and how long they mean to stay. Jud is a regular visitor.

"Well, you know anything about this?" Frank shakes the grocery bag. "There's enough contraband in here to lock you both up for a good long while, friend. I got beef jerky, beer, a goddamn steak, you shithead. You think you're gonna just sneak this shit in here under my watch?"

Behind him, Jud shakes his head violently, subtly telling him to keep his mouth shut.

Igor hates this. He does not want Jud to take the rap for this. After all, this is entirely Igor's fault. He never should have asked Jud to bring him this stuff. He should have known that Jud would try to be nice and bring him some meat and beer, and he should have told Jud that Frank was an overzealous douche who checked everyone's bags, even if they've been coming for months.

This is all Igor's fault, and he is sick and sweaty with that knowledge. He starts to tell Frank exactly that, but then he remembers Elli. Scared, tiny Elli, hiding in his bedroom. What will happen to her if he's arrested? She won't be able to stay in his trailer, all by herself, at least not for very long. She'll have to leave eventually, and when she does, the Moonlight Runners will be after her, eager to eliminate their victim, who can probably identify them all.

"I don't know, Sir." Igor keeps his tone respectful. "I don't know anything about that."

Jud nods behind Frank, looking relieved.

Igor frowns, hating himself, exasperated with Jud, but grateful to him as well.

"So, your friend back there just thought he'd bring his groceries with him to your place, is that right?"

Igor shrugs. "I guess."

"You don't think that's kind of a weird thing to do?"

Igor would like to reach out and grab Frank by the collar and pull him in close for a hard, brutal punch. But Frank is armed with pepper spray and a gun, and all the other guards would be on Igor in seconds if he dared assault a security officer. It would not be wise. But damn, it would feel good.

"I guess it might be. I really don't know anything about it," Igor says through, clenched teeth.

Frank stares at him for a long time, as if hoping that his penetrating gaze will make Igor crack. Little does he know, his gaze is not penetrating, it is glazed and piggish, and Igor is not at all intimidated by it.

"Well, alright then," says Frank. "I guess we'll be putting your buddy there under arrest, while you go back into your house and jack off to cannibal porn or whatever you sick assholes do. Good to see what kind of friends you barbaric fuckers make."

That hurts Igor more than it should. He has always prided himself on being a good and loyal friend, and in fact, until this moment, he would have been right to do so. Now, he watches from the doorway as the police arrive. They relieve Frank of his grocery bag, keeping it for evidence, he supposes. They arrest Jud and force him into a police car like a common criminal.

Igor closes the door. He is running out of options.

CHAPTER FIVE

"So, you know where the phone is?"

"Yes."

"And you can use the can opener?"

"Yes."

"And you can reach the water faucet and all that?"

"YES!"

Igor is nervous. He is leaving Elli home alone, venturing out into the city, and the idea of leaving such a tiny, helpless thing all by herself in a compound full of reformed cannibals makes his chest tight. He himself struggles with self-control, and he is a very strong-willed individual. He knows his neighbors might not be able to help themselves if they see a small, juicy, unattended child roaming around. Worse, she's uninfected. Everyone knows that uninfected meat tastes best.

"If I'm not back by tomorrow, you have to call this number." Igor hands the girl a slip of paper with Helen's number written on it. He figures that if he doesn't come back by tomorrow, that means he's dead, and if he's dead, he doesn't have to worry about Helen having him arrested for consorting with a minor.

Helen seems like the kind of lady who would be good with children.

Elli takes the paper and holds it, looking at it closely.

"Will you be ok, Elli?"

Elli looks up at him and rolls her eyes. "Yes, Igor. I'm a big girl."

He smiles. She's the smallest girl in the world, but her self-assurance is charming.

It's time for him to go.

Mothers Against the Cannibal Takeover Headquarters is located in a small cottage, donated to the cause by a deceased mother who had evidently been against the cannibal takeover. Now it's an oddly homey place, full of country-style throw pillows and shades of peach. Igor sits in the headquarters, on a plush, well-worn couch, his giant limbs spilling out of it awkwardly. He is waiting for an audience with Faith Gregory, the chapter president.

MACT has been an active voice in cannibal suppression, ever since its formation near the beginning of the virus crisis. It was MACT who pressured Congress to pass the Containment Center laws, and they were the driving force behind the push to keep the infected away from children, regardless of relationship. Their weapons of choice are petitions, protests, and lengthy letters written to congress to further their agenda. They speak loudly, and carry a big stick, too.

Igor knows that if he goes to the police and has them arrest the Moonlight Runners, the problem will be handled swiftly. He also knows that the public discovery of a group of relapsed cannibals who kidnap and eat children will set off a mass panic, and mass panics never turn out well for disenfranchised groups. Like cannibals.

Igor is forward-thinking enough to see the consequences of going to the police. Neighborhoods everywhere will demand stronger monitoring for Containment Centers. Some groups will call for mandatory prison sentences. Some will call for executions. And a few will take it upon themselves to go cannibal hunting, "for the good of society."

That's why Igor has come to MACT today. In many ways, it's a terrifying place for him, infected as he is, surrounded by spiffily dressed office workers who would have him arrested in a heartbeat if they knew he was infected. But he doesn't know what else to do. He needs help to shut down Moonlight Run. As the driving force behind Containment Center policies, he is hoping that Mothers Against the Cannibal Takeover might have some ideas about how to contain this cult. Maybe there are zoning laws or something. He is not sure.

Of course, there is the possibility that MACT will go public with the Moonlight Runner scandal. But he has reason to believe that Faith Gregory might be amenable to hearing him out, and might be willing to keep things on the down low. In fact, he is quite certain of it.

The woman herself emerges from behind a beige door. There is a sign on it with a little haiku written in faux-Japanese style calligraphy.

We are the guardians

Mothers who protect their young

Nothing's more sacred.

Faith Gregory is blond and polished in a suburban housewife kind of way. She is well-scrubbed and sun-pressed. Igor imagines she has baggies of cheerios in her purse.

"Igor Fenenko?"

He stands and extends a hand for shaking. She is frozen, staring at his tattoo. He sighs and lets her take it in. Conversation will not be possible until she overcomes his appearance.

She unfreezes and flicks a smile at him. "Come in."

He walks into her "office," which had obviously been a young boy's bedroom at some point. It's painted a pale blue with a sailboat wallpaper border. A Winnie the Pooh mural is plastered to the wall behind her desk.

"Big Winnie the Pooh fan?" He smiles at her, trying to break the ice.

She grins back and waves a hand. "I know. I really need to get around to redecorating, but things keep coming up. You know how it is."

Igor nods, as if he does indeed know how it is, as if he is always thwarted in his redecorating efforts by office administration duties.

"So tell me how we can help you, Mr. Fenenko."

Igor leans forward, then sits back, realizing that his body language might be seen as intimidating. He is going for friendly, not scary. "It's about a group of cannibals who have... relapsed."

Faith sits forward and grabs a pen. Her smile is gone now, and she's all business. "Relapsed, huh? Yeah, that happens a lot. But first, who are these guys? And why do you think they've relapsed?"

He exhales. This is it. No turning back now. "I've seen them."

"You've seen them eating human flesh?" She lowers her voice, serious.

He nods.

"How did you see this?"

"I went out to visit an old friend of mine, to check up on him. He was living down at Moonlight Run with a bunch of others. They had kidnapped a little girl—an uninfected girl—and were planning to eat her."

"Oh my God," she breathes. The pen she is holding has snapped and ink spills out all over the place.

"Oh! Oh my God!" She grabs some tissues from a box and dabs at the ink. Igor helps, blotting the desk.

"I'm so sorry about that," she laughs. "God, what a mess."

"It's alright. It's a shocking story."

"It certainly is. What happened to the girl?"

"I kidnapped her back," he explains with a little half-smile. "I snuck her out in the middle of the night, while everyone was sleeping."

Faith exhales. "Good. Good. Where is she now?" She looks up at him with shining eyes. She thinks he is a hero. He is sorry that he's going to have to disprove that notion.

"Back at home with her parents," he lies smoothly.

"Excellent. So, have you gone to the police?"

This is going to be the tricky part. Igor sits back in his chair. "I was hoping to solve this without the police."

She frowns. "Why?"

"You know why. If this gets into the press, there will be widespread panic. Persecutions, maybe even killings. We've finally managed to get some peace between the infected and the uninfected, and this thing could blow all that up, set us back ages."

Faith raises an eyebrow. "If these guys are kidnapping children and eating them, don't you think that warrants a little concern? Maybe people would be right to be worried."

Igor shakes his head. "These are just a few nutjobs, Ms. Gregory. They don't represent all of the infected. Also, I'm not convinced they've actually eaten a child. At least not yet. I think these guys can be rehabilitated if we give them a chance."

She nods, pensive. "I see your point, but I respectfully disagree. They've already kidnapped a child. That, in and of itself, is enough to tell me that these aren't reasonable folks. I think it'll be better if we go to the police. They're the best ones to handle this kind of thing."

Igor opens his bag and rifles around. "Alright, Ms. Gregory. I was hoping it wouldn't come to this, but..." He pulls a photo out of the bag and shows it to Faith. "You recognize this guy?"

She looks at the picture, which shows a young man wearing the required rehab jumpsuit, sitting next to Igor, arm slung over his shoulder.

"Where did you get this?" She snaps. She tears up the picture, immediately, face red and blotchy.

Igor tries not to laugh. "There's more where that came from Ms. Gregory. There's these things now, called computers?"

She throws the remains of the picture into a trash can that's stuffed neatly under her desk. She glares at Igor.

"You're one of them. A nasty, disgusting, savage, cannibal. And you come in here and think you can—"

"Can we please drop the name calling? I know how you feel about the infected. I watch the news. But whether you like it or not, we're on the same page here. We both want these guys stopped. We need to work together here."

"What do you want?" Faith looks like she needs a hundred beers.

"I already told you," Igor shrugs. "I want your help to take out the Moonlight Runners. I remember hearing about those guys who were squatting in that abandoned school building, and how you got them all kicked out and put in Containment Centers. Something like that. I mean, there has to be zoning laws about living by the river, right? I'm happy to help, of course. And I want you to keep this out of the media. No reporting of any kind. No leaks. Just go down there, make some threats, and scare everyone away."

"And if I agree to this?" Faith looks weary and pained, like a headache is silently creeping around behind her eyeballs.

"Then nobody will ever find out that your son is infected. I'll destroy every picture I have of him. You have my word."

Faith exhales. "I suppose I have no choice."

Igor wobbles his head left and right. "Well, you always have a choice. But, yes, I see what you mean."

"Hey, how did you get this picture anyway? Aren't phones and cameras prohibited in rehab?"

"Lots of things are prohibited in life. Doesn't stop people from doing them."

"Ain't it the truth." She raises a wry eyebrow.

"So do we have an agreement?"

She presses her hands into the desk in front of her. "Sure. But only if you do something for me."

"What is it?"

She throws her hands up in the air, exasperated. "Why the hell do you have a spider tattooed on your face? Why a spider? Why on your face? Why?"

Igor can't help it. He laughs.

He barely remembers the night he got the tattoo. It was a rough time in his life. It was after the incident at the lab, after the hearing, after his social and professional disgrace. He'd gotten good and drunk off tequila, so drunk he could barely walk straight, so drunk his eyes couldn't stay focused on any one thing, so drunk he was almost ok with his new status as an infected and dangerous person.

But it wasn't enough that he knew himself to be a danger. After all, people were stupid. They didn't know what was good for them most of the time. That's why they needed signs, signs to tell them that there's downed power lines, wet slippery spots, bumps in the road, coyotes and bears.

Cannibals.

He'd wandered into a tattoo parlor next to a bar, where the tattoo artist tried to talk Igor out of the tattoo, get him to come back when he was sober. But Igor wouldn't be dissuaded, and nobody tried to dissuade a man of Igor's size for long, or too insistently. He'd chosen a scary-ass giant red spider, and got it emblazoned across his face. A warning to others, not to come to close, not to let him hurt them.

The next day, and every day after, he'd regretted it.

He looks at Faith behind her desk, with her stiffly hair-sprayed blond hair, her neat, tidy appearance, her obvious conviction that she is Doing Right, her need to hide the truth of who and what her son is, in order to preserve her hard-won self-respect and dignity and career. He will not confide in her.

"What can I say? It seemed like a good idea at the time."

She shakes her head, and Igor can't tell if she is amused or disgusted or both.

She looks up at him, gaze set to neutral. "I'll be in touch."

After Mr. Fenenko leaves, Faith sits at her desk, still and shaken. She presses her palms flat into the wood in front of her and takes several deep, soothing breaths. There. That's better. It's been a rough day with all the cannibal encounters and blackmail, but she's got it together now. She's always been good in a crisis. It's part of why she's such an effective leader at MACT.

Nobody is certain what caused the man-eating virus. Various theories have been floated around, circulating on the internet, repeated in harsh tones by suspicious grandmothers. There is a large and vocal segment of the population who blames immigration in all legal and illegal forms, claiming that the poorer and dirtier peoples of the world brought their bad habits and terrifying pathogens with them. A particularly racist minority claims that the virus has been active in Africa for centuries, causing its unfortunate inhabitants to dine on each other regularly.

Mothers Against the Cannibal Takeover subscribes to none of those views. They have long held the position that the virus was caused by a genetic mutation, which had likely been caused by a minor nuclear "incident" that occurred some years before the first cannibals were reported; the spillage seeping into human DNA, wreaking havoc and altering brains on a cellular level. Nuclear power, in MACT's view, is one of the great dangers of the civilized world, and the virus its main threat.

The designers, safety inspectors, and upper managers of the Silverstone Nuclear Power Plant are all gone now. Many of them met with unfortunate accidents. Some of them became infected themselves and are now quarantined in one of the many Containment Centers that dot the land. Some of them have simply disappeared.

Naturally, Mothers Against the Cannibal Takeover denies all responsibility for these deaths and disappearances, and no charges have ever been brought on the organization or on any of its members. There has never been any proof of wrongdoing. The mothers are crafty, and they are careful.

Faith is the craftiest and most careful of them all; it's how she has managed to attain and maintain her position of power all these years. She is not a stranger to coups, both the non-violent kind and the kind where people die.

Igor Fenenko has presented her with an interesting opportunity, and an exciting challenge. A part of her hates the man for his insolent blackmail, but frankly, she welcomes his request as an exciting change of pace. As of late, her duties have been administrative, paper-based, and dull. It will be nice to get her hands dirty again, and she is sure her girls will agree.

It's been too long since they've taken out the trash, and now, things are starting to go rotten. It's time to clean up.

CHAPTER SIX

Igor carefully prunes a bonsai tree in his garden, mentally preparing for tonight's coup on the Moonlight Runners. He has already received some threatening calls in the three days since he brought Elli home, sinister calls from unknown men, all along the lines of "If you've been meddling in our business, we'll find out and make you pay."

Clearly, Igor is under suspicion, and so the coup cannot be postponed any longer. Any minute now, the Runners might come snooping around, and that, he cannot abide.

Faith Gregory has been in touch, and despite her general distaste for cannibals, he feels confident in her abilities, and he trusts that she will not fuck him over. He has to.

He cannot leave Elli alone in the trailer, not with all the nasty phone calls. Nor is he comfortable taking her along to the scene of her kidnapping and near devouring. He is no child psychologist, but he knows better than to do that, at least. He has a better plan.

He finishes his pruning, the scent of broken stems warm on his fingertips, his mind cooler for the exercise. He begins to put away his pruning shears, but then thinks better of it, and puts them in his pocket. The more sharp objects he has on his person, the better. He doesn't anticipate massive violence. After all, the plan is just to show up, threaten everyone with zoning laws and police officers, and scare everyone away. But he knows it's better to be safe than sorry. Nobody likes getting kicked out of their homes, after all. Angry people can be unpredictable.

Igor does not like violence; in fact, he hates it. That being said, he is very, very good at it, owing to his massive size and years of practice.

Unsurprisingly for a man with a spider tattooed on his face, his childhood had not been a pleasant one. After his mother died, leaving him and Karl alone with a severely depressed father, he had been a sad, melancholy boy. His father's depression had turned to alcoholism, and then into a raging methamphetamine addiction, and finally, into a violent psychosis with which he tortured his small sons on a regular basis.

Igor has many scars on his back, his ass, and his legs. His left arm, though still quite strong, will never match the strength of his right arm, because it was weakened after a particularly bad break he suffered at the age of six, at the hands of his paranoid, feverishly angry old man.

Karl was younger than Igor, and smaller. Though he certainly suffered his fair share of beatings, Igor was always careful to protect Karl. Sometimes he hid the boy in closets and bushes. Sometimes he sent him on long scavenger hunts around the neighborhood, hunts that kept the kid occupied until their dad's anger was spent. Sometimes Igor provoked his dad on purpose, taking the brunt of the old man's anger, saving Karl from the worst of it. Their father was a sadist, but not a discriminatory one; he would beat whatever was in his path.

But, like most child abusers, the old man was short-sighted and small-minded. He forgot that children grow up. And as Igor matured into a freakishly tall, strapping young man, he did not forget the many hurts he had suffered as a young boy. No, he did not.

Instead, he secretly learned to fight. First, he joined the school wrestling team and learned basic holds and grips and throws. He found a boxing club near his home, and there he honed his skills further. And finally, he was recruited to join a real, actual fight club, where he learned the dirtiest and most effective fighting techniques available.

He bided his time, steering clear of his father whenever possible, slinking around with the hunched shoulders and submissive posture of a whipped puppy. If his father noticed Igor's shiny new bulging muscles, he said nothing about them.

It was a late night when Igor emerged from his bedroom, hearing a loud banging coming from the living room. Still half asleep, he wandered in in his boxers, a sixteen-year-old boy, but already much larger than most men. Karl was away on a sleepover. Igor often arranged sleepovers for his brother when his dad went on a meth bender.

His dad was bashing holes into the wall with a hammer, a quick, steady stream of words emanating from him in a fast incoherent babble.

"Dad, could you not?"

The old man ignored Igor, continuing his work.

"Dad, what the hell are you doing? You're messing up the walls." Igor did not enjoy stating the obvious, but he could think of nothing better to say.

"DAD."

Finally the man turned and looked at his son, as if seeing him for the first time. His eyes widened, and he held the hammer out, pointing at Igor with it. "Why?"

"Why? Why what?"

"Why you want me to stop?"

"Because it's three in the fucking morning, Dad. I need to sleep."

"Yeah, I bet you do, I bet you need to sleep."

Igor sighed. "Yeah, Dad, I need to sleep. So can you cut it out, please?"

He spun around and threw the hammer at Igor, narrowly missing his head. Not missing a beat, he strode toward Igor and grabbed him by the throat. "You let the DTF in here, you little piece of shit? You the one who let them put all these wires and shit in here, spying on my every goddamn move? You're a traitor. A fucking worthless traitor, and I got your number you son of a bitch."

Igor could not breathe. He could feel the pressure building up in his face, painful and tight.

And that was the day Igor grew up.

He thrust a meaty fist directly into his dad's stomach, hard enough to knock the wind out of him, hard enough to crack a rib or two. His dad let go of his throat, and Igor breathed in gasps of sweet, sweet air. He didn't have time to overindulge, however, as his dad was already coming back for him, arms reaching to hurt him in some undefined way.

Igor would not allow that. Not anymore. He grabbed his dad's shoulders and neatly swept his feet out from under him, sending him flat on his back on the ground, gasping.

"You goddamn piece of—"

Igor had heard enough, and he kicked the old man in the side, to shut him up. Suddenly, every unkind word, every punch, every cut, every terrible thing his dad had ever done to him came rushing back to him. He remembered being a small, five-year-old child, crying and scared as the monster in the house devised new and horrifying ways to hurt him. He remembered when his dad set fire to the teddy bear his mom had given him; the last thing he had of hers. He remembered the time his dad had put him in the trunk of the car and threatened to drive it into the river, laughing as the small boy cried to be released, mocking him ruthlessly in the aftermath upon discovering that the boy had wet himself from fear.

He remembered all of that shit, and he was going to make his dad pay.

He reached for the hammer. In a nice story, this is where Igor would remember his humanity, and he would be the bigger man, leaving his father to think about what he'd done. In a nice story, Igor would have calmly set the hammer down next to his father, just to let him know that he *could* have hurt him if he'd wanted to, but that he was choosing the high road.

But Igor's story is not a nice story, and Igor pinned his father to the floor, took that hammer, whacked him in the side with it. Then he hit him in the arm. It was quick and efficient, and over so fast that Igor didn't feel entirely satisfied. It was the hammer, the hammer was too cold, too impersonal. He set it aside, and punched his dad in his sick, sadistic head. It was wonderful, a feeling of freedom he had never felt before.

He beat his dad unconscious that night. And even after he woke up and stayed on the floor for a full day, obviously very severely injured, moaning and swearing, Igor refused to call an ambulance. He left his father to suffer on the floor, in horrible pain. He was no doctor, but he guessed his dad had bruised ribs, a nasty concussion, and possibly some internal injuries. He was also missing his two front teeth. Igor did not care. He used his dad's temporary immobility to flush his crank down the toilet.

Karl came home from his sleepover, and Igor refused to let him in the front door. He told him to go stay at his friend Mike's house. Karl heard the moaning coming from inside the house and did as he was told. He did not ask questions.

When the old man's withdrawals started, he had trouble pulling himself to the bathroom, and he shat all over himself and the floor. Several times, during the worst of it, Igor nearly caved and called for medical help. But then, he would remember the time he'd had a stomach virus, and accidentally vomited on the carpet, and the old man had made him eat up every bit of that vomit with a spoon. Or he would remember being shot in the head with a BB gun, nearly losing his eye. He would remember these things, and then he would go on about his business, leaving his father to his own devices, only deigning to bring him glasses of water and crackers, to keep him alive.

Well, eventually the old man healed enough that he could get up and walk. Igor was nervous, expecting a terrible reprisal, and he slept with a knife under his bed, in anticipation of a sneak attack.

But the attack never came. In fact, the old man never laid a hand on Igor or Karl, ever again.

Igor's story is sad. He knows that. But the fighting skills he learned, and the rather terrifying ability to turn off his emotions entirely, will serve him well tonight, if necessary. Not only for the coup, but for what is coming before. The hardest part of all of this.

He is going to have to say goodbye to Elli.

One of the many strange symptoms of the virus is a heightened sense of smell. The virus hijacks the olfactory system and makes it hypersensitive to human odors—sweat, urine, hair, the oils on skin. An infected person can detect these odors—and many more—

with far greater accuracy and at much greater distances than the average human. Because of this, all rehabilitation centers focus on ways to deaden the sense of smell—air fresheners, incense, lavender sachets, things of that nature.

Igor does not like synthetic fragrances. They give him a headache. Instead, he gardens and presses wildflowers, preferring the natural scents of herbs and foliage. The problem is, those scents are not as strong as the nasty spray-bottle garbage, and so when he enters his small, cramped trailer after pruning the bonsai tree, he is overpowered by Elli's smell, so much stronger after spending time outdoors, in the fresh air.

His eyes dilate. His mouth fills with saliva. He should have prepared himself mentally for this, but his mind had been elsewhere. His pulse is faster than normal, he consciously breathes deeply to try to slow it down, but that does not help, for obvious reasons. He breathes through his mouth instead.

He goes to the sink and pours a bunch of dish soap into it, running water at full blast, filling his nostrils with lemony bubbles. That's good. Lemons are safe. Dish soap is safe. He breathes deeply and clears his head.

"I already did the dishes," says Elli, looking at him, puzzled.

Igor's heart sinks, hating himself for putting her in danger, just by existing. "That's good, Elli. Thank you."

He looks at her, sitting on his couch, watching some cartoon about a teenaged girl who turns into a superhero. She's so cute he can't stand it. And he almost ate her, like a goddamn monster in a fairy tale.

It sickens him, but it also galvanizes him, makes him feel better about what he needs to do.

"So, Elli? Tonight I'm taking you somewhere."

"Where?" She doesn't seem alarmed or upset. That's good.

"To a friend of mine. Her name is Helen, and she'll take good care of you." He doesn't like how his voice sounds, all wooden and robotic. Like he's fucking Siri or something.

"What do you mean, she'll take care of me?"

Now she looks concerned. Dammit.

He runs a hand through his hair. "Well, you know, you can't stay here much longer. It's illegal, for one thing. And also, you know I'm infected. I'm... not safe to be around."

Surprisingly, she grins at him. "Don't be stupid, Igor. You won't hurt me."

God this is hard. "Not on purpose I won't. Not ever. But, you know... sometimes people like me, we can't help it. Sometimes we do bad things, and we don't mean to. It's a sickness."

Elli is not grinning anymore. "You can stop yourself from doing bad things if you want to."

"I know, I know. But the thing is... there's maybe some bad things that are gonna happen soon. Those people who kidnapped you, they might come back for you. And I can't let them get you. I need to make sure you're safe, with a safe person who can take care of you."

"You take care of me!"

Now Elli is angry, pounding her little fists on her legs. Igor can't look her in the eyes.

"I do the best I can, but I'm not good with kids. Elli, I don't even have a spare room for you. Someday, you're gonna have to leave the house, go to school, get a job, all that. You can't do that if you're living here with me."

"Why not?" Elli is wailing, her eyes running tears.

"Because I'm not allowed to keep you, Honey." The term of

endearment slips from his mouth, without him consciously using it.

"But why?"

"Because it's against the law. It's the same reason your parents couldn't keep you, right? You need to stay with a safe person, someone who isn't infected. Do you understand?"

"No. I don't understand anything."

Igor sighs. "I know. It's hard. And believe me, if you could stay here, I would let you. You're a great kid. But you can't stay. And that's all there is to it."

Elli is shutting down now. She will not look at Igor. She will not talk anymore. She stares blankly at the TV, but she's clearly not watching it.

"Elli?"

She does not respond.

"Elli?"

Nothing.

Igor goes into his bedroom. The girl obviously wants him to leave her alone.

Igor peels Elli away from his chest, out of his trench coat, where she stayed hidden on the long, tense ride to Helen's condo. He'd half expected the girl to slide out of his grip and jump off the motorcycle, or to scream and make a fuss and draw attention to herself. Instead, she wept quietly, soaking the inside of his jacket with hot, steamy gasps and tears, which was much worse.

Helen's condo is in a brown building, large and modern, with white trim. It is perfectly ordinary, in a nice way. He spoke to her on the phone before coming over, to verify that she is home, but he did not tell her the real reason for his call. She is expecting him but does not know why.

Quickly, he carries Elli to her door, where he knocks twice with his unencumbered arm. She answers the door, and he can't help but smile. She is not in her usual boxy pantsuit or skirt suit, and her ugly shoes are nowhere to be seen. Instead, she is delightfully barefoot, wearing a snug tank top and tight, tight jeans. Her hair is piled on top of her head, with little curls springing out in places. She's wearing makeup, and her lips are plump and shiny. Through the open door, he can see that candles are lit on a coffee table. Shit. She must be expecting a boyfriend or somebody. Igor feels a clench of discomfort in his shoulders.

He swallows. He remembers the crying child in his arm. He looks at Helen's face and realizes that he's been ogling her body, completely missing the expression of shock on her face.

"I'm sorry Helen. Were you expecting someone?"

Her mouth opens and closes. She looks oddly hurt for some reason. She frowns, gesturing to Elli. "What's going on, Igor?"

"Right. Yeah. Can I come in? I'll explain."

She steps aside and lets him in. He is greeted with the sound of music. He listens for a few beats and identifies it as "Minor Swing" by Django Reinhardt. Excellent. Helen has good taste.

Elli stands next to the door, refusing to come any further into the room.

Helen ignores Igor now, and turns her attention to the girl. "Hey, sweetie. What's your name?"

"Elli," she sniffs.

"Looks like you've had a rough day. Can I get you something? Juice? A cookie?"

Elli shakes her head, still sad. But Igor feels better, seeing Helen's kindness to the girl. He's making the right decision.

"Let me get you a tissue, anyway, ok?" Without waiting for a response, Helen gets a box of tissues and brings them to the child. Only then does she look at Igor.

"Alright. Tell me."

He runs a hand through is hair, nervous. "I don't know where to begin."

The music and candlelight lure him into a soft state of mind. It makes it a little easier to talk.

"See, there's these guys, bad guys. And Elli needs protection from them."

Helen shakes her head. "What bad guys?"

"They're reformed cannibals who've fallen off the wagon. They want Elli. I can't keep her at my place. You know why. So I was hoping you could help her out."

Helen sits on a wooden chair opposite Igor and looks at him intently. "But why do they want her? Why this specific kid? That doesn't make any sense."

"I know it doesn't. And I'd tell you more if I could, but I'd like to keep you out of all this. All you need to know is, she's a nice kid, and she can't stay with me."

"Well why not take her back to her parents? Oh shit—I mean, shoot—" she glances at Elli, who is staring at her shoes. She whispers to Igor, "Are her parents the ones who are trying to hurt her?"

Igor shakes his head. "No, but they're infected. They can't have contact with her."

"Jesus," Helen presses her lips together, tense. "So these people—did you call the cops on them? Where are they? Who are they?"

Igor stands. "That's all the information I have for you, I'm afraid. Will you take care of Elli? Keep her safe?"

She shakes her head, lost. "I mean, I'll do the best I can, Igor but—"

"Good," he says, turning away. He needs to say goodbye to Elli now, before he loses his courage and wusses out.

"Elli," he goes to her and kneels down, so he's more or less at her eye level. "I just want to say that it's been great getting to know you. You're a good kid. If things were different—" his voice cracks, and he hates himself for this weakness.

Elli throws herself at him, wraps her frail little arms around his neck. "Please don't leave me here, Igor. I won't call you Igor anymore. I'll call you whatever you want. I'll call you—Mr. Hero Guy. Ok? I'll do all the dishes, and I'll be so quiet, all the time."

Now Igor is crying like a little bitch. He keeps his face away from Helen. He can't let her see him like this.

When he has composed himself, he stands up. Helen is watching them, arms crossed over her chest.

"Igor, can I speak to you in the kitchen, please?"

Igor hesitates for a moment, wanting to leave as soon as possible. But he nods his agreement.

Helen goes to Elli and gets her set up on the couch with the remote control and a glass of milk and a plate of Oreos. The child taken care of, the adults go into the kitchen.

CHAPTER SEVEN

Igor and Helen sit at the table. It's a small, light, wooden one, the kind you buy at IKEA when you're fresh out of college, furnishing your first place.

"Can I get you something to drink?"

"Tequila, if you have it," Igor smirks at her.

She rolls her eyes. "Very funny. Anyway, I don't have any. I'm a strict beer drinker."

"Actually, me too. I hate tequila. Had a bad experience. Though I think everyone has a bad tequila story. Usually from college."

"I don't."

"Really?"

"I went to a dry campus. BYU."

Igor processes this new information. "You're Mormon?"

She shrugs. "Not anymore." She looks ashamed, like she admitted to not brushing her teeth anymore, or not using toilet paper anymore.

"Water is fine," he tells her. She grabs a glass for each of them and sits down with him.

"You need to be straight with me," Helen says, leaning forward onto her forearms. "How did you find that little girl?"

"I can't tell you that."

"And why didn't you go to the police?"

"I can't tell you that either."

She sits back in her chair and folds her arms over her chest. "I'm disappointed. I thought maybe you just didn't want to talk in front of the girl. But now I can see you just don't trust me."

Igor says nothing. This makes Helen more upset, and her face shows it.

"You know, I got into this job because I think it's the best thing for the infected. I want to make sure you guys are able to live on your own, not in prisons or camps or whatever. I want to see you—people like you—succeed and do well once you get out of rehab."

"Okay..."

"My point is, I'm not the enemy, Igor. God, what do I have to do to convince you? Remember when I found that can of tuna in your cupboard?"

"Oh God, not this again." Igor closes his eyes.

"See, that's what I mean!" Helen looks ready to tear out her hair. "You act like I'm the bad guy. But did I turn you into the police for having contraband in your house? No. Did I write you up? No. All I did was give you a little lecture, and you act like I'm some psycho tuna nazi. I've tried so hard..." She breaks off, biting her lip. "You know, when you called today and asked if you could come over, I thought..."

Igor looks at her, amazed. He has never seen her express any real emotion before. She's always been so guarded and grim and nervous. This strange and startling bit of vulnerability is both off-putting and charming.

He reaches out, intending to pat her hand, but retrieves it at the last minute. She won't want him to touch her. "Hey. Hey. You're not a tuna nazi. I never meant to imply that you were. But you have a job to do, and I respect that. I don't want to get you involved in anything that might hurt you. You're a good person, a nice person. The less you know about some things, the better."

"Ok, but how am I supposed to explain to people that I've got a little girl in my house? What am I supposed to tell them? That I took her in off the streets? That she's hiding from the mafia? What?"

Igor shrugs. "Sure. If that's what you want to tell them. It doesn't matter much, as long as she's safe. If you can't keep her yourself, I'm sure you have connections; you can get her into a nice home with a nice family somewhere. She's not infected."

Helen's mouth gapes. "So you've been running around with an uninfected child? Are you for real? Do you know how much trouble you could get in for that?"

"That's why I brought her here!" His voice is louder than he wants it to be. He breathes deep. "Look. According to basically all of society I'm a danger to that girl. And hell, maybe they're right. But that doesn't mean I don't want her to be safe. And I might not be around here much longer to make sure she is."

"What do you mean you won't be around? What are you talking about?"

Igor sighs. This is harder than he'd thought it would be. "I have a thing to do. I'm pretty sure it's all going to be fine, but it might not be. I might make some people really pissed at me. And if that happens, I'll need to leave town for a while."

Helen throws her hands up in the air and shakes them around in frustration. "And that's all you'll tell me about what's going on?"

"Correct."

"And you won't call the police?"

"No."

"Well, what if I call the police?"

Igor looks Helen in the eyes, pleading and dark. "I'm asking you to keep the police out of this. Without knowing why. I'm asking you to trust me."

"You understand that I'm your caseworker, right? I'm assigned to keep tabs on you, and report on your health and activities. What am I supposed to tell my boss if you skip town? That you vanished into thin air?"

He nods. "Actually, that would be fine. Just tell them the truth. You don't know where I am."

Cannibal disappearances are treated much in the same manner as missing children. A dispatch will be sent out, alerting the community that an infected person is unaccounted for. His picture will be sent around from person to person, his picture put up on walls and bulletin boards. People will be on the lookout for him.

He would like to ask Helen to lie for him; to say that he'd gone to visit an ailing relative, or taken a vacation to Hawaii. But of course, cannibals cannot travel outside their designated towns without a government-issued permit, so that lie would never hold up to any kind of scrutiny. Maybe she could tell them that Igor was dead? No. Igor does not want to ask Helen to lie, at all, for any reason. He will have to take his chances, and hope nobody looks for him too hard.

Helen looks back at him for a long time. She seems to sense his internal struggle. Finally, she exhales. "Alright, Igor. I'll keep the police out of it. And I won't tell my boss about any of this. But you better not make me regret it."

He shakes his head and stands up. "I won't."

"You know, this whole situation is pretty fucked up," she mumbles, looking down at the table.

"I know, and I'm sorry. I know it's a lot to ask of you, to take care of her, with no warning like this."

She waves a hand. "I don't mean the kid. I mean, this whole situation with the virus. Like, we have this whole segment of society that is basically infantilized. You're kept in tightly watched communities. You're monitored. We tell you what you can eat and what you can watch on TV. You aren't allowed around kids. You don't have jobs; we all take care of you, the taxpayers, I mean. But you're not children." She glances up at him, looking him in the face. "It makes me sick inside most of the time. All this wasted potential I see in you guys, every day. But, then again, sometimes one of you goes and eats somebody's face, and then all this babysitting makes sense."

She peers into his eyes, searching. "Is it wrong, what we do? Monitoring you all, like kids? I mean, I would hate being treated the way you all are treated. But then again, we can't just let you run around biting people and eating their bodies, right?"

Igor's mouth opens, unsure what to say. Finally, he croaks, "I don't know."

"Right?!" Helen slams her palms into the table. "Right?! I don't know either. What are we supposed to do? What's the answer?"

Igor is silent for a moment. "I don't have an answer. Not yet."

And then he turns and leaves.

Faith's guys are dressed all in black, with bank-robber face masks. They look like legit ninjas, and Igor is both impressed and amused. His own black T-shirt and jeans look less than polished in comparison. He wonders why they felt the need to dress like this, just to threaten a bunch of cult members with zoning laws. He guesses it must be for dramatic effect.

None of the ninjas speak, which is just fine with Igor.

Faith does not want Igor there, would prefer to handle all of this herself, with her men. But Igor has insisted. After all, this is all happening because of him. He is responsible for the outcome, and because of that, he needs to be responsible for the execution.

It is nearly impossible for a cannibal to get a gun. It's illegal to purchase one through above-ground channels, of course, and the underground channels are mostly peopled with the uninfected, who, perhaps fairly, are not comfortable weaponizing man-eaters. All too often, a reformed cannibal relapses, and when he does, any illegal items found in his home will be seized, catalogued, and probably traced back to the source. Not good for business.

Because of this, Igor is limited to knives and bear spray. His ninja accomplices, however, are not so constrained, and he can see the glint of metal flashing from the odd hip and boot. He worries that they look too combative, that it will immediately put the Runners on edge, and make them more likely to fight.

"Hey guys? Maybe we should leave some of these weapons. Or like, hide them a little better. We don't want them to think we're there to attack them."

The ninjas ignore him, which is annoying. Though, he supposes, they might be right. Maybe it's better for the Moonlight Runners to see that they mean business, that they're not to be fucked with.

The plan is simple. Igor has already identified Karl, and Faith has distributed a picture of him to all her ninjas, a fairly good one found on the internet. As the leader, Karl is the main target. They will seize Karl and tell him he is in violation of Zoning

Code Whatever, and that he and his cult members must disband, immediately. If Karl refuses to cooperate and disband the Moonlight Runners... then they will threaten him with the police. An empty threat, but an effective one. If he still refuses... they will forcibly remove the cannibals from the teepees and set the shelters on fire. They will destroy any and all rations and munitions.

Igor is certain it will not come to that. He might not approve of Karl's recent activities, but he knows that deep down, Karl is a reasonable man. He doesn't want to go to prison. He doesn't want to die. He just wants to live free. Igor is fine with that. Just not if that freedom involves kidnapping and eating children.

He smells cooking human meat, and it is pure torture. He is unsure if he can commit violence while surrounded by that delectable smell and still maintain his abstinence. In a moment of frenzy, he might slip up and bite somebody. And if he bites somebody, it will all be over for him. He hopes very much that everyone can just be reasonable.

He looks at the ninjas. None of them are infected, he's sure. Faith Gregory wouldn't voluntarily work with cannibals, her son's condition notwithstanding. They can't possibly understand the hunger roiling around in his stomach, the way his pulse is popping in his neck, how his mouth is a sack of saliva. And he can't explain it to them. They would only be disgusted. It's amazing they've even allowed him to be part of this.

Igor hasn't eaten human meat since the incident in the lab. Back when he was working on his PhD in microbiology, studying under the illustrious Dr. Jesse Tran.

He'd become infected accidentally, by sipping the wrong drink at a party. The most efficient way to infect someone with the virus is a deep, skin-breaking bite, because the saliva goes directly into the bloodstream, but a healthy amount of backwash will do the trick, if ingested. Unfortunately for Igor, he drank most of the beverage in question before realizing his error. He'd found his own drink, also in a red solo cup, where he suddenly remembered leaving it, next to the television set. Looking down at the cup he'd been drinking from in horror, he'd thrown it out immediately.

Still, he hadn't been too worried. After all, what were the chances that the original cup owner was infected? Surely, cannibals weren't so careless as to leave their unfinished drinks lying around on tables, unattended. Nobody would be so thoughtless.

But somebody was that thoughtless, and within three days, Igor began experiencing symptoms. The reduced body temperature, the heightened sense of smell. And finally, the cravings.

Igor believed himself to be a rational, solid man, with reserves of self-control. He realized he was infected, and he was upset about it. But he truly believed that with determination and good common-sense, he could keep himself abstinent and stick to a socially acceptable diet.

But a microbiology lab, located in a medical school, is not an ideal place for a freshly infected cannibal to practice his self-mastery. It was a bit like teaching a toddler to read using Karl Marx's *Das Kapital.* He was in over his head.

The cadaver lab was often unattended, and Igor often worked late into the night, long after everyone had gone home for the evening. If the bodies had been embalmed, it wouldn't have been so difficult to resist. The smell of an embalmed body was off, sort of like bacon dipped in gasoline. Not very appetizing, even though you know there's bacon in there somewhere.

But when the bodies came in fresh... that was the tricky part.

To Igor's credit, he avoided the lab when he could. He avoided contact with people in general, living or dead, as much as he was able. It was safer that way. Still, there were nights when he was alone, and the odor from the bodies was so strong, it overwhelmed him, and he was forced to stick his head out the window for relief.

One night, he slipped up.

The body was fresh, of course. That intoxicating, pungent smell rolled into him, sneaking in under his closed door, tickling his nostrils, calling to him.

There was nobody there to stop him.

And after all, the body was dead. He wasn't hurting anybody. He wouldn't take all the body, just a bit, just the tiniest bit, to satisfy his massive hunger. That's all he needed. Just a taste.

He carved a small, thin, minute-steak sized slice from the man's buttock. He brought it back to his lab and turned on the Bunsen burner. He roasted it, using test tube tongs, turning it this way and that as the fat sizzled and dripped. And when at last he placed the delicate morsel into his waiting mouth, it was like God had exploded on his tongue. It was better than the best orgasm. It was tastier than a thousand cakes. It was the greatest thing he had ever experienced.

Until it was gone, and all that was left was the crushing guilt, and a craving for more.

He vowed it would be the last time. Never again. He was done with that life. He would never set foot in the cadaver lab, not if his life depended on it.

His resolve lasted two days.

It wasn't long before someone noticed that pieces were missing from the cadavers. Igor never took much, but still, it wasn't the kind of thing that could stay hidden for long. Of course, nobody knew who had done it, but everyone knew it was a cannibal.

Questions were asked. The idea of mandatory cannibalism testing was floated, and dismissed as a violation of privacy. Instead, the university put up cameras in the cadaver lab, in the hopes of catching the flesh-eater in the act, or at least deterring him from trying it again.

And it did deter Igor. For a while. But eventually he was so hungry and out of control that he lost his head and entered the lab anyway. He'd disguised himself with a wig and a hat, and though this was in the time before the facial tattoo, he was still Igor, tall and muscular and obvious.

The hearing had been quick and easy. He'd been dismissed from the program and sent on his way. Fortunately, the school had declined to press criminal charges, so he had that to be grateful for, but all the same, it was, at that time, the lowest point in his adult life.

Of course, things would get much, much worse, but he didn't know that then.

Igor thinks of these things as he waits to confront the Moonlight Runners. He remembers the Bunsen burner and the taste of flesh, and he smells the meat roasting down below. He clutches his bear spray. If he uses his bear spray, he won't have to touch anyone, and if he doesn't have to touch anyone, he can't bite anyone. And if he can't bite anyone, he won't relapse.

He holds his bear spray to his chest, clutching it tightly like a talisman. In a way, it is a talisman. He is counting on it to keep him safe.

The head ninja gives the hand signal. It's time to go.

As they creep closer to the camp, the scents grow stronger. Now there's a faint sickly tinge to the meat, vaguely gangrenous and very unwholesome. The ninjas don't seem to notice, intent on their mission, eyes forward.

Igor knows which teepee is Karl's. He saw the leader go into his home earlier in the evening, and he has yet to reemerge. There are no prisoners that Igor has seen, but he will keep his eyes and ears open, just in case.

They are close now, close enough to be seen, if anyone looks. But Igor and the ninjas are stealthy and graceful on their feet. Nobody hears them approach.

Karl's teepee is quiet. Igor thinks maybe the leader is resting, or reading by flashlight. He was always a big reader, always staying up late to finish whatever book he had. The entrance is blocked by a thick quilt.

"HEY!"

Igor has been spotted in the process of lifting the quilt. That's not good.

Slowly, he turns around and sees his old friend Nevin. He is still short, and still angry.

Igor holds his hands up in a placating gesture. "Hey, just coming to visit. Nothing to—"

There is a soft thud as something is brought down on Nevin's head, and the short man crumples to the ground, unconscious. At least, Igor hopes he's merely unconscious, and not dead.

One of the ninjas, standing behind Nevin's crumpled body, gives Igor a quick thumbs up and reholsters his gun.

Jesus. This isn't how it's supposed to go. Igor is supposed to get Karl, take him aside, make him see reason, disband the group.

But all around him, ninjas are attacking, slipping into teepees, dragging people out by their hair. A few who had been gathered around one of the fires try to run away, but ninjas seize them, dragging them away under their armpits.

"HEY! Not like this!" Igor's shout is loud and commanding, but the ninjas don't give a shit, and the Runners are too scared to care.

Igor needs to stop this. He needs to get everybody calmed down.

"Karl," Igor reaches into Karl's teepee and pokes the sleeping man. "Karl, come out here. We need your help."

Karl is obviously unwell. He smells like eight kinds of death, and all he does is moan in response to Igor's plea. Shit. Igor knows, of course, that his brother suffers from Crohn's disease. But it was easy to forget, when he was in remission.

Apparently, remission is over.

Exasperated, Igor leaves Karl alone. He can't be reasoned with when he's sick like this. He'll have to figure something else out.

The ninjas are now setting fire to things. One of them is pouring a jug of gasoline onto a picnic bench, while another holds a lighter.

"NO!" Igor runs to them, knocking them both down. But the bench is already on fire, roaring and angry.

He grabs the closest ninja by the shirt. "Why are you doing this? This isn't how it's supposed to go."

The voice that answers him is calm and a little condescending. "No. This isn't how *you* wanted it to go."

Igor releases the man, disgusted.

The ninjas have lined the cannibals up in rows, close to the riverbank. It's easy to see them and their terrified expressions with all the new fires springing up everywhere. The air is a few degrees warmer, and it's getting harder to breathe.

Igor heads to where the people are assembled, meaning to talk to them, though he's not sure what exactly he's planning to say or do.

As he approaches, there is a loud BANG, and one of the cannibals falls over.

Screams echo all through Moonlight Run, and Igor runs to the fallen victim.

There is another bang. And another. Igor realizes now why the ninjas made the Runners line up. It's a firing squad. They are going to execute each and every one of them here tonight. Right now.

Before he can change his mind or consider the stupidity of his plan, he jumps on top of the flaming bench and screams his loudest, most primal scream.

"RUN! RUUUUUN!"

His clothes are on fire now, of course, and he runs directly into the river to extinguish the flames. He shouts "RUN" the entire way.

It was idiotic, what he did, and as he smells his own burnt clothing and hair and skin, he regrets it deeply. However, it was effective, and now infected are running everywhere, in a mad scramble, like bugs when you lift a rock off of them.

The ninjas act quickly, shooting whoever they can. There are gut-wrenching thuds and screams and bangs, and Igor knows that some of those shots are successful. He emerges from the water, soaking and hurting, and very unsure what to do.

Karl has stumbled out of his teepee, and he spots Igor dragging his feet over the rocks, like some terrible burnt swamp thing. He calls to him.

"Igor?"

Igor doesn't know what to say. Should he apologize? Explain that it wasn't supposed to be like this? What is there to say?

He takes a few steps closer to Karl. His movements are slow and painful.

Arms grab him from behind. A knife is at his throat.

"You didn't think you were getting out of here alive, did you, biter boy?"

One of the ninjas is attacking him, and Igor realizes all at once how deeply, profoundly stupid he has been.

He twists out of the ninja's grip and judo flips him onto the ground. He lifts his steel-toed boot and stomps the ninja into the rocks, crushing his face into pulp. It is fast, and it is brutal, and it is efficient. His ankle throbs and his breathing is fast.

Karl watches, his face a strange mixture of sickness and confusion and excitement.

"Karl," Igor croaks. "I didn't mean any of this. You gotta know, it wasn't—"

"You best get out of here now, Igor," Karl's voice is strangely calm, his eyes twinkling with demonic lights. "You'd better go now."

"Let me explain."

"There'll be time for that later. Trust me."

Two ninjas see Karl and grab him. Another sees Igor and the dead ninja under his boot and takes out his gun, meaning to shoot.

Skin bubbling, clothes wet and sooty, and full of a terrible, all-consuming guilt, Igor runs.

CHAPTER EIGHT

The GI tract of a cannibal is especially twitchy. It's one of the side effects of the virus. Stress, unusual foods and drinks, high altitudes, and any number of things can cause intense stomach distress.

As it turns out, murdering a ninja is one of those things, and Igor is sicker than he's been in ages by the time he gets back to his trailer. Walking is agony. Speaking is out of the question. He rummages in his medicine cabinet for some kind of remedy, finds an old container of Tums, and chews a handful of them, wincing at the flavor, hating the repulsive feel of chalk melting on his tongue.

That chore handled, he now has to get out of town. Karl saw him. Karl knows he was involved in this raid, one way or another. The ninjas know that Igor killed one of their men. He knows they won't go to the police, given the nature of their activities at the time of thc killing—but he doubts they are the sort to turn the other cheek and let Igor go on about his merry business.

The Moonlight Runners and Mothers Against the Cannibal Takeover are now out to get him, with certainty. He is extra glad that he had the foresight to take Elli to Helen's. He is glad he got at least one thing right in all this mess.

He throws some clothes and deodorant into a duffel bag. He has a bit of cash stored in a shoebox under his bed; he adds that to the bag as well. He can't pack much, or he'll make the guards suspicious. He is not allowed to travel.

Where should he go? Canada? Mexico? He no longer has a passport, because the infected are not allowed to travel internationally, so those are not good options, unless he wants to border jump, which he does not. He wishes he'd had the forethought to get one of those fake IDs that Jud was always saying were so necessary in "this climate."

He thinks of Jud, locked up in a jail cell, all because Igor wanted some goddamn groceries, and he feels even sicker. He clutches his abdomen, runs to the bathroom and vomits up bile and a few bits of undigested beef jerky. Is there anything he doesn't fuck up? Is there anyone who is safe from him?

He thinks of Elli and Helen, cozy in their little condo, probably watching a movie and eating popcorn together. He has no idea if this is true or not, but it could be, and the thought soothes him. His girls are safe.

He realizes he is thinking of them as "his girls" when he has absolutely no right to do so, but he doesn't dwell on it.

His grandfather's wedding ring is around somewhere. He has no sentimental attachment to it; he'd never known his grandfather, after all, but he would like to find it before he leaves. He might be able to sell it, or trade it, if it comes down to that. Where did he put it?

It's not in any of the drawers or hiding under the pile of junk mail on the counter. He slides aside books and peeks into closets. He is rummaging around behind the couch when his fingers connect with a piece of paper. He pulls it out into the light of the trailer, curious.

Igor,

I don't know why you aren't answering my emails...

And just like that, Igor knows where he is going to go.

Igor waits in the bus station, watching the communal television set, blasting the news. He has always wondered why public televisions are so often set to news stations, as if that were the most inoffensive, crowd-pleasing option.

Everything smells musty and old, and none of his fellow travelers look happy to be there. They mostly look homeless and hopeless. Bus travel is not a popular option these days; not after several people claimed to have been infected after bus trips. Of course, the virus isn't transmitted that way, but the rumors were enough to damage the bus industry. As a result, buses are the last remaining mode of transport that does not check ID.

Igor does not want his ID to be checked. Nor does he want people to see him on his motorcycle, driving out of town. Igor wants to be as inconspicuous as possible for a man of his size and skin choices. He pulls the hood of his sweatshirt over his head tightly, obscuring as much of his face as he can. He adds some sunglasses for good measure.

The news anchor is a middle-aged woman with a blond bob and red lips. "And in other news, a local infected man, Doug Erickson, has been arrested on charges of murder, conspiracy to commit murder and kidnapping. Sources say that Mr. Erickson had been running a 'Santa training school' to train unemployed and underemployed men to work as mall Santas. Posing as a non-profit, he lured dozens of unsuspecting men into his classes... only to kill them and consume their body parts."

A fat woman in a white tank top cries on screen. "I told Henry that this wasn't a good idea, that he should just go back to school. But he'd always loved kids, always loved Christmas. He thought it'd be a good way to make a little extra money for the holidays. And now look. Just look what happened to him."

The news anchor shakes her head, looking grim. "Authorities say that Erickson had no criminal history and was not living in a surveilled community."

"I didn't even know he was infected," says a young man in a baseball cap. "Lived next door to him all those months and I had no idea. Not that those people advertise it, you know."

The news anchor is back. "This is the latest in a string of scams intended to lure in the disenfranchised and use them for meat. Some politicians are now saying that the laws we have in place are not enough."

The mayor flashes on the screen now, large belly pushing against the podium in front of him, patchy beard climbing over his red cheeks. "It is clear that we live in dangerous times. And I, for one, believe it is our duty as public servants to act as necessary to protect our families, and our children. That is why I am introducing a new city ordinance that requires blood testing for all of our citizens in order to receive or use public services."

He looks directly into the camera now, glaring. Igor feels like he is glaring directly at him. "For those of you who feel you can hide from justice, who feel you can sneak around our community and harm the good people of this town, doing whatever you please, I say to you this—not on my watch."

There are cheers from the crowd who have come to watch the mayor speak.

The news anchor is back, but she has moved on to another story now.

Igor looks around at his fellow travelers. An older woman with a wheeled suitcase, wearing a thick puffy jacket and a knit beanie, despite the warm temperature. A lazy-eyed, scratchy looking man who is clearly nodding off due to some recent opiate use. A pair of young kids, dressed in black, looking surly and mean, peering at their phones.

Any of these people might have been Erickson's victims. Or, if not Erickson, someone like him. The news was full of stories like the one he'd just heard: con artists, cults, crazed violent rampages. The details change, but the story is always the same. Cannibals are dangerous. Cannibals must be contained. Cannibals must be punished. Cannibals cannot be allowed to live among decent, good, uninfected people.

Normally, this sentiment frustrated Igor. After all, why should he be blamed for the actions of a few bad apples?

But now, all Igor has to do is remember the crunch of ninja skull under his boot, and he can't summon even the tiniest bit of offended outrage. Igor *is* dangerous. Igor *does* need to be contained.

He thinks about his destination, the home of Dr. Jesse Tran. If, by some miracle, she is actually on to something, Igor is willing to offer his services. He will just have to exercise extreme caution around any human body parts. And if it doesn't work out, Igor is prepared to do what needs to be done. He will turn himself in to the police, and never look back. He does not want to go to prison, but it's the only option.

Igor is dangerous. Igor must be contained. Igor cannot be allowed to live among good, decent, uninfected people.

Jesse Tran's house should be hideous, but it isn't. In fact, it's exquisitely beautiful. A classic Victorian confection, painted in various bright colors, it resembles a giant, inedible cake, with curving shingles, turrets, and a large, wrap-around porch, looking for all the world like a cake stand.

The door knocker is an oddly creepy one, a wolf's head with a vaguely pornographic tongue lolling out of its mouth. Igor pinches the tongue between his thumb and first finger and gives it a rap.

It's not long before a man answers the door. He is six feet tall, and solidly built. His hair is silver and slicked back away from his face. His beard is white against tanned, leathery skin. Eyes twinkle up at Igor. Igor has not been twinkled at in a very, very long time.

The man extends his hand. "Igor Fenenko! We were hoping you'd come by. I am Esteban Zappa, and you are very welcome. Come in, come in!"

Esteban Zappa did not react to Igor's appearance with fear or disgust.

Esteban Zappa is already walking back into the house, though walking is too tame a word for what he is doing. Esteban Zappa is striding manfully into his lair, and for the first time since reaching adulthood, Igor feels like a little boy, trailing along after the grownup. It is unsettling, but after his ordeal, not entirely unwelcome.

"The laboratory is in the basement. I know, such a cliche, to have an underground laboratory, but frankly, there is no better place for it. It is quiet, large enough to contain all of the necessary equipment, and of course, private."

"How do you know who I am?" Igor asks.

"Ah. Jesse told me she had invited her former protege to assist us, and, well. We do not have many visitors who fit your description."

"Right."

Esteban Zappa stops walking and turns to Igor. "I feel I must warn you that much of our research and many of our methodologies are... unorthodox. And not entirely legal. Rather, they exist in a murky legal gray area. If you are uncomfortable with any of this, you must let us know right away, and we will discuss it."

Igor nods, unsure what to say. He needs to see the lab before he knows if he will be comfortable with it or not.

"Excellent. Come with me."

The stairway leading to the basement is dark, and the wooden stairs are creaky beneath their feet. The wood is fragrant in the way that old houses are always fragrant—warm, spicy and well-loved.

"So, how do you know Dr. Tran?" Igor asks.

Esteban Zappa chuckles a little. "Ah. We met at Harvard University."

"Oh, I see."

"We were doing research on the underground lizard colony. I don't need to tell you that such intense conditions forge intense friendships. Together we have done much important research. She is a truly brilliant and luxuriously inventive woman."

They reach the bottom of the stairs, and Igor shivers a little. It's much colder under the house, which is to be expected. As the lights flicker on, he looks around. Tables and test tubes and glass tanks and computers are set up everywhere. Sinks and flashing lights and charts on the walls. A life-sized model of the skeletal system stands in a corner. For some reason, it is wearing a unicorn horn on its forehead.

Igor's eyes light on the microscope and his jaw drops. He walks to it in a trance. He reaches out a hand to touch it, then draws back. Surely, he will not be allowed to touch it.

"Is this a high-resolution TEM?" His voice is reverent. His eyes do not move from the gorgeous piece of equipment before him.

"It is," says a woman's voice.

Igor whirls around and sees Dr. Jesse Tran, standing in the doorway. Short, with a neat black bob, in neat black clothes, she is exactly as Igor remembered her .

"Dr. Tran!"

Igor grins wider than he's grinned in a long time.

Dr. Tran smiles back and strides to him, wrapping him as best she can in a small-armed hug.

Igor is unexpectedly moved by the sudden physical contact. He supposed he thought Dr. Tran would be afraid of him. But she clearly isn't, and the relief is an expansive, warm feeling coursing through his lungs.

"It's so good to see you again, Igor," says Dr. Tran.

"You, too."

"And you've met Esteban Zappa."

"Yes."

"Great!"

"Dr. Tran—"

"Jesse."

"Oh, ok. Jesse. How the fuck did you get a high-resolution TEM? These are crazy expensive. I've never heard of anyone having one in their house."

"Yes, well. I have my resources."

Igor turns and looks at Esteban Zappa carefully. Then he looks at Jesse again. Are they up to some sketchy black-market shit?

He suddenly decides he doesn't care. Igor wants to work in this lab, more than he's wanted anything in his life. He wants to find a cure for the virus. He wants to save the world.

CHAPTER NINE

Igor's room is comfortable and lovely in an exotic, disturbing way. There is a rug made of some kind of brightly colored woven rubber next to the bed. The walls are adorned with taxidermized alligators—three of them.

He'd asked Esteban Zappa about the alligators, and the man had replied that he had, at one time, been employed to rid the New York City sewers of alligators and had helped himself to some of the carcasses, choosing to have them stuffed, rather than consign them to the crematory at the local pet hospital.

"Alligators are noble creatures. And though these few had the misfortune to find themselves inhabiting a most unsanitary and undignified domicile, they maintained their inherent worth, as fearsome and interesting animals."

Jesse had nodded enthusiastically, and Igor wondered if many scientists worked with underground lizards as a side gig, and why.

He had nodded politely, but in truth, he was a bit grossed out that sewer lizards were stuck on his walls. He hoped they'd been washed thoroughly before they'd been mounted.

Still, he couldn't complain. The room had its own adjoining

bathroom, with a shower nozzle that was high enough for Igor to fit underneath it comfortably, which was a luxury not often afforded to men of his height. There were no televisions in the house, but the library was extensive, and as promised, Igor was allowed to borrow anything he wished.

Jesse Tran's "cooking adventures" turned out to be gourmet culinary feasts, the likes of which Igor had only ever tasted in the very occasional fancy restaurant.

"At one time, I wanted to be a professional chef," she explained. "I actually trained in France for a while, until my lover and I had a falling out, and I was forced to take measures." Her eyes went dark and faraway, and she stood silently in the kitchen, holding her knife aloft. She did not explain what she meant by "take measures" and Igor did not care to ask.

Best of all, most important of all, there was the work. Igor hadn't felt professionally fulfilled since the lab incident, and it was good to flex his mental muscles again. It had been far too long.

Esteban Zappa and Jesse were indeed very close to a breakthrough, and as Igor reviewed all the data, he grew more and more excited about the very real possibility of a cure. A cure for the virus.

And so now, Igor spends his days in Esteban Zappa's home, eating scrumptious meals, and doing real, important work. There is only one problem.

The bed.

There is nothing wrong with the bed, exactly. In fact, it is a huge, beautiful bed, carved from oak, complete with soft quilts and fluffy pillows. But ever since the incident with the girl, Igor has not allowed himself to sleep in a large bed. The temptation to fill it with another person is far too strong. Igor does not like to sleep alone. He is a cuddler and sleeps best with a body close to him.

After the incident with the girl, and his subsequent stay in rehab, he'd thrown out his old bed and purchased a slim twin bed, large enough for him alone, and not even him, as his feet dangled off the edge of the mattress. Any time he was tempted to bring a woman to bed, he reminded himself that there was no room for her; no woman would agree to sleep in his tiny bed, squeezed up against the wall, or dangling precariously over the edge.

His bed in Esteban Zappa's home is huge. It is inviting. Any woman would be pleased to sleep in it, if she could get past the creepy sewer alligators staring at her.

He remembers the woman. It was the week after his dismissal from the lab. His tattoo was healed up, and he had not stopped drinking in any serious way since his last day at work. He was desperate to do anything he could to ease his pain and sadness and despair. Taking a woman home would be a perfect, if temporary, solution.

He'd picked her up at a bar. He'd found a bad girl, smacking gum, wearing too much eyeliner and too few items of clothing. He could tell she liked his tattoo, liked his muscles. It had been easy to get her to hop on his motorcycle, easy to get her in bed. So easy.

Of course, he would not kiss her. Even in his drunken, desperate state, he'd been principled enough to refrain from that. In fact, ever since the virus, most casual sex was kiss-free. Kiss-free sex was the new equivalent of condom use. Once, people had worried about genital sores. Then, they'd worried about broken immune systems. Now, they worried about becoming cannibals.

Still, even without kissing, they could still have a good time.

And they did. Until they didn't.

Igor will never forget the poor woman's screams as she ran naked from his apartment, streaking down the hall, blood beaded on her pretty leg, while neighbors poked their heads out of doors, and cell phones were retrieved from pockets.

When the police came, Igor hadn't put up any resistance. He was too shell-shocked, too horrified to defend himself. And what defense could there be? He'd lost control of himself. And now that poor woman was infected, if she hadn't been before. It was all his fault.

He reclines uncomfortably in his comfortable, large bed. He gathers some pillows to himself and wraps his arms around them, taking comfort in their softness and their bulk.

The alligators stare at him with judgmental, beady eyes.

"Fuck you," he mutters to them.

He tries to sleep.

Igor wakes to the smells of butter and baking bread and rich, roasting coffee. A gentle, tinkling laugh wafts up the stairs. Intrigued and hungry, Igor gets out of bed and heads downstairs.

In the kitchen, Jesse is sautéing onions and garlic in a pan. She adds a dash of dried red chili flakes and tosses them expertly to mix. Esteban Zappa is squeezing oranges, making orange juice.

Two stunning women in their fifties sit at the breakfast bar, watching their hosts work. They are each wearing one of Esteban Zappa's dress shirts, bare legs extending from underneath, warm and soft looking on the wooden chairs.

"Ladies, the secret to a truly magnificent breakfast is butter." Jesse adds an extra dollop to the sauté pan and it sizzles enticingly.

Lady number one inhales and moans. "God, that smells good." Her braids sway gently as she leans toward the food. Jesse pulls playfully on one of the braids and uses it to move her face closer, and she plants a kiss on her lips.

"Seriously," says Lady Number Two, a redhead with a fresh, freckled face. Her legs are almost the same shade as the shirt she's wearing, creamy and white.

Igor moves a little closer, but says nothing, unsure what the etiquette is in this situation.

"Ah, Igor, welcome! Dr. Dayton, Dr. Ellis, this is my trusted assistant and lodger, Igor Fenenko."

The women turn around in their chairs to greet the newcomer and gasp. Igor stifles the urge to roll his eyes—barely. Yes, he has a tattoo on his face. Yes, he is large.

"Nice to meet you."

Lady Number One—Dr. Dayton—regains her composure first. "Esteban Zappa and Dr. Tran have been telling us a little about your research. It sounds fascinating."

"Is it true that you may be on the precipice of a cure for *Pestis Manducans*?"

Igor nods, uncertain. Is it safe to tell these women what they've been up to? It must be, or they wouldn't have invited them here and told them all about it. But then again, the dick wants what the dick wants. And the pussy too, he imagines.

"Doctors Dayton and Ellis work in the oncology lab at University Hospital," Esteban Zappa explains.

"We do," says Dr. Ellis. "And... we understand the constraints you're working under. And we're happy to help."

Igor tilts his head. He had no idea what the woman is talking about.

"Doctors Dayton and Ellis have kindly agreed to procure some tissue samples for us," explains Jesse.

Igor's eyes widen and he almost jumps. For this latest experiment, they are desperately in need of human tissue samples, particularly samples with inactive or severely weakened immune systems. Tissue that has been exposed to chemotherapy would be perfect.

"Wow, I—thank you!"

"No need to thank us," says Dr. Ellis. "We like to think we're doing our part to save the world." She looks at Esteban Zappa from dilated pupils, licking her lips slightly. Igor recognizes the look.

There's so much food in the kitchen. So much sexual energy. So much talk of human tissue specimens.

Igor's mouth is a swamp of longing and saliva. And then his brain is a swamp of worry about how he'll handle himself around the specimens. He hopes Jesse and Esteban Zappa will handle them, removing the temptation. If not... maybe he'll have them gag him while he works.

Esteban Zappa sets down his oranges and moves to Dr. Ellis. He leans in and kisses her, deeply. He stops, as if realizing his rudeness, and turns to Dr. Dayton and gives her an equally long kiss, with the distinction of her biting his lip playfully as he pulls away.

"Ladies, perhaps we can save breakfast for later. I've always preferred brunch to breakfast, anyhow."

The doctors giggle like silly sorority girls, Jesse included, and they all get up and run—yes, run—out of the kitchen.

Igor sighs. This is going to be a long-ass day.

He helps himself to some toast and heads down to the lab.

Dear Helen,

I hope everything is going well with Elli and all that. I can't tell you where I am exactly, but you can write to me at the address below, and I'll get the letter. I'd like to hear how Elli is, and know that she's alright.

Things got messy back home, and I had to leave. I can't explain, but I hope you'll understand and trust me when I say I had a good reason for everything I did. For now, please take care of Elli, and yourself.

I'm working on a project. Again, can't really say much about it, but I'm hoping that if it all works out, I can come see you again, if you don't hate me too much.

Take care. I hope your feet aren't hurting you too bad.

Sincerely,

Igor

CHAPTER TEN

After working with Esteban Zappa and Jesse for several weeks now, there was no question that they were geniuses. But they were also pretty damn kooky. All day it was science, and all night it was strange visitors and weird games and endless stories about their wacky adventures. It was a side of Jesse that Igor had been unaware of when he was working as her assistant at the university. He was glad he was getting to know it now.

But sometimes it could be a bit much. For instance, this morning, the two of them were writing and reciting poetry about Blackbeard. Yes, that Blackbeard. No, Igor has no idea why. But it is apparently a loud, alcohol-fueled endeavor, and Igor needs to be far away from it. And so he's going into town.

It's nice being in a town where nobody knows him, because nobody knows that he's infected. He doesn't have to live in a Containment Center, he doesn't have to stay out of burger restaurants. He can see an action movie anytime he wants to, and no one will bat an eyelash, much less report him to the authorities.

Of course, he still attracts a fair amount of attention because of how he looks, but no one knows his history, and the fact that he lives with Esteban Zappa and Jesse Tran—who are apparently much-beloved minor celebrities in town—is enough to vouch for him to the townspeople.

Today, he is going to deliver a letter to Helen, and he also plans to stop by a little locally owned scrapbooking shop, and then he will hit up the gym. Now that he has a nice, stable place to live, a job with a sense of purpose, and a small sense of pride, he is beginning to heal from his past traumas and disappointments. He is reemerging from his mental hibernation, and he is ready to take up some of his old hobbies.

He feels pretty good in his new clothes. He'd come to Jesse's with hardly anything, and so Esteban Zappa had brought in his own personal tailor to make clothes especially fitted to Igor's unusually sized body. He'd never had anything fit him so well, and he hopes that one day he'll be able to pay Esteban Zappa for what must have been a rather large expense.

He catches sight of himself in a window and is pleased with what he sees. He stands up a little straighter. He doesn't have to hunch into tight shirts that strain at his neck anymore. His pants flow elegantly down to his shoes, not flapping around his ankles, as they used to. He'd never known that new clothes could make a man feel so good.

The woman who works in the store smiles and waves at him. He waves back, flustered, embarrassed at having been caught checking himself out in the window, like some kind of prima donna. He hurries on past the brick storefront.

Now he's walking past one of the many parks that dot the town. It's a cute park with duck ponds and lots of benches. Today, there is a man standing in front of a crowd, speaking into a microphone.

"We must end this scourge now. Not tomorrow, not next week,

not next year. Today! The CRA is not welcome here, nor will they ever be welcome here!"

The crowd claps and cheers.

The CRA? Igor has never heard of them.

"That's why, my promise to you, as mayor of this town, is to enact strict city ordinances, restricting where the CRA and their members can gather, what types of activities they can engage in, and how and where their materials may be distributed."

Igor scans the crowd. Everyone is listening intently. He has never seen a mayor give a speech in a park before. Is this some new, grassroots style of organizing?

"As you all know, the CRA is crafty. They have members who are skilled in computer hacking, psychological manipulation, and terrorism. They will stop at nothing to increase their numbers and strengthen their group. But there are things we can do, as individuals, and as a community. If you own a local restaurant or business, do not allow the CRA to congregate in your spaces. Do not rent your banquet and meetings halls to them."

Igor is part of the crowd now, if only at the perimeter. He nudges a woman standing close to him. She has frizzy brown hair and is holding the hand of a toddler. She looks kind. When she turns to look at Igor, she squeaks in fright, then calms herself.

"Ma'am? Why is he doing this in the park?" He keeps his voice to a loud whisper.

"CRA took out the mayor's computers this morning, with some kind of virus. He can't send out a normal press release, or emails or anything."

"What's the CRA?"

"Cannibal Rights Association."

Jesse's computer is full of amazing surprises and shocking information. When Igor first turns it on, he is greeted by messages from "Vindicator937," with whom Jesse and Esteban Zappa are apparently planning a stealth attack on an offshore drilling operation. After Igor gets the gist of the plan, he respectfully declines to read further.

There is a recipe folder, which Igor can't help but open and read. A folder dedicated to the "Demon Hunting Society," which he most definitely does not want to read. He is tempted to look at the search history because he is beyond curious about what other treasure he might find, but he doesn't.

Instead, he pulls up boring old Google and searches for "Cannibal Rights Association."

It's been a few months since Igor came to Dr. Tran's, and in all that time, he has hardly touched a computer, and hasn't paid attention to the news at all. He didn't want to know if the attack on Moonlight Run had been reported. He didn't want to hear about it. He didn't want to think about it. He just wanted to concentrate on his research and work out and eat Jesse's cooking.

Now he can see that his hibernation impulses had been misguided at best, and downright dangerous at worst.

The leader of the CRA is none other than Karl Fenenko, formerly of Moonlight Run. Apparently, he had survived the attack on his camp, and had started his community anew, this time with grander aspirations. Igor looks at his slightly smirking face, staring straight out at him from the screen, as if sizing Igor up, judging him for his wrongdoings.

Igor navigates the website, learning about the organization. Membership is estimated to be nearly five thousand, and growing every day. They are politically active, motivated, and fiercely vocal.

There are several CRA centers around the country, where its members can work and live.

Igor looks through some of the pictures. The centers look nice. Nice, clean houses, where cannibals pose with each other, watching TV, splashing around in a pool... barbecuing in the backyard...

He shakes his head, unbelieving. It must be an inflated number. There's no way Karl could have recruited five thousand people to his cause in only a few short months. Could he? Maybe he's been recruiting for much longer, since before Moonlight Run, even. But how did he get the money to buy all these properties?

There is a tab on the site called "Our Demands." Igor clicks on it.

We, the members of the Cannibal Rights Association, are committed to the protection and promotion of the cannibal way of life. As part of this commitment, we will work tirelessly to secure the rights of the infected, both feasting and non-feasting, and we will fight to introduce anti-discriminatory legislation at every level of government, to secure our safety and to promote harmony in our communities.

Namely:

We demand an end to the dehumanizing and infantilizing forcible containment at government sponsored "Containment Centers."

We demand an end to forcible testing for Pestis Manducans, both by government agents and by private employers and corporations.

We demand an end to ineffective and costly rehabilitation centers, which do nothing to cure the virus, and which imbue its inhabitants with a needless and cruel sense of shame.

We demand an end to the separation of the infected from their children. As part of this demand, we require that previously separated children be reunited with their parents at the soonest practicable time.

We demand an end to food and entertainment restrictions on cannibals.

We demand an end to laws that criminalize the eating of human flesh and body parts.

Only when these demands are met can we hope to achieve a society where cannibals are accepted and appreciated for their unique worldview, abilities, and gifts. The scientific evidence is clear; the need to consume human flesh is part and parcel of the Pestis Manducans virus; it cannot be eradicated through criminalization, rehabilitation, or fear tactics.

Join us in the fight for cannibal rights!

Cannibals today! Cannibals tomorrow! Cannibals for all time!

Igor sits back in his chair and bites his lip. Many of the demands the CRA is making sound fine to Igor. In fact, the end to food and entertainment restrictions is downright sensible. Others are questionable. For instance, the end to the Containment Centers sounds nice, but where will all those cannibals go? It's not as if employers are knocking down their doors to employ them. Without the centers, and without jobs, they'll be forced to live under bridges, like cannibalistic trolls.

Or they'll have to live at one of Karl's centers.

It's the end of the laws against human flesh consumption that really concerns Igor. If the CRA gets what they want, will the infected be allowed to murder humans for their meat? Or do they just mean to decriminalize the grave-robbing, cadaver-lab-snacking kind of feasting? It doesn't say, which gives Igor a pretty good idea of that their intent is.

Igor has been happy these last few months, in his hideaway. But now the outside world is intruding, and Igor can't ignore it any longer.

———

(Letters to the Editor, in The Echo Tribune)

My Fellow Americans,

There comes a time when each and every one of us must take stock of our country and our place in it. Right now, we are in the midst of a moral and cultural war, the likes of which I have not seen in my lifetime. We must each choose which side of that war we want to be on. I, for one, choose to be on the side of decency and common sense.

These wicked cannibals calling themselves "The Cannibal Rights Association" are the greatest threat today to our liberty, our safety, and our lives. The fact that there are so many of them, and that their numbers are growing every day, should scare the living daylights out of everybody. I know it scares me. In their little manifesto, they actually demand the right to eat human flesh. They're not even trying to pretend anymore. They have stated their intentions loud and clear.

In case you are unaware, let me share some facts with you. Because of these monsters, my kids can't walk home from school anymore, for fear of being attacked and bitten. Statistics show that bite attacks are up almost eighty percent, just since last year. These guys aren't changing their ways; they're getting worse.

Because of these monsters, my own dear mother was kicked out of her trailer park, because the government converted it into one of the "Containment Centers" these freaks get to live in rent free. And not just my mother! Old folks and decent Americans everywhere were "relocated" just so the liberals' feelings wouldn't get hurt because we stuck cannibals in jail, where they belong. The cost to the taxpayer is astronomical. Just look at the horrifying cutbacks we've seen in military funding lately. It's a miracle nobody's attacked us.

Because of these monsters, we've got hordes of unsupervised children roaming the streets, while their parents hide away in their taxpayer funded houses, munching on eyeballs and Heaven knows what else. And these kids, who nobody seems to give a care about, are at risk of becoming cannibals themselves, with nobody to protect them. And many of them get involved in drugs and theft, as well.

There was a time, in the not-so-distant past, when cannibalism was a rare and sickening crime, the kind of thing we talked about in hushed voices, disgusted that anybody would consider doing such a thing. Nowadays, thanks to groups like the Cannibal Rights Association, cannibalism is celebrated. They call it an "alternate lifestyle." Well, I call it garbage.

I know. There's those people out there who claim that this behavior is because of the "virus," but I call hooey. There are hundreds of free, effective rehab centers all over the country to teach these folks how to control their urges. If these guys go to a rehab center, they have the tools and the know-how to keep themselves from eating people. They just aren't using them. Not because they're "sick" or because they're "victims," but because they're weak and immoral, and they just plain like being cannibals.

Friends, the United States is going to Hell in a hand basket. The Bible tells us that in the final days, the great Babylon will fall. She will be judged for her sins and will be destroyed by plague and by fire. There will be a terrible reckoning for all who dwell within her. That's not my opinion, that is Biblical fact.

We have two choices. We can act now and rid our society of these deviant criminals. We can stop the madness that is the Cannibal Rights Association and put these guys in prison or give them a merciful death. Or we can do nothing and watch our country burn.

Sincerely,

Angelo Zimmerman

To the Editor:

I write to you in support of the Cannibal Rights Association. As a non-infected individual, I feel it is my duty, and the duty of all of us, to stand in solidarity with those who suffer from this very real illness, and to defend their rights.

Pestis Manducans, the virus which causes cannibalism, while vicious and difficult to treat, does not impair the judgment of the infected in any way. These are still thinking, feeling human beings, and their rights are being trampled by a misguided government.

Take a look at the restrictions on meat eating. There is very little evidence to support such a restriction, and in fact, many experts believe that meat consumption, particularly red meat such as beef, can help to curb the appetite for human flesh. The laws against the infected consuming meat are unnecessary, silly, and downright cruel.

As a Christian, I ask that we all take a look at our fellow humans who are suffering from disease, and see them with kind, Christlike eyes. Would Jesus force the infected to live in dirty trailer parks? Would he shun them for cravings that they cannot control and did not choose? I don't think he would.

And if you think about it, wasn't Jesus the first supporter of cannibalism? As he said in Matthew 26: "While they were eating, Jesus took bread, and when he had given thanks, he broke it and gave it to his disciples, saying, 'Take and eat; this is my body.' Then he took a cup, and when he had given thanks, he gave it to them, saying, 'Drink from it, all of you. This is my blood of the covenant, which is poured out for many for the forgiveness of sins.'" He was literally offering up his body to be consumed by his followers. If that's not setting an example for cannibal tolerance, I don't know what is.

Now nobody is saying the infected should be able to run around murdering people. That's insane, and against the law, both God's and man's. But if they can live in society without killing anybody, we need to embrace them and show them the same loving kindness we would like to be shown if we were in a similar situation. As they say, "There but for the grace of God, go I."

Sincerely,

Marsha Jackson

CHAPTER ELEVEN

Jesse reclines in her office, reading a biography about Cleopatra, a snifter of brandy next to her on the end table. Everything in this room is old-fashioned and interesting. An antique globe perches on the desk, a number of pins sticking out of it. One wall is devoted to books in a variety of colors, sizes and languages. Shelves contain strange artifacts: a shrunken head, a compass, a pitch helmet, an amulet meant to ward off demons, a terrifying looking taxidermized shark.

Igor doesn't want to disturb her, but he doesn't have anyone else to talk to, and the idea of being alone with this is unthinkable. He needs help. He needs perspective.

He knocks on the open door.

Jesse puts her book down on the desk, giving Igor her full attention. "Hello, Igor. I take it you're here to discuss the last batch of skin samples?"

"I wish that's all I had to think about right now." Igor sits in a chair opposite her, rubbing his temples despondently.

"I see." She retrieves a snifter from a shelf and pours Igor a healthy dose of brandy. "This is Hine Triomphe Cognac. It's a mouth full of citrus-glazed creme brûlée, and it eases the pain of existence."

Igor takes a sip and suppresses a moan as the flavors caress his tongue. It's really good.

"So what's up? Lady problems?"

Igor smiles a little. "No, nothing like that. Though you'd be the first one I came to for advice in that regard."

She tips her glass toward Igor in acknowledgment of the compliment.

"No, it's all this stuff with the Cannibal Rights Association. Have you heard of them?"

"Of course."

"What are your thoughts about them?"

"Have I ever told you about my friend, Nambuka-Titip?"

"No." Igor would have remembered a name like that.

"When I was trekking through Papua New Guinea, along the Sepik river, doing dissertation research, I got lost. I was supposed to stay with the group, obviously, but you know how it is."

Igor nods as if he knows exactly how it is, getting lost in Papua New Guinea.

"I was tired and hungry, and really stressed out. I had some weed on me—"

"Naturally."

"And so I got my pipe from my jacket and took out a lighter, to light it. And that is what drew my friend, Nambuka-Titip."

"He wanted to smoke with you?"

Jesse's eyes crinkle. "No, it was the lighter. You see, at the time, in the seventies, there were still tribes along the Sepik River who had never encountered lighters. The ability to light a fire with a flick of the thumb, well. It seemed magical to him."

"Of course, when I explained how it functioned, and took it

apart and reassembled it, the magic was gone, but still, he was obsessed with it, and offered to purchase it. Of course, I required no payment from him, but I did request a meal. I was really hungry."

"Wait, how did you talk to this guy? Did he speak English?"

"At first, we communicated with hand gestures and facial expressions. It's not too hard to convey a sense of wonder with the eyes, or to express hunger by patting your belly and miming putting food in your mouth. Later, I became fluent in Asmat, and we spoke that way."

"Really?" Igor is intrigued by the idea of Jesse Tran as a young explorer, befriending isolated tribes in faraway lands. It seems appropriate. This story has nothing to do with the CRA, but it's taking his mind off things, at least.

"Yes. Though it took some time before the tribe was comfortable talking to me. They were suspicious of outsiders, and when Nambuka-Titip brought me back to the village, their first instinct was to cook me and eat me."

Igor sets his drink down and sits back. Now he understands where she's going with this.

"They were cannibals."

"Indeed," she smiles. "Some of the last remaining cannibalistic humans on the planet. And I can tell you, from first-hand experience, that they were nothing like the primitive savages you might expect. They were polite, charming, and hospitable, once my friend convinced them not to eat me."

Igor tilts his head side to side. He is not sure he buys the whole "charming, polite cannibal" description. But then he realizes that he himself is technically a cannibal, and feels bad for being so judgmental. Presumably, this is Jesse's point.

"Nambuka-Titip brought me into his hut and allowed me to

stay with him and his family for several weeks. He showed me every imaginable hospitality and became one of my dearest friends. I still make it a point to visit him, when I'm in the Papua New Guinea area."

Igor likes how she says "when she's in the Papua New Guinea area," as if she's talking about a trip across town.

"My point in telling you this, is that it is perfectly possible to befriend a cannibal. The problem is not cannibalism as such; rather, it is the fact that viral cannibals lack self-control. In the Asmat culture, cannibalism is restricted to certain situations, and is sanctioned by the society in which they live. Cannibals in the Unites States have no such model to follow, and the virus has eroded their ability for self-regulation. As such, they are a danger to others, which is problematic."

"So... you don't support the Cannibal Rights Association?" Igor sighs.

"It's not as simple as supporting them or not supporting them. We are in an untenable position with regard to the infected. We don't want to oppress living, thinking human beings. But neither do we want to be eaten or bitten by them. Suppression and punishment is not the solution. Neither is allowing them to run rampant, biting and chewing."

"So what is the solution?"

Jesse looks at him as if he's lost his mind. "Well, a cure, of course."

Igor flushes, feeling stupid. "Of course."

"But why does the CRA upset you so much? I don't understand."

And so Igor tells her. He tells her all about Karl, and the Moonlight Runners, Elli and Helen, and the terrible violent attack on the camp, and how he'd had to leave town to escape vengeance. It is a long story, and when he is finished, he takes a large drink of cognac, swallowing down the last bit.

"My, my, my. That is quite the story!" Jesse looks exuberant, and she gazes at Igor with new respect. "I am impressed."

Igor frowns. "What about that is impressive? I completely fucked everything up. And now Karl is basically taking over the country."

Jesse nods with enthusiasm. "Exactly. He sounds like a worthy adversary. You're a person of adventure and rare courage, like me."

Igor smiles in spite of himself. He likes that description.

"But what should I do? The CRA—it's led by Karl. He's my brother. And he's bad news. I don't think he's just interested in letting the infected watch scary movies. I think he wants a world where the infected are in control, where they can kill and eat whoever they want."

"You're probably right."

"But more than that, I think what he really wants is power. You didn't see the Moonlight Runners, but I did. They were all living in teepees, taking part in these made-up ceremonies, just because Karl told them to. He likes that. And always, even when we were kids, he was always the one in charge of his little buddies, the guy who everyone came to for advice. I think there's some part of him that really gets off on that, on getting people to do what he wants."

Jesse nods and refills Igor's glass. "And if he finds you, he will likely want revenge."

Igor nods.

"And he'll have an army of people to help him."

He nods again.

"And if he succeeds in spreading his message and recruiting masses of the infected, the uninfected of the world will no longer be safe."

"Right."

Jesse taps the book on her desk. "You know, when Cleopatra's brother-husband, Ptolemy XIII, ran her out of Egypt, she didn't just take it lying down. She fought for herself. She never gave up, and now she's remembered the whole world over, and Ptolemy XIII is about as famous as Billy Joel's cousin, Andrew. And how did she do this? She joined forces with Julius Caesar, and she defeated him in battle."

Igor presses his lips together and blinks. "And in this metaphor, Julius Caesar would be..."

"Science, of course."

"Of course."

"And on that note, let's get down to the lab."

For unexplained reasons, Jesse and Esteban Zappa get their mail delivered at a house that is not theirs, located two cities over. They instructed him to use this house for his own mailing address, should he require anything be mailed to him.

Igor had shrugged, not caring, and not eager to start receiving junk mail again. But then, he had sent the letter to Helen.

And now, she has written back.

He holds the envelope in his hands, taking in the little sticker in the top corner that contains Helen's name and address in a curly, feminine font. He imagines her holding the paper in her hands, sealing the envelope with firm pressure from her fingers.

Finally, he opens it.

Dear Igor,

I got your very weird letter, and I'm a little angry at you. There's absolutely no reason for you to be so darn cryptic. You can tell me what's going on. You can trust me.

Anyway, my plan was to take Elli and hand her over to Child

Protective Services. I'm not set up for a kid, and I wasn't sure my house was the best place for her. But after talking to her for a while, we both decided that she can stay at my place for now. I'm not sure how long, or what will happen, but for now, she's with me, and she's safe.

I'm not sure what you know about her background, but I've been able to get a little bit of information out of her, and it's not good. After her parents got infected, she was taken away from them and sent to live with some cousins in "the country" wherever that is. The dad was a really crazy racist, who blames the virus on illegal immigrants, or "wetbacks" as he so charmingly called them. He was always talking smack about her parents, telling her that if they hadn't been hanging around with "dirty wetbacks" they never would have been infected.

Nice, right? Well, that went on for a few months or so, she's not sure how long she lived there, but then things got worse. Her cousin and his wife were part of those folks who patrol the border, looking for border crossers. Which wouldn't have been SO bad, but these guys took it to another level. They really, truly hate Mexicans, and they think there wouldn't be any more cannibals if we could just deport them all.

Long story short, they caught a woman trying to cross the border, said she was infected, and brought her back to the house and shot her. Just shot her, right out in the cow pasture.

I know. It sounds insane, but I believe her. You should have seen how shook up she was when she was telling me this story. I think her cousins really did murder a woman, trying to prevent her from coming into the country and spreading disease.

If you look online (I did) there's actually a growing number of people who blame immigrants for the virus, and they have all kinds of sick solutions to solve the problem. Some of them say we should do genetic testing on everybody and force out anyone who has Latin American heritage. Some of them are saying we need to go to war with Central America. Some are advocating stronger criminal penalties for those who cross illegally, as well as a halt to all legal immigration as well. It's all bananas, and it sounds like Elli had to hear and see a lot of that crap.

After her cousins killed the Mexican woman, she ran away. The farm where they live is pretty far away from town, so she had to walk a long ways until she got to the nearest farm. She snuck into the back of their pickup truck and hid there until he drove into town. When they got to town, she hopped out of the truck and never looked back.

She's a smart, resourceful girl. And even though I'm still a little mad at you for how you've gone about things, I'm glad you brought her into my life. We're getting along great. She has fantastic taste in movies.

I hope you decide to come back soon. And if you don't, I hope you at least write again.

Helen

CHAPTER TWELVE

Igor is enjoying a plateful of Jesse's extra-spicy chilaquiles. They are the best he's ever tasted, luxurious with tomatoey, mole-infused sauce, poached eggs oozing their bright yellow richness onto the perfectly salted tortilla chips. Chilis burn his tongue in the best way possible. He tries not to moan, which would probably gross Jesse out.

The doorbell rings.

"Oh!" says Jesse, setting aside her plate, dabbing her lips with an embroidered linen napkin. "That must be our guest."

Igor swallows his bite, reluctant to let go of the flavors. "Guest?"

She nods and smiles. "Yep. Now, before I show the man in question into our home, I think I should warn you about the particulars of this visit."

Igor sits back in his chair. "I'm listening."

"The mayor will be joining us for brunch today."

"The mayor? You mean Fred Gault? The cannibal hater?" Igor cannot imagine why Jesse would want such a man in her home. In addition, he is concerned about his own safety. He doesn't imagine the mayor is the type to overlook an unregistered, fugitive cannibal living in his town. "Should I hide?"

The bell rings again.

"On the contrary, Igor. I need your help."

"What do you need?"

She taps her chin. "I don't have time to explain. So just... stand nearby, look as menacing as possible, and let your instincts guide you."

"Wait, what?"

But she is already moving out of the kitchen, toward the front door.

"Mayor Gault, thank you for stopping by today. Come in, come in." Igor hears her cheery voice, and he slinks along after it, reluctant. He knows that the mayor won't be able to tell that he's infected just by looking at him, of course, but it's possible that a man like him checks the missing cannibal registers regularly. He seems like the type.

Remembering what he was told, he straightens to his full height and scowls, an expression that comes quite naturally at the moment. He tenses his muscles, making his posture rigid. He enters the foyer, just in time to see Jesse remove a knife from her belt and throw it at the mayor. The knife goes through the mayor's jacket, right at the shoulder, pinning him neatly to the wall.

"Jesus Christ!" Mayor Gault screeches.

Jesse takes another knife from her belt, and flings it at the mayor again, this time pinning him by the baggy crotch of his pants. Gault looks like he might faint.

Igor shakes his head. He supposes he should have asked questions when he noticed that Jesse had a number of knives strewn about her person this morning, but he'd thought it was just a fit of stylistic whimsy. She's a weird lady.

"Mayor Gault. Again, thank you for coming today. I apologize for the manner of your detainment, but I have always had a penchant for the dramatic. And one does feel such a thrill when throwing knives, doesn't one?"

The mayor is busy trying to remove the knife that is nestled near his testicles, using his one free hand. It is embedded quite firmly into the wall, and Igor is impressed.

"Igor? Would you mind terribly restraining our guest, so he can't mess with the knives? I'm afraid he might run away before we've had a chance to chat. There's some rope in the armoire, just there." She gestures to the armoire.

Igor is shaking a little. He has no idea what's going on, but he doesn't imagine this is going to end with a lovely brunch. "What are you doing?"

She smiles. "You'll see. In fact, I think you're about to have a lot of fun, if you can get past this little bout of jitters."

"I... I don't want to hurt him." Igor finds that he is a little ashamed of himself for saying that.

"You won't. But you'd better hurry—"

The mayor has managed to unstick himself and is making for the door, his old-man shoes sliding on the hardwood floors.

"Dammit," Jesse sighs. She moves toward the mayor and extends her forearm, clotheslining the old man neatly. She sits on the mayor's chest and gestures to Igor. "The rope, please, Igor."

Igor doesn't want to get the rope. He gets the rope. Then he ties the mayor's legs together, which is quite the process, as the man keeps kicking and wiggling.

Still, the tying gets done, and though the mayor is quite loud and shouty, he isn't moving anywhere.

"Mayor Gault, now that you're settled, let's talk."

"You know, my wife knows where I am, you bitch. You won't get away with this. In fact, I—"

Jesse punches the mayor in the face. It does the trick, and Gault quits shouting.

"There. That's better. Now, Mayor Gault, it has come to my attention that you are, in fact, a cannibal."

Igor starts. Fred Gault, the same guy he just saw giving an anti-cannibal speech in the park, is a cannibal?

"I'm no savage man-eater, you psycho! What the hell are you—"

"Two days ago, you were spotted buying Clamato in the local Save-R-Mart."

"Um... maybe he just genuinely likes Clamato," says Igor.

Jesse turns to Igor, rolling her eyes. "Nobody likes Clamato, Igor."

"That doesn't prove anything," protests the mayor. "I'm no cannibal. Just look at all the legislation I've introduced, all the city ordinances. Why would I do that if I was infected?"

Jesse chuckles. "You're not speaking to some country rube, incapable of understanding political maneuvering, Mr. Gault. Now, the longer you protest, the longer this meeting will take. You might as well answer my questions truthfully, because I already know most of your dirty big secrets anyhow."

The mayor glares but says nothing.

Igor shifts uncomfortably. He doesn't know how he feels about all this just yet.

"Tell us what you know about the Shadow Lake Kin."

Igor watches the mayor's face carefully, and sees his eyes widen with horror, for just a split second. Jesse must have seen the same thing, because she says, "I see you know exactly what I mean. Excellent. Now tell me more."

Igor has never heard of the Shadow Lake Kin. For all he knows they are a club full of schoolchildren who make candy on the weekends. But, judging from Jesse's manner of tackling the subject, he doubts it.

"I don't know anything."

"You are a member." It's not a question.

"I'm not a member of anything."

"Igor?"

Igor tilts his head, listening.

"Igor, I'm afraid our guest is being unpardonably rude, and after we have extended to him the hospitality of our home. Perhaps we will need to teach him some manners."

"You... you want me to..."

Jesse throws her hands up in the air and exhales. She turns to the mayor. "Mr. Gault. I'm afraid I need a moment alone with my associate. We'll be right back. Please, enjoy the frescoes on the ceiling. I've always liked them. If you look closely, there's a jolly horse gamboling about in a field, right there."

She puts an arm around Igor's shoulder and escorts him out of the foyer.

"Igor, what in the fuck are you doing?"

"What the fuck are you doing?" Igor nearly shouts. He is stressed.

"I am interrogating Fred Gault, one of the highest-ranking members of the Shadow Lake Kin. I am trying to learn more about his fucking cult and those involved in it. And I need your assistance."

"What is the Shadow Lake Kin? Why do we care who's involved in it? And where's Esteban Zappa?"

Jesse frowns, her brown forehead crumpling like a paper bag. "Esteban Zappa had a submarine emergency, so he can't help right now."

"Naturally," snarks Igor.

Jesse ignores his tone.

"Haven't you ever wondered what happens to the wealthy when they become infected? Haven't you noticed that there are no wealthy cannibals in the prisons, even when they offend repeatedly? When was the last time you ever heard of a rich cannibal being arrested?"

Igor shrugs. "I guess I never thought of it."

"Well, you should. Because it concerns you directly. These rich ones, they've formed a club, secluded somewhere deep in the forest. There, they can indulge every flesh-consumption-based whim, whenever they please. A fresh supply of undocumented immigrants, orphans and homeless people is shipped in regularly, just for them."

"Jesus," Igor breathes.

"Exactly. And if these wealthy cannibals continue to gain power and grow their numbers, there's no telling what damage they'll do. And people like you, Igor, who do their best to refrain from doing harm—will be among the first casualties of their reign."

"But? Me? Why?"

"Because you're a threat to the new world order they're trying to create, a world where the infected are completely free to do as they please, where all is excused on account of their disease. You are proof that there is another way. You are proof that the disease is not destiny."

Igor thinks for a moment. "I see. And how do you know the mayor is involved?"

"After you told me about your encounter with him in the park, I got a niggling feeling. It wouldn't let up, and so I followed my instincts, and began surveilling him. My instincts are never wrong.

I discovered that he is a member of this group, and that there are plans to expand into other territories. We need to know where those territories are, and who's in charge. Once we have that information, we can decide what to do."

Igor nods. "Alright. Let's find out what he knows."

Jesse pats him on the back. "Good man."

"But, Jesse? In the future? A little advance warning would be nice, if you want me to help you take a man hostage and whatnot."

She nods in response. "Noted."

Together, they return to the foyer. The mayor has evidently been trying to roll toward the door, but he is not an athletic man, and now he is stuck on his stomach, wriggling back and forth like an overturned beetle.

"Such a shame. You never got to see the little horsey frolicking on the ceiling. Oh well. We have more important things to discuss."

"That's right, asshole." Igor administers a kick to Gault's butt, rolling him over onto his back again. He squats down low, so his face is closer to the mayor's. "You think you and all your rich little buddies can do whatever the fuck you want, just 'cause you got some money and some land? Maybe you bought off a few judges? Huh?" Igor gives the man a little push on the shoulder. Not enough to hurt him badly, but enough to let him know how strong Igor is, how badly he *could* hurt him, if he felt like it. "We know all about it. And if you want to get out of here and go back to your nice, comfy life, you better start talking."

"I just... I just..." Igor realizes, with mounting panic, that the mayor is near tears. He doesn't like that at all. God, what is he doing?

"It's not easy, to be infected. I guess you don't know about all that. But the cravings, they're so strong sometimes. It's like..."

"I don't care," snaps Igor. "You hypocritical piece—"

"I believe what my associate is trying to say," interrupts Jesse, "is that we have no interest in hearing about your experiences with the virus. This is not some maudlin weeping program on NPR. We need to know about the Shadow Lake Kin. Where is their current location? Also, we need to know about their plans for expansion. Where is the next location? Has land been purchased? If so, by whom? You will tell us all of this, and you will tell us now."

"I can't tell you that."

Igor slaps the mayor's face. He doesn't feel bad about it. He's getting better at this. He remembers his dad, his dad's drunk, bullying face. The mayor and his dad are the same. The mayor has power over his city. His dad had power over his house. They both are the kind who abuse their power, who use it to hurt people, to take their paltry, small-time, two-bit authority and throw it around like a weapon.

"You'd better start talking." Igor's voice is calm and icy. He hears it and he likes it. He should talk like this all the time.

"No, you don't understand. I swore an oath. If they find out I talked, they'll kill me."

"And we will kill you if you don't talk. A bit of a quandary you're in, huh?" Igor smirks down at the small, fat man.

"In times like this, it's best to do the most sensible thing," pontificates Jesse, her voice conversational. "On the one hand, you face a possible death if your buddies discover your treachery. On the other hand, you face certain death if you don't do what we say, right now. Possible death, certain death, possible death, certain death." She weighs her hands side to side, as if her body is a scale. "If it makes it any easier, we have no intention of revealing to the Shadow Lake Kin that you're our source." And then she winks at the mayor, an exaggerated, goofy wink.

"But it's just, you don't understand, you can't—"

Jesse sighs. "Igor, will you go into the kitchen and get the bleach from under the sink?"

"Alright, alright. OK. Look, I don't know everything. I swear. But I'll tell you what I do know."

Jesse and Igor look at each other. Then, simultaneously, they sit down on the floor, listening to the mayor like kindergarteners at story time. It's an interesting story.

The main location of the Shadow Lake Kin is deep in the mountains of Appalachia. Isolated enough that nobody hears the victims' screams, far enough from civilization that nobody is likely to stumble upon it by accident. The only people who *might* stumble on it would be hillbilly mountain people, not the kind of folks who run to the police over every little murder and escaped cannibal they see.

It was founded by a man named Kerry Cain, of the shipping Cains. After his infection, he found the restrictions placed upon his person to be quite the drag, and so he used his family's money and influence to have those restrictions loosened. He recruited several likeminded and like-wealthed individuals, and Shadow Lake Kin was formed.

The kin employs several "headhunters" whose job is to bring in fresh meat. They scour the country, picking up hitchhikers, lurking around homeless shelters, snatching hungry, abandoned street kids. Igor thinks of Elli and restrains himself from punching Gault again.

Gault is not certain where the new compound will be established. He doesn't think it's been decided yet. He knows that the new location will have a new leader, some guy who just signed on with the kin, after his own, similarly minded group, was liquidated by vigilantes.

The new guy's name, of course, is Karl.

They let Fred Gault go, with the understanding that if he squeals on them, they will squeal on him.

Igor and Jesse return to the kitchen, where their chilaquiles are now cold and unappetizing. Bummed, Igor picks at the remains on his plate, while Jesse tidies up.

"So, what are we gonna do about this?"

Jesse turns on the water at the sink. It's one of those fancy faucets with the hand-held attachment that can be adjusted to spray a variety of sprays. She chooses a strong, loud spray, and blasts the dish in her hand. "I don't have a plan, yet. Your thoughts?"

Igor frowns, concentrating. "When I tried to take down the Moonlight Runners, that was a disaster. I tried to enlist the help of Mothers Against the Cannibal Takeover, and they turned the whole thing into a bloodbath. Also, they tried to kill me."

Jesse nods, as if this were the most normal story in the world. "Yeah. Extremists can be a great help when you need extreme action. But you can't count on them to keep their actions within normal parameters. Still, I see your point. An ambush is likely to end badly for us, particularly if this group is as wealthy and well-protected as I imagine them to be. They likely have top-notch security. No, an ambush won't work."

Igor sighs, and takes his chilaquiles to the stove, turning on the burner. He is going to try to reheat them in a pan, hoping to save them. He was hungry when he left the table, and all the kidnapping and violence and threats have made him hungrier still.

There is a smell of smoke, and he realizes there is a bit of cheese stuck to the burner. He idly brushes it off with a spoon.

The smoke gives him pause.

"Jesse? Have you ever heard of Thomas Farrinor?"

He pauses in his dishwashing for a moment. "No. Why?"

"He was a baker in the seventeenth century, in London. He started the great fire."

"The Great Fire of London. Right. Why do you mention it?"

"It was such a small thing that caused such great destruction. This one baker forgot to put out his oven fire, and because of that, the whole city burned down. It spread so far and so wide, there was nothing anybody could do to put it out."

Jesse turns off the tap and whirls around to face Igor. Her face is lit with a bright smile. "Are you suggesting we burn down the Shadow Lake Kin's compound? Because if so, I am delighted! It's been ages and ages since I've set a good big fire."

Igor grins back. "No, we're not gonna burn it down. We're gonna do something even better."

"Oh, and what's that?"

"We're gonna infect those motherfuckers."

Because Igor and Esteban Zappa and Jesse have been working on a cure for the virus, their lab is already well suited for the kind of work they need to do. Except now, instead of focusing on a cure, they are doing the opposite. They are creating a new virus.

It's difficult, challenging work. Live viruses are no joke, and keeping one contained is about as easy as creating an atom bomb. The virus they are creating has to be easily transmissible, preferably through respiration. It has to be fast acting, with a very short incubation period. And, of course, it has to be deadly.

Their plan is dangerous, and there is much that can go wrong. First, they will infect their friend Fred Gault. They will somehow have to do this just before he enters the compound, so as to avoid transmission to the general public. Then, they will have to cordon off the compound, again, to prevent transmission to innocent people. Then, after each and every Shadow Lake Kinsman is dead, they will burn it down, ending the virus forever.

Igor isn't sure what to do about Karl yet. Will taking down the Shadow Lake Kin end Karl's ambitions? He doubts it. Even if he quits his alliance with the rich folks and their "Most Dangerous Game" cult, he still has the Cannibal Rights Association, and they're possibly just as dangerous. He's beginning to see that Karl will never stop his machinations. He is working constantly, with a determination that would be impressive if it weren't so terrifying. He is stirring many pots, sticking his fingers in all kinds of pies. Which means, that sooner or later, Igor is going to have to deal with him. But not now, not today. He will fight one battle at a time.

Biological warfare is nothing new, but it is new to them. None of them has ever done anything like this before, and they hope to never do it again. But despite his moral squeamishness about killing people, Igor finds that he rather enjoys the work. The problem solving, the puzzles, the joy of mental stimulation are all intoxicants for him, and he is beginning to like his life again.

He spends two hours per day lifting in the well-manicured backyard. He thrusts the weights high above his head, victorious, proud and strong. He flexes and squats, raises and drops. He is growing.

He doesn't want to kill people. At all. But he does want to fight for justice, and he does want to protect the innocent. And he is willing to do the work to make that justice happen.

He is getting stronger every day, mentally and physically. Soon, he will be ready.

CHAPTER THIRTEEN

"So, Jesse, how did you manage to find out all that stuff about Mayor Gault? Are you a spy or something?"

They are working in the basement laboratory. They had been listening to Igor's favorite band, Napalm Death, but Jesse has replaced it with her own favorite, Django Reinhardt. Igor doesn't mind Django, in fact he kind of likes it, but the quiet, magnetic quality of the music pulls him out of himself, makes him talkative.

Jesse moves her face away from the microscope and surveys Igor. "Are you sure you want to know?"

Suddenly, Igor is not sure he wants to know. "How about this? Just give me the highlights."

"OK. After the nuclear mishap known as 'Three Mile Island' I was tasked with researching the causes and potential consequences of the accident. I, along with several other scientists, was given a high security clearance. The government has never rescinded these permissions, and I just... never told them about the error."

"Wait, so all this time, you've had some kind of high-level security clearance you can use to spy on people? That's super sketchy."

Jesse throws back her head and laughs. "It is! Still, it comes in handy for me, and, as it sometimes happens, for society too."

"But, I don't understand. Why would you be given the ability to surveil ordinary citizens, just to investigate a nuclear accident? That doesn't make any sense."

Jesse smirks. "And that, my friend, is a question to which you do not want an answer."

"Understood." He kind of does want the answer now, but he lets it be.

A thought occurs to him.

"So, hey. Do you think you could use your... abilities, to help me find someone?"

"Possibly. Who are you looking for?"

"Karl Fenenko."

"I see. Your brother. The guy who's trying to take over the world."

Igor spins on his barstool, away from his slides. "I need your help to find him. Before we do this thing, taking out the Kin, I want to talk to him. I need to give him one last chance to do the right thing. I owe him that much."

Jesse nods. "I respect that. I'll find him for you."

Igor sighs, satisfied. He is glad to have this burden somewhat reduced. He's going to give Karl an out, give him a way to make things right. And if he refuses to cooperate, well then. At least he tried.

In the first video, taken by a shaky smart phone, Karl is standing on top of a burning car. The crowd gathered around him is eerily silent, listening to every word that comes from their leader's mouth. It's dusk, very nearly dark, and the flames show loud and furious on camera.

"And this, ladies and gentlemen, this is what comes from ignorance and hatred. Look around you."

The camera obediently swings around. Igor recognizes the landscape at once. It's Moonlight Run, or what's left of it after the ninja/MACT attack. Smoking teepees lie in pieces on the ground. There are injured people lying and sitting on stumps and rocks. The phone swings around and shows a body floating in the water, his shirt stuck on a log, preventing him from floating downstream.

Igor swallows down vomit, refuses to give in to his distress, refuses to look away. He is the cause of this. He will absorb these terrible consequences. He is man enough for that.

"Not one of you here today is deserving of this carnage. Not one of you is anything but what the great spirit has made you. And if these bigoted assholes can't control their violence, then we will control it for them."

The crowd breaks its silence to cheer for this speech.

"Friends, there are other places, other ways of being. Come with me. Together, we'll rebuild, we will literally rise from the ashes. Together, we'll create a new and better world, where we and others like us can live in freedom, without fear."

Karl doesn't look so good. Igor remembers how sick he'd been on the night of the coup d'état, lying in his teepee, moaning and weak. He remembers how slowly he'd moved that night, when he finally emerged into the night.

Now, in the video, he's sweating profusely, though Igor supposes that could be from the fire. He is pale and there are deep hollows under his eyes. He has lost a lot of weight, Igor notices for the first time. Still, his eyes are feverish and bright with intelligence, and his voice is strong and magnetic.

In one graceful movement, Karl leaps down from the car and strides into the center of the crowd. He spins in a circle and gestures around. "These assholes haven't heard the last of us."

More cheers.

The video stops.

Igor clicks to the next video, one of several that Jesse found for him. She also found Karl's current place of residence, his social security number, his passwords to his various email accounts, and a number of other highly personal bits of information, including his medical history.

The next video shows a group of people dressed in what look like makeshift togas, twirling and swirling around in a field. It's daylight in this one, and there are drums beating somewhere off camera. Whoever is filming this time has a steadier hand, which is nice for Igor's eyes and head.

Karl stands to the side, dressed in a loincloth, like he's fucking Tarzan. He is narrating the dancers' dancing.

"And when the first bite desecrated first flesh, then was the dawn of the first transformation."

One of the dancers dips the other, as if they'd been doing the tango, and pretends (Igor assumes it's pretend) to bite his partner on the neck. The way they do it makes it look like a sexy, romantic thing, beautifully choreographed, and Igor laughs in spite of himself. It's just so ridiculous.

"And as our numbers grew, so too did our strength."

Other dancers join the dance, nuzzling each other's necks and shoulders, pulling each other close, moving to the beat of the drums.

Igor doesn't recognize the location. It could be a field anywhere, in any part of the country. Hell, it might not even be in the USA, for all he knows. But he recognizes Karl, and he knows exactly what's happening. This is some kind of recruitment tactic. At Moonlight Run, he tried using Native American heritage to bind everyone together, to keep them loyal to his little cult. Now he's trying something different, creating a completely new mythology for the infected to rally around. It's still creepy as fuck, but at least he's not doing cultural appropriation anymore, which Igor supposes is a tiny step in the right direction, morally speaking.

Still, this interpretive dance nonsense seems asinine to Igor, and he can't believe how well it seems to be working. But it is working, great. The dancers are all super into it. Nobody appears to be going through the motions, nobody is standing still, glancing around awkwardly, which is what Igor would have been doing in that situation.

"The day will come when all of our kind can abide together in peace and harmony, living as we were meant to, in accordance with the will of the spirit inside us."

The dancers all stop their twirling and form a circle, holding hands. They raise their arms and chant in unison. "So be it." They walk toward the center of the circle until they are all clustered together. They hug and sway together, keeping time with the rhythm of the drumming.

It's sort of moving in a twisted, fucked up way. And as messed up as it is, Igor has to admit, he gets it. It would be nice to have that kind of belief, that kind of comfort, that kind of validation. It would be fantastic to believe—truly believe—that the virus was meant to be, that it made you special, that if conferred on you a special status, with a special destiny.

Igor is not a believer, but he gets it.

Karl is currently living in Cleveland, Ohio, staying at a hotel, while plans are made for the new compound. Igor has the address of the hotel, and a list of aliases he might be using. Karl is careful and smart, but in this day and age, it is nearly impossible to keep yourself hidden for long.

Igor shuts the laptop and gets up from the desk. He heads back to his room. He needs to pack.

The hotel Karl is staying in is nice, much nicer than Igor had expected. It's the sort of old-fashioned, towering residence that you can imagine Cary Grant and Audrey Hepburn patronizing in their heydays. There are a number of well-dressed people moving in and out of the rotating doorway, buspeople handling luggage, shiny black cars with opened doors that reveal flashes of the soft gray luxury within.

Igor is dressed in jeans and a worn T-shirt. He is sweaty and wrinkled from his long bus ride. He misses his motorcycle. Showing up at a place like this, getting off a bus, looking poor, is sobering and slightly embarrassing. Showing up at a place like this on a motorcycle, wearing leathers—well, that would have been cool.

He squares his shoulders, refusing to be intimidated. After all, the money that paid for Karl's little vacation here isn't exactly clean. He might be rolling in the dough because of his new friends, but Igor knows what's what. If Karl belongs here, then Igor does, too.

He strides into the hotel, past gawking porters and cabdrivers. He pushes through the revolving door and walks straight to the front desk. According to Jesse's research, Karl is checked in using the name Marcos Schultz.

"I'm here to see Marcos Schultz," says Igor.

The front desk clerk is a young dude, staring intently at a computer screen. He does not look up from it when he speaks. "What room?"

"I don't know the room number. I was hoping you could tell me."

The kid exhales, exasperated. He still will not look up. "I can't give you the room number if you don't know it. It's our policy to protect our guests' privacy."

Igor slams his fist onto the counter. It's loud and startling in the quiet, classical-music-infused atmosphere, and finally the kid looks up from the computer.

And gasps. Igor raises an eyebrow and enjoys the show as the kid's mouth opens and closes, as his eyes widen, as his face reddens. Sometimes it's good to be Igor.

He leans closer to the clerk and uses his most menacing, sinister voice. "Listen to me. You're gonna give me that room number. You're gonna do it right now, quickly, or there's gonna be trouble. For you, I mean. Not for me." He grins.

The kid nods and swallows. He types on the keyboard for a moment and says, "Mr. Schultz is in our penthouse suite. You'll need a key to access the elevator."

Igor rolls his eyes. Of course Karl is in some exclusive penthouse suite. "Give me a key."

The kid doesn't need telling twice. He scurries away and locates one and hands it over to Igor, not making eye contact.

"Thank you for your help," says Igor, now using his best manners. "Have a nice day."

He spins on his heel and walks across the highly polished mosaic-tiled floor, his dirty sneakers leaving little black marks as he goes.

CHAPTER FOURTEEN

Igor knocks, listening to the muffled voices coming from behind the mahogany door. The knocker is heavy brass, highly polished, in the shape of a vicious-looking, fanged snake. He thinks it's a bit dark for a shiny happy hotel like this one, but hey, what does he know about the dens of rich cannibals?

Karl answers the door in front of a cloud of opium smoke the likes of which Igor has not encountered since college, when a pretentious roommate declared himself a Buddhist, grew a Fu Manchu, and briefly turned their dorm into an opium den, inviting his friends over to puff and speak in asinine platitudes.

Igor did not figure Karl for the type.

Karl's eyelids are droopy, and he smiles at Igor lazily. "So. You've come to talk."

Igor looks behind Karl and sees two men and two women sitting on cushions on the white carpeted floor. The curtains are drawn and the light is dim. Soft sitar music plays in the background and Igor rolls his eyes internally. What the hell is Karl up to now?

"I have."

"Well, come on in."

Karl steps back and lets Igor enter. The pipe the people are passing around is stunning, an absolute work of art. The silver engravings, the delicate pattern painted onto it, the charmingly decorated little damper—Igor wants to snatch it up and keep it for himself. He could. These people are puny and high. He won't. But he could.

"Guys, this is Igor. I believe you might have heard me mention him?"

One of the men looks up at him with new interest. "Your reputation precedes you," he says. It is not a compliment.

One of the women gets up from her cushion. She is small and brunette, her hair knotted and messy. She approaches Igor without a hint of fear or nervousness. At first, Igor is charmed by her lack of trepidation but then she reaches up and slaps him. She tries to get his face but can't reach, and so she settles on his neck, slapping it with all the righteous fury she can muster in her groggy state.

Igor sighs.

"Could you please not do that again?" He looks down his nose at her, making a stern face.

"You motherfucker. After what you did to Karl, you're lucky that's all I did. You deserve worse."

She closes her eyes for a moment, then returns to her cushion.

For a moment, he wishes Jesse had come with him. Or Esteban Zappa. They would know how to handle this. They would be sitting on a cushion, taking a pull off the pipe, chatting the women up and charming everyone in the room. But instead, they're back at home, working in the lab, so as not to lose momentum.

Igor wishes he was charming.

He turns to Karl. "Look. I hope we can talk civilly. Will you hear me out?"

Karl nods, grinning. "Alright guys. I'm gonna need you all to clear out. Me and Igor need to talk."

The assorted opium smokers begin the long, slow process of extricating themselves from their cushions, putting away their belongings, finding their shoes, and then finding the door.

"We'll meet again tomorrow," says Karl, hugging each one in turn as they exit. "We have a lot of planning to do, and I'm so glad to have you on my team."

After they leave, Igor and Karl are alone in the hotel room. The smoke is clearing out, but the smell remains, clinging to the creamy drapes, swirling around Karl's head.

Karl speaks first. "Alright, then. Let's sit."

Igor follows Karl into the sitting room, where striped sofas are arranged around a black coffee table. Igor sits down opposite Karl and watches him closely. He doesn't think Karl's been feasting, at least not today. He looks glazed and calm, not giddy and manic. He's better dressed than he used to be. Igor guesses his new friends must have pimped out his wardrobe.

Igor wishes he'd thought to pack some of his new clothes, the ones Esteban Zappa had tailored for him. But he'd been thinking of comfort and utility, not fashion.

"Sorry about the opium," Karl gestures around at the smoky air. "Helps with my Crohn's. That and feasting are the only things that really help. Plus my new associates seem to like it." He shrugs.

"I don't care about that. I just came to talk."

"Shoot." Karl holds him with level, watching eyes. Even through the drug-glaze, it's an intense, intelligent gaze, and Igor remembers why it's so easy to fall under this man's spell, so easy to do what he wants you to do. Igor will not be making that mistake today.

"First of all, Karl, I want to apologize for what happened at

Moonlight Run. That's not what was supposed to happen. At all. Those ninjas... I didn't know what they had planned."

Karl smirks, and for a moment, Igor doesn't recognize him. Karl never smirks. Except now he is smirking.

"Really? So, you hired Mothers Against the Cannibal Takeover—a known anti-cannibal hate group—to come into my village and, what? Talk to us? Join us for a picnic? Be serious, Igor."

"I am serious. The plan, as far as I knew, was to gather you all up and evacuate you. I was going to try to talk some sense into you, Karl. Try to get you to see how fucked up all this is." Igor gestures around the room. "Nobody was supposed to get hurt."

"You expect me to believe that?"

Igor sighs. "It's the truth."

Karl looks at him for a long time. Then he laughs. Loud, aggressive laughter. "You know what, Igor? I think I do believe you. Jesus Christ, if anyone in the world was stupid enough to think that Mothers Against the Cannibal Takeover would treat a rogue camp with fairness and dignity, it would be you. You stupid, stupid, motherfucker."

He continues to laugh, while Igor sits uncomfortably, watching him.

Finally, Karl stops laughing. "Alright, then Igor. I'm not gonna say I forgive you. Fact of the matter is, it's not for me to forgive. A lot of people got hurt that night, and some people even got killed. It's them you have to answer to, not me."

Igor crosses his arms over his chest. He knows that Karl is right. He is responsible for a lot of damage, and he hates it.

"But here's the deal. I think that maybe, just maybe, there's a chance for you and me to put this shit behind us. Bury the hatchet, so to speak. We're brothers, and that means something. You feel me?"

Igor nods. "I'd like that, Karl."

"You gotta join up with the cause."

"The cause." Igor blinks fast.

"That's right. Moonlight Run was only part of the plan, Igor. Fact of the matter is, it was small potatoes compared to the other things I got going. The Cannibal Rights Association—I'm sure you've heard of them—they're gaining strength and speed by the day. Membership is up. We have a few members on city councils, too. In small towns, but hey, it's a start. Before you know it, we'll get some guys elected to higher offices, get some legislative power behind us." Karl looks like he's sobering up now, his eyes wider, his posture straighter.

"And now, I've got some new interest in the project. These rich fuckers with too much money and time on their hands. Well, they don't like the way we've been treated either, and they don't mind funding some of my more ambitious plans."

He leans forward onto his knees, looking at Igor intently. "You can be a part of all this. You can be on the ground floor of the new world we're trying to build."

"But... why would you want me? You know where I stand on all this shit. I don't think it's right to kill people, Karl. I just can't accept that."

"How did you find me, Igor?"

Igor cocks his head to the side for a second, confused by the non-sequitur. "What do you mean?"

"Jesus Christ, man. I'm here in a hotel under a fake name. I haven't told anyone where I was. I haven't used my phone or computer in weeks. How. Did. You. Find. Me."

Now Igor is cautious. He doesn't want to drag his friends into this. He shrugs. "I needed to talk to you. So I figured it out."

Karl claps his hands. "See! That's what I'm talking about. You might be naive as shit, but you're also one of the smartest fuckers I know. I remember you talking about all that research and geeky stuff you did back before you got infected. In all honesty, the guys I got on my team... well, let's just say none of them are gonna be short listed for a Nobel Prize anytime soon."

"You don't need anybody with brains," says Igor, half smiling. "Not for what you're trying to do. You just need money and power."

"That's where you're wrong." Karl shakes his head. "Maybe you just don't understand what I'm trying to do."

"No, I think I understand it perfectly," insists Igor. "You're trying to make a world where the infected have equal rights with the uninfected, which sounds great, in theory. Hell, I like my beef jerky as well as anyone. But you also want a world where cannibals can kill and eat whoever they want, whenever they want. And that's the problem. For me, anyway."

Karl presses his hands down in an elaborate "calm down" gesture. "Ok, ok. I get it. You don't like the killing thing. So don't do it! Nobody's saying you, personally, have to kill anybody. We just want the right to live the lives we are destined to live. And the idea that we'd be just running around eating whoever is wrong, and ignorant. When we attain power, yes, we will be able to eat our natural diet. But it would be a restricted diet. We will only feast on criminals, the terminally ill, the suicidal. There would be laws and regulations. Good God, man, what kind of monster do you think I am? I'm not suggesting some kind of free-feasting anarchy! You know me better than that."

Karl looks hurt. Igor doesn't care that much. He remembers Elli—sweet, innocent little Elli, in that monstrous cage. He's glad to hear Karl talk like he has some scruples, but Igor fears it's all just lip service. Yes, Karl is his brother, and yes, Igor loves him. But that doesn't mean he has to like him, or be sorry for his hurt feelings.

"I don't understand what you want from me."

Karl stands and begins pacing now, all traces of his former opium-induced languor gone. "I don't know if you've been following the news much lately, but there are scientists working every day to create a vaccine for the virus. Or a cure for the virus."

Igor nods slowly. "Yes. I've heard that."

"Now, they've all been dead ends so far, but who knows what the future will bring? It's only a matter of time until somebody hits a breakthrough, and then I'll be totally fucked. Everything I've worked so hard to build will be destroyed."

"But don't you want to be cured, Karl? I get that you've put a lot of time and effort into this... movement, or whatever you want to call it, but still. Don't you see how a cure would benefit everybody?"

He glares at Igor for the first time. A real, hateful glare. "It would not be better for me."

Igor is frozen in the face of Karl's anger. Suddenly, he remembers something from when they were kids. A cat, a random cat that Igor used to feed, had scratched Karl, when Karl was ten years old or so. Igor had tried to calm Karl down, but it didn't work. Karl threw the cat out the window.

Karl's face looks exactly as it did then, before he tossed the cat.

Then, Karl thaws. His facial muscles relax into his old, normal expression. His shoulders inch down. "Look. You have doubts. That's ok. I would expect nothing less from you. But Igor, I need your help."

"How? What do you want?" Igor is growing frustrated. Why won't Karl just say what he wants?

"I want your scientific skills," he shrugs. "I need you on my team. I've got financial backers now, with real, serious money. They'll build you the best, most highly sophisticated lab that money can buy. You can hire whoever you want to assist you. You'll have the run of the place. And all I ask in return is that you do what needs to be done to strengthen the virus."

"Strengthen? The virus?"

Igor has never, ever considered such a thing. It's insane. Karl is insane.

"That's right. You know, mix it up in a test tube, make it indestructible. Make it mutate so fast the scientists can't ever pin it down. Keep things interesting." Karl winks.

Igor shakes his head and stands up. He's heard enough. He'd come here hoping to convince Karl to come around to his point of view, but the man is obviously so far gone, so enmeshed in his power-mad fantasies, that he'll never back down.

"I'm sorry Karl. It was a mistake coming here."

"You might wanna sit back down," says Karl, smirking again.

Igor sighs and runs a hand over his head. "I don't think so. I don't think we have anything left to discuss."

"Oh yes, we do. Sit."

Karl sits, exhausted. "Fine. What?"

"What happened to that little girl? The one who escaped from Moonlight Run? Don't bother lying to me, I know it was you who broke her out."

Igor's blood turns to antifreeze. He can't feel his lips. "What?"

"Did you take her back to her parents? No, you couldn't do that. She doesn't have parents, does she? Or, anyway, none that can take care of her. So, what did you do with her Igor? You didn't just drop her off at a police station somewhere. That kind of idiocy would get you arrested. You didn't send her back out on the streets. If you had, we would have found her by now. So... what did you do with her, Karl?"

"None of your goddamn business." Igor is ready to snap. He is done being polite. His fists are clenched, ready to punch. His mouth is watering, ready to bite. Karl isn't a small guy, but he's smaller than Igor. It wouldn't be much of a challenge.

"Calm down, boy," smiles Karl. "We're just having a chat, alright? Now listen, my guess is, you've got the little girl with you somewhere. You're hiding her in whatever little bungalow or apartment you've been staying in. Am I right? Actually, never mind. It doesn't matter. Because if you agree to come work for me, I'll forget all about her. I won't look for her. I won't give her a second thought."

"What makes you think I give a shit about the kid?" Igor snaps. He tries to look as mean and fierce as possible, like the kind of guy who hates children and cats, who punches women and calls gay people slurs. With his face and body, it should be an easy task. But it doesn't fool Karl.

Karl laughs again, a deep belly laugh. "Oh God, Igor. You're forgetting, I know you, brother. Underneath that scary-ass exterior, you're a fuzzy little puppy dog."

Igor glares at Karl. He wants to throttle him, just to prove him wrong. But he keeps his cool.

A part of him wants to tell Karl what he wants to hear. It wants to say, "Yes, I'll come work for you, just leave the kid alone." But another, more honorable part of him, cannot do it. He cannot give this sleazebag the satisfaction of feeling superior, feeling like he's won. He has not won, and he will not win. Not while Igor draws breath.

He stands again. This time, he will leave, no matter what Karl says.

"Igor, you owe me. After Moonlight Run, you owe me, and you know it."

Igor turns and heads for the door.

"If you walk out that door, I'll have my guys hunting for you and that girl, night and day until we find you both."

Igor stays facing the door. "Leave me alone, Karl. Find another scientist. If you leave me alone, I'll leave you alone. Let's just go our separate ways."

A hand on Igor's arm turns him around. "Igor, don't you dare—"

Igor pushes Karl to the ground with one meaty hand. "Don't you fucking touch me, you prick. Now listen up. I've had it with you and your bullshit. I'm not gonna be your goddamn science monkey. And if you come after me, or mine, I'll make sure you regret it."

Karl scoffs, trying to look tough from his spot on the floor. "And what can you do? You're nothing. You're nobody. Your shoes are fucking gross."

Igor scowls at his shoes for a second but recovers. "I will make Moonlight Run look like a damn church picnic. I will unleash a shit storm on you and your little compound that will make you wish you'd never been born. You aren't the only one who's ever thought of using science to infect people, Karl. Not by a long shot."

And with those parting words, Igor leaves.

From: John Cena

To: Helen Wade

Re: Some new complications

Helen -

I don't have time to write you a letter, because this is urgent. I have set up this email account, in case my normal email is being monitored or hacked. It's unlikely, but I feel it's better to be safe than sorry.

It's possible that you, and everyone in your home, is in danger. I am doing everything in my power to protect you and keep you safe, but know that it is a very real possibility that someone might be looking for something in your home. Something small, that needs to be protected.

I'm sorry for being cryptic. I know I'm coming across as paranoid. I'm not asking you to do anything crazy. Just keep your eyes open for anything suspicious. If you don't have a bug-out bag, I suggest you get two.

If you need to contact me, you can reach me at this email address. I will check it as regularly as I can. Please keep me posted, and let me know you're safe.

Sincerely,

John

Igor reads his email a few times, hating every word of it. Is he doing the right thing? Is he making a colossal mistake? What if Karl and his minions are monitoring Helen's email as well? Would they think to do that? Will she remember that she once said he looked like John Cena? He had tried to think of another name that might tip her off, but couldn't think of anything better.

Igor doesn't think they will be monitoring. Karl has no idea who Helen is, or where she lives. He thinks as long as he only contacts her using an alias, she will be safe. But he wouldn't have been able to rest if he hadn't given her that warning. The idea of Helen and sweet little Ellie roaming around the streets, unprotected, unaware, is enough to make him nauseated and sweaty.

Even if his email has upset her, he is glad he sent it. He wants her on her guard. Safe and upset is better than dead and happy.

He remembers watching one of those prepper shows with Elli, how they'd talked about bug-out bags. They'd chatted for a long while about what should be included in one. Igor had mentioned things like beef jerky, extra clothes, a flashlight. Elli had suggested pixie sticks, jolly ranchers, and Hershey's kisses.

He smiles, imagining Elli helping Helen craft an emergency supply bag. He hopes Helen lets her have a few goodies.

Igor arrives home late at night, tired from his trip, and emotionally worn out from the fight with brother. He is happy to see the doors of his house, and happier still to open them and step inside. He is also determined. Determined to conquer evil, defeat Karl, and save the world.

Igor does not know why a number of heavily tattooed Japanese gentleman are gathered in the sunroom, or why they go silent as Igor passes them on the way upstairs. Nor does he know why Jesse is petting a gigantic Newfoundland in front of the fireplace in the library. Nor why Esteban Zappa is also in the library, wearing a loincloth, like Tarzan. Igor lives with weird people now.

But at the moment, he doesn't have time to indulge their weirdness. He needs to talk to them. He marches into the library and speaks loudly.

"Esteban Zappa, Jesse, we might be in trouble."

Igor notes that the tattooed Japanese men don't seem troubled by Igor's appearance, and he takes a second to be grateful to them for their good manners. But only a second, because he has pressing things to discuss.

"Ah, Igor. You have returned to our humble abode. It's wonderful to see you again. Here, have some brandy." Esteban Zappa pours with a practiced hand. Igor waves the drink away, which makes Esteban Zappa frown.

"Is there a problem, Igor?" Jesse speaks from in front of the fireplace.

"I just said there was." Igor is frustrated. "I went to talk to Karl. It didn't go well. In fact, he might be planning on attacking me, which means I can't stay here anymore. If he or his men find me, it could bring you trouble, and I don't want that."

Esteban Zappa spins in his chair to face out the window. He strokes his beard pensively for a moment, and takes a drink of brandy. "I see. Well you mustn't run, Igor. You are welcome to stay here as long as you like. We mustn't give in to bullying and threats. We will stand strong, together, like the bold men we are."

Igor shakes his head. "You don't understand. He has the backing of some really rich dudes who have resources. He can find me. He might have someone following me right now, as we speak. I think it's best if we pack up the lab and head out, someplace secluded. Are there Yakuzas in the sunroom?"

Esteban Zappa stands and strides manfully toward Igor. He places a hand on his shoulder, staring at him with intensity. "My boy, until now, you have shown remarkable bravery. You fought against the Moonlight Runners. You rescued that little girl, at great risk to your life and liberty. You moved to a new place, moved in with a man you didn't know and a woman you only knew professionally, and put your talents to use, helping to work on a cure for the virus, even though you stood to lose your freedom should anyone have recognized you or if Jesse and I were up to something unscrupulous. And even though this Karl person is clearly a threat to you, you sought him out and did your best to deal with him, face to face. You are one of the least cowardly men I know. Will you flee now, because of one man's silly threat? That is not the Igor I have come to know."

Igor runs a hand over his head, not able to look Esteban Zappa in the eye.

"And yes, there are Yakuza in the sunroom."

Igor laughs. Esteban Zappa smiles.

Jesse abandons the dog and hugs Igor.

"Ditto what Esteban Zappa just said. Now come down to the lab with us. We have some remarkable things to show you."

CHAPTER FIFTEEN

"*Desmodium Ciliata*," says Jesse, holding up a tiny plant with emerald-green leaves, the tips rimmed in sharp black triangles, like pointy antlers. The roots dangle down, globs of dirt clinging to them. "Otherwise known as deadly blackhorn. These small plants grow in only the darkest and driest of places. Toxic to humans, as the name suggests, but—"

Jesse rushes into Igor's face, reaches up, plugs his nose, and stuffs the plant into Igor's mouth. Reflexively, Igor pushes her hand away and spits the plant out.

"What the hell are you doing?"

Jesse sighs. "You have no sense of drama, Igor. You were supposed to swallow the plant, remain well, and then realize the implications of what just happened to you. It was gonna be a lovely scene. But the moment is gone now. Ruined."

Igor scowls. "You can't just shove a poisonous plant into my mouth and expect me to swallow it."

Jesse scowls back. "Apparently not."

"But, I see what you're getting at. The infected can eat the plant and not be hurt. That's what you mean to tell me, right?" Igor looks at the blob of saliva-moistened leaves on the ground by his feet. Gross.

"Correct." Esteban Zappa is full of cheer and enthusiasm. "The mechanism by which humans are harmed when consuming deadly blackhorn is simple. It attaches to red blood cells, inhibits their ability to release carbon dioxide, and causes the person to die of asphyxiation. As you can see here—" Esteban Zappa leads Igor to a set of Petri dishes situated on their own table, away from their other research. Igor peers into a microscope, which is trained on a slide. "This mechanism is disabled when applied to the red blood cells of an infected human."

Igor knows all about deadly blackhorn. It's one of the plants he studied during his botany phase, back at the Containment Center. He wishes he had his scrapbooks—he means notebooks—with him now. Igor examines a few slides and Petri dishes, confirming Esteban Zappa's statement, refreshing his memory about the plant's appearance and molecular structure.

"How did you discover this?"

Esteban Zappa grins. "Like most of the best scientific discoveries, it was part inspiration, part happy accident." He gestures to the wall behind him. Igor sees now that a small deadly blackhorn plant is sprouting from a crack in the wall. He'd never noticed it before.

"A small leaf fell into one of our tissue samples as I was working with it. I meant to throw it out and start anew, but decided at the last minute to examine it, just for fun, in case it might lead to something. After all, waste not, want not."

"And you saw that the red blood cells were unaffected. Remarkable." And it is. Still, he wishes Esteban Zappa and Jesse had spent their time doing something more useful in the lab. So,

Igor can eat deadly blackhorn, and the uninfected can't. So what?

Jesse scowls.

"You're not impressed. But you should be, because there's more."

Esteban Zappa twinkles at him, excited to see Igor's reaction to whatever's coming next.

Jesse continues explaining.

"Look at this. These are uninfected tissue samples that have been exposed to our little plant. And these are the tissue samples after exposure to the plant, and then again, after exposure to the virus."

"Did you... find a cure?"

Jesse gestures to the microscope, face carefully blank.

Igor looks at the samples, his heart pounding, palms sweaty. Then he sighs as he realizes what he's seeing.

Esteban Zappa has not found a cure. Nor has he found a vaccine. But he has found a way to make the virus less virulent. The tissues that have been exposed to both the deadly blackhorn and the virus are infected, but the virus is far less active, and replicates at a much slower rate than in a typical infected sample.

It's not a cure. But it's something. It's a way to slow the progression of the disease. And maybe, with a little more research, they can find a way to stop it in its tracks.

"But of course, there is a problem," says Esteban Zappa. "Namely, that uninfected humans cannot ingest deadly blackhorn without dying. And this would need to be ingested before the infection becomes full-blown, in order to be effective. We need to find a way to disable the mechanism that harms red blood cells in order for this to do any good."

Igor bites his lip, hard. Yes. It's going to be quite a challenge to get over all these hurdles. Challenging. But not impossible.

On impulse, he throws his arms around Esteban Zappa and

Jesse, engulfing the smaller people in his meaty embrace. They make strangled sounding chuckles and Esteban Zappa pats Igor on the back. "Yes indeed. We have much to celebrate, Igor. Let's return to the main house. I expect our guests are growing hungry as well."

There is a terrible thump from above as they ascend the stairs. This thump is followed by loud shouting in Japanese.

"Um, should we do something?" Igor hesitates on the stair.

Jesse turns and looks at him, considering his question. "No. Best to let them handle their own affairs. I imagine once their bellies are full, they'll settle down."

Igor nods, and together, they go into the kitchen. Together, they prepare a fantastic meal, which pleases the Yakuza and does indeed calm their tempers. They have a splendid evening, Esteban Zappa and Jesse chatting animatedly in Japanese, Igor nodding and smiling and drinking warm sake, which he doesn't like but drinks anyway, out of politeness.

As Esteban Zappa said, they have much to celebrate.

The Yakuza are gone, Igor never receiving any explanation as to why they were there in the first place, and the house is quiet. Igor has fallen asleep reading a book about Norse mythology and is dreaming that he is Thor, using his mighty hammer to smash in Karl's face. Seeing the exposed brains peeking through the fractured skull, Igor gets hungry. Really hungry. He scoops a handful of the slimy gray matter out, like an otter, and pushes it into his mouth.

It tastes terrible, like warm sake. He turns around and sees a fire burning in a trash can, and decides to use it to cook the brains, reasoning that they probably taste bad because they are raw. A glass of Clamato appears in his left hand. He throws the brains into the trash can, and the smell intensifies. It's so smoky. It gets smokier. He can hardly breathe.

He wakes up and coughs. His nightlight is still on, the Norse mythology book still resting on his chest. His room is filled with smoke, billowing in under his door, the tendrils rising up to the ceiling. He leaps from his bed and runs to the door. The brass handle is scorching hot, and he pulls back his hand in horror, blisters forming on his skin.

He looks around, frantic. He has to get out. He opens one of his windows and takes a gasp of fresh air. It feels so good in his lungs, clean and cool.

His room is on the second floor, and he doesn't want to risk jumping to the ground. He takes the sheets from his bed, quickly knots them together, ties them to the bed frame, and tosses his makeshift rope out the window. It's not ideal, but it gets the job done.

He hits the ground, barefoot, wearing nothing but his boxers. The grass is damp and cold under his feet. A stick pokes him between the toes and he skitters off it. The chilled air washes over him, and his skin prickles to attention. He looks.

The house is aflame. Such old, dry wood is easy to burn, and Igor can see that the building is probably beyond saving. At this point, the fire department will only be able to make sure the flames don't spread.

He is frantic, worried about Esteban Zappa and Jesse. He prowls around the house, searching for them. A siren wails somewhere nearby. Good. The fire department is on the way.

A tap on the shoulder startles Igor. He turns around and sees Esteban Zappa, wearing long slacks, wingtip shoes, and a smoking jacket. He looks impossibly dapper and amazingly calm.

"Esteban Zappa! I'm so glad you made it out!" He hugs the

man, desperately.

Jesse rushes around the corner, crazy-haired, but wearing an elegant robe with fuzzy slippers.

Igor throws his arms around her, gladder than he thought he could be to see a living person. Esteban Zappa and Jesse's delicious scents don't even tempt him. At least, not very much.

"Of course, of course. One must always be prepared for this sort of thing, mustn't one?" Esteban Zappa says.

Igor can feel Esteban Zappa judging Igor's lack of preparedness, his bare feet and partial nudity. He doesn't care much though. There are more important things to worry about.

"What are we gonna do? All our research is in there."

"And someone knows it," says Jesse.

Igor's blood runs fizzy, as all at once, he knows exactly what has happened, and why.

"Jesse, I—"

"It's fine, Igor. But I think for now, we need to separate. It's clearly too dangerous for us to continue working together, here."

"But, what are we gonna do?"

"We separate," says Jesse, shrugging sadly.

"I have nowhere to go," says Igor, realizing all at once how very true this is. With no home, and no research, on the lam, his options are extremely limited. His entire life is extremely limited.

"Here," Esteban Zappa reaches into an interior pocket in his smoking jacket and retrieves a small, burlap bag.

"For you, Igor. If you find a reputable coin dealer, this should fetch you a tidy sum. Enough to get you back on your feet and start a new laboratory."

Igor opens the bag and examines the jingly contents. He sees fistfuls of coins. The fire light is enough that he can see them, but not enough that he can see them well. "Coins? What are these?"

"Pirate treasure," says Esteban Zappa, because of course it is.

"Pirate treasure," Igor repeats.

"Yes."

"Your house is burning to the ground, and you're giving me a bag of pirate treasure to start a new lab."

"Yes, precisely."

"I see."

"It has been wonderful working with you, Igor," says Jesse. "You'll start a new lab, recreate the research we began. Esteban Zappa and I will head north and try to get funding from one of our partner organizations in Toronto. We'll be in touch."

"Why are you both so prepared for this?" Igor is truly baffled.

Esteban Zappa and Jesse laugh.

Esteban Zappa claps Igor on the shoulder. "This is not our first rodeo, as they say."

"It happens," agrees Jesse.

Together, they turn to face the billowing smoke emerging from the remains of what was once a beautiful house.

"It was a beautiful house," says Igor.

"It was," says Esteban Zappa.

The wailing of sirens is closer now.

"Igor, you'd better get hidden, before the authorities find you here," says Jesse.

Igor nods, choked up. He hates this ending.

Esteban Zappa turns and strides manfully away from the burning wreckage of his home, into the darkness. The fire trucks arrive, sirens blasting, hoses unfurling.

Jesse gives Igor one final hug and scurries toward the firefighters, heading them off before they can see him.

Igor slinks into the shadows as best as a man his size can slink. He has lost everything. He is depressed, frightened, and utterly sure of one thing.

Karl must be stopped.

Igor is leaving the antique dealership, his head down, his mood somber. Everything about the building is old-fashioned, right down to the escalator, which is made of wood and creaks menacingly as it lowers him back to the pavement below.

The antique dealer had not been able to help him with his pirate treasure. In fact, she'd been downright suspicious of the bag of coins Igor had shown her, and even more suspicious at his state of undress, and he'd left in a hurry, afraid the woman would call the police on him.

Igor is now homeless, jobless, shoeless, and hopeless. All that research, gone. All his hard work and effort, gone. Karl is still at large, making his plans, expanding his reach. Jud is still in jail, probably. He has no family, no girlfriend. His clothes are all ashes. He hasn't brushed his teeth and his mouth is rancid and sour.

Igor is not happy, and he has no idea what to do about it.

He supposes he should try to find another antique dealer, or a rare coin dealer, but he has no idea how to find one, and no way to look one up with no phone and no computer. He guesses he will walk around town, hoping to see something promising. It's not a great plan, but it's the only one available to him at the moment. He wishes he had his motorcycle, which would at least speed up the process.

He is hungry. Very hungry. He reaches instinctively for his beef jerky, but of course, there is none. He'd left it all behind at Esteban Zappa's. He needs something to chew, something salty and meaty.

He walks. There is a nursing home up the road a little; he has seen it many times. Old people sitting outside in the garden in their wheelchairs, attending nurses dutifully pushing them along well-worn paths.

Igor will go there. Not because he's going to bite anyone, obviously. But it won't hurt to look. And that's all he's going to do. Look.

It takes him twenty minutes to get to the nursing home, its pale, creamy yellow paint giving the place a sense of prim cheer. It belies the misery and sickness within.

Igor can smell the meat clearly. Juicy and tender, muscles soft from disuse. He imagines the long ropes of meat that lie just beneath the skin.

He comes a bit closer. He peeks into a window. An old man is in the room, alone, watching TV. It's a private room; the man must have some money. He has wisps of white hair on his head, and he's wearing a blue robe over comfortable looking pajama pants, even though it's three in the afternoon. Igor supposes there's no point in getting dressed at his age, in his condition. He wouldn't bother, either.

There is nobody around. The residents are not outside today. No nurses are helping the elderly gentleman with his blood pressure or anything. It would be quite easy to smash the window, jump inside, and help himself. The old guy is frail; he wouldn't be able to put up much of a fight.

Igor places a hand on the window. If he pulled back his arm and punched forward, he could do it. He could do it right now.

The old man is nearly dead anyway. He can see from looking at him that the end is just one flu season away. It wouldn't be murder, exactly. It would be more like euthanasia. Speeding up the long, slow, painful process of dying. It would be a kindness, really.

Igor's skin tingles. His pulse races. He has never eaten fresh human before, unless you count the tiny taste he got of the woman from the bar, which he doesn't, because it wasn't even a proper mouthful of flesh. Just a bit of blood, and that's all. The meat he'd taken from the cadaver lab had been exquisite, wonderful — but it had been tainted with embalming fluid, not at all fresh.

The old man would be fresh. He would be delicious. He would satisfy Igor's every dark, desperate craving.

Igor brings back his hand, ready to smash the window. Then he sees a picture hanging behind the old man's bed. A picture of a small girl in pigtails, sitting on a bike, her face covered in chocolate. A happy child, watching over the old man. Maybe it's his granddaughter. Igor doesn't know. But he does know that he can't murder an old man with the picture of a small child staring down at him. He just can't.

Igor backs away from the window and runs as fast as he can in the opposite direction. He needs to get far, far away from this place, with its nearly dead residents and their soft, tasty flesh.

It's just like he'd learned in rehab. Stressful situations can stimulate the appetite, especially in the infected. He supposes that losing his job, having his house burn down, and the destruction of his life's work could be considered "stressful" and he knows he needs to get a grip before he loses control of himself completely.

He needs something to eat. Not human meat. Something socially acceptable, something to fill his stomach. He will find something, right away.

CHAPTER SIXTEEN

Igor tries, unsuccessfully, to barter his pieces of "pirate treasure" for food. Perhaps unsurprisingly, no one is willing to take him up on his generous offer. Most people think he's joking. Some people think he's a very incompetent con-artist. But nobody is willing to sell him anything, not even at the hipster waffle and lollipop cafe where they serve leftovers to the homeless. They are obviously thrown off by the fact that he is almost naked, but there is nothing he can do about that fact.

Igor is faint and shaky. With his exceedingly large body mass, he requires a lot of calories, and it's been many hours now since his last meal. He is tired. He is stressed. His feet are black from dirt and covered in blisters and every step is agony. He is so, so, hungry. He is ripe for a relapse, and if he doesn't do something about it soon, he might lose control and bust into a hospital and start gulping down babies like chicken nuggets.

He wanders toward a park, the same park where he'd heard the mayor give his anti-cannibal speech. Today, it is filled with little white tents, arranged in two neat rows on the grass. People carrying reusable, cloth shopping bags wander through the aisle, peering and poking and chatting.

A farmers market. Perfect.

Igor is not aimed at any tent in particular. He knows that most of them will refuse to do business with him anyway, so he just goes to the one that is closest to him.

As luck would have it, the first tent he approaches is a husband-and-wife team, selling homemade jerkies. Igor reads the sign. Beef jerky, elk jerky, deer jerky, even something made out of dried mushrooms called "vegan jerky."

The wife takes one look at Igor and jumps. Her face doesn't change expression, and she doesn't scream, but her quick, physical recoil is hurtful all the same. Igor presses his lips together, grim. Her wide blue eyes gulp him in. She clearly wishes she could seal off the tent like a panic room, to keep Igor and his terrifying muscles away from her. He keeps his voice gentle.

"Ma'am, I know this is a weird request, but..." he reaches into his little cloth bag and pulls out a golden coin, "would you be willing to do business with me if I trade you one of these coins?"

The husband comes up behind the wife. He is in his fifties, clean-shaven, in a red plaid shirt. He looks like the sort of man who builds model trains and takes it very seriously. He tries to snatch the coin from Igor but misses as Igor quickly draws his hand back.

The husband is annoyed and insulted. "I wasn't gonna steal it. Can I take a look at it?"

Igor considers refusing until the gentleman says "please." *Somebody* should teach him manners. But it won't be Igor. Not today.

Igor lowers his palm and lays the coin flat upon it. He does not hand it over to the husband.

Husband is obviously very, very curious about it. He peers

down at it intensely for a good long minute, then quietly asks Igor to flip it over, so he can see the other side. Igor complies.

Husband whistles. Then he stands up and remembers himself. He straightens his face and tries to look unimpressed.

Until this moment, Igor had not been certain if the coins were actually worth anything. But based on this man's reaction alone, he now knows that he has a bag full of something quite special.

He wonders briefly how Esteban Zappa managed to get his hand on a bag of real, valuable pirate treasure.

"So. You wanna use this old coin to buy some jerky, huh?"

Igor nods. He is so fucking hungry.

Husband looks at his wife, giving her look of suppressed glee, not a full smile, but a tight twitch of the mouth.

Igor knows that this man has paid sticker price for every car he's ever bought, and that he has never won a game of poker, ever.

"And, how much jerky were you looking to buy? We've got all kinds. Even got some ostrich jerky, if you're looking for something a bit exotic."

"Beef please. All the beef jerky you have."

Husband waggles his head a little, considering. Igor wants to punch him in the mouth. *Dude stop fucking with me and acting like you don't know you're getting the better end of this deal. Douchebag.*

The husband grins in a rueful fashion. "Ah well. I guess I can make you a deal. All the beef jerky, coming right up. But first we'll need to see your ID."

Igor startles. "ID?"

"Well, of course," says Husband. "I mean, I'm sure a gentleman like you isn't one of those nasty people-eater folks, but you understand, it's the law. I can't sell meat to the infected."

Igor swallows. He pats his bare chest and legs, theatrically, if unrealistically. "Dang it. You know, I don't think I brought my ID with me."

Husband pulls a face. "Oooh, that's too bad, buddy. Well, tell you what, maybe this one time, I'll make an exception. I won't tell if you won't." Husband winks at Igor. Igor, despite his earlier crankiness with the man, winks back.

"You don't have your ID, huh?"

Igor hears the question and turns around, only to be confronted with half a dozen young men, all staring up at him with hardened, impassive faces. Surprised, he answers them.

"Yeah, I guess not."

The guy in front, obviously the ringleader, steps a foot closer to Igor, uncomfortably close. "You know it's against the law to go out without your ID."

Igor shrugs. "My mistake."

"I don't think you have an ID," says Mr. Tough Guy, who, Igor notices, has blond curly hair. Igor wants to laugh. It's difficult to look badass when you have a mop of lovely bright angelic ringlets on your head. Instead, he keeps his calm and answers.

"What makes you say that?"

One of the thugs holds out his smartphone and shows it to Igor. On the screen, is a picture of Igor's face, coated with red spider parts, a surly set to his jaw.

He glances at the website, "cannibaltracker.com," and flinches. He'd been so stupid to wander around town so much. He couldn't be safe here. He couldn't be safe anywhere, probably not ever again.

He sighs, buried under the weight of his many disappointments.

"The fact that your ass is all over this website, and probably a million other ones."

Igor smirks down at the kid. He needs to be careful. Goldilocks might be small and stupid, and his friends might be a bunch of short weaklings too, but there *are* six of them.

"So... you guys just walk around, looking up cannibals online and trying to ID them in public? That's... a pretty weird hobby."

"Shut the fuck up," snarls Goldilocks. "Listen. You're gonna pay us every penny you have in your pocket, and then we're gonna take a little field trip to your house, and you're gonna pay us everything you got in there."

"No, I don't think I will," Igor smiles down at the guys.

"If you don't, we're gonna call the cops and tell them exactly where you are. And you won't be able to run, because me and my friends here are gonna keep you right where they can find you."

Igor is finding this less amusing by the second. Are these fuckers serious? He looks around at each young man and sees nothing there to reassure him that these guys are not in deadly earnest.

"Look, I'm not gonna give you my money. In fact, I don't have much to give you, because my house actually just burned down, so..."

"He's lying," says Goldilocks, "and we don't take kindly to liars, do we Vin?"

The guy with the phone, presumably Vin, agrees that they indeed do not take kindly to liars.

Igor is not proud of what he's about to do, but he's going to do it anyway.

He reaches out a fist and brings it into the side of Goldilocks' head, whose knees crumple and whose body wobbles to the ground, arms reaching up to protect his pretty face.

Vin and two other guys come at him, encircling him to get him from all sides, to hit him at all angles.

Igor sticks out a leg and sweeps the feet of the guy in front of him. He backhands the one to his right, sending his tough, hard forearm into his nose. Guy at his back jumps onto it, in a painful, aggressive game of piggyback. His fists land on his head and Igor spins around to try to shake him off. It doesn't work, and so Igor jumps into the air and throws himself to the ground, landing directly on top of his assailant.

The other guys, who have not, up to this point, participated in the fight, now join their injured comrades.

Igor is annoyed. Why won't they just leave him the fuck alone? His head throbs where it absorbed those punches. He's going to be sore tomorrow.

He spins and throws elbows. He kicks and stomps. He is a fearsome giant, surrounded by boys, and he is doing his best to look the part. He is getting tired, suffering under the weight of the punches and attempts to knock him over. He is so goddamn hungry.

A siren wails.

"Shit!"

Igor's attackers scatter. He himself is not feeling up to scattering, which he supposes means he lost the fight.

Instead, he is relieved when Husband and Wife motion to him to come into their tent. Hurriedly, they hide him behind a stack of coolers, Wife standing in front of them to aid in the visual illusion.

Igor remains still and quiet, lying flat on the ground. He can hear the sounds of the police, asking questions.

"Who were they?"

"Where did they head?"

"Did anybody here get hurt?"

Husband and Wife don't rat him out. They stay quiet, and when the police come to their booth and ask if they're ok and tell them to call if they have any problems, they just send the cops on their way.

From in front of the coolers, Wife says "I'll tell you when they're gone."

Igor doesn't know why these two have chosen to help him, and he doesn't much care at the moment. He's just grateful.

Igor lies there a long time, throbbing and silent. When Wife comes to say that the coast is clear, he gratefully springs to a sitting position, rubbing his sore arms. He stands. He has to duck because of the tent's low hang. His skin is pocked with a strange, concrete-induced pattern.

"Thanks," he tells the jerky merchants.

"Don't worry about it," says husband, waving a dismissive hand. He turns to look directly at Igor. "Look. We don't like cannibals. We don't like what you do, and we don't like how you live. But we don't like bullies either, and those kids have been coming around here for weeks now, harassing everyone they can, acting all righteous like they're out here doing the Lord's work or something."

"They scare away business," says Wife. "We've lost a lotta money because of them." She smiles. "But I guess they won't be coming around much anymore."

Igor nods. "Well, thank you, anyway."

The wife approaches him, and Igor is shocked that there is no hesitance in her step. She seems to have gotten over her fear of him, which is strange, given the whole cannibal reveal. Maybe seeing him get attacked by thugs served to humanize him.

"Here," she holds out the coin. Then she hands him a stick of beef jerky. "Now don't go telling anybody where you got this, you understand?"

Igor nods, smiling a little.

"I gotta tell you, it was fantastic seeing somebody sock it to those assholes. Where'd you learn how to fight like that?"

Husband gives Igor a brusque pat on the back. "Alright, Una. Let's send this guy on his way."

Husband looks at Igor pointedly. Igor tilts his head in acknowledgment. It is indeed time for him to go.

"Hey there. Spider-Man."

Igor turns and looks at Husband, whose arms are now folded defensively across his chest. "You wanna sell those coins, I know a guy who can help you out. Don't go around trying to buy snacks with them—they're worth something. Alright?"

Igor is shocked at this strange turn of events. Isn't this the man who just recently tried to take one of the coins in exchange for dried meat?

Husband hands Igor a business card. "This is my guy. I'm a bit of a collector, you see."

Igor does see. The husband isn't evil, exactly, just greedy. He's probably got a massive collection of coins sitting in a coin collection safe somewhere, and when he saw Igor's treasure, he just lost his head for a moment. Could happen to anyone.

"Thanks, sir."

"Don't mention it. And for god's sakes, put some clothes on."

Igor now has more money than he has ever imagined he would have. Bills are stuffed into the pockets of his new clothes, strapped to his body with tape, crammed into the folds and sacks in his new backpack. Husband's coin dealer had indeed been a fair man and had paid Igor handsomely for his coin collection.

Now he is holed up in a cabin in a ghost town, somewhere outside county lines. He'd read about this place a long time ago in one of those magazines designed to inspire learning and a sense of adventure in pre-teen boys. He'd always wanted to see it, though perhaps not like this—infected with a cannibalism virus, on the run from the law, having just lost everything in a house fire.

The ghost town, Violent Ridge, had been an outpost for settlers, back when the country was first being settled by Europeans. Legend has it that the whole town was killed by the barmaid known as Mary McGee, who had gone mad and poisoned the cask of beer from which everyone had been drinking.

It is a strange story, and Igor doesn't know if it's true or not. Regardless, it's been a safe haven for him because it's ugly, uninhabited, and far enough away from civilization that he doesn't need to worry too much about being discovered.

The only cabin that is still standing is almost destroyed, with holes in the roof and a nasty dirt floor. The other structures are mere piles of rubble, collapsed walls tilting over, toppling to the ground in inelegant heaps. It's not a romantic ghost town with a saloon and a church and a few cute houses, and Igor understands why the place never caught on as a tourist attraction.

He can't sleep in any of these places. It will actually be more pleasant to sleep outside. But that's ok, he won't be here long. He just needs a quiet place to think while he plans his next move.

He opens his backpack and retrieves some crackers and a bottle of water. He has used some of his newfound riches to stock up on some basics, and he will be ok here for a few days, at least.

After his snack, he does some pushups, pressing himself high into the air, clapping his hands, and returning to the ground, his full weight slamming into his wrists. He flips upside down and does handstand pushups. He is feeling better now, the fresh air and exercise having boosted his mood considerably.

Money isn't an issue anymore. He can go wherever he wants. In fact, if he wanted to, he could probably buy membership in one of those rich enclaves like the one Karl is dealing with. The idea, though repugnant, makes his stomach rumble.

No, he won't be joining any murder cults anytime soon.

He has money. He has knowledge. He has a goal, even though that goal has been set back. Now he just has to figure out how to achieve that goal, given his constraints.

He thinks he knows how to get this done. But he's going to need some help.

CHAPTER SEVENTEEN

It's evening when he arrives, dark already. He knows he is probably too late for dinner and that he shouldn't expect to be fed anyway, but he is monstrously hungry and hopes for food. He climbs the stairs, one by one instead of his usual two at a time method. Despite all that he's been through lately, it is this that makes him afraid, and his progression is slow.

He raises a finger to ring the doorbell but stops. The loud, aggressive ding of a bell would be too startling, too intrusive. Instead, he gently raps on the wooden door, three times, quickly. Maybe no one will answer. Maybe no one is home. He prepares to turn around when the door swings open.

"Igor!"

Elli has jumped onto him, arms and legs clinging to him in a massive full-body hug. He pats her back, desperate to get her off of him. He's happy to see her, but he is also starving. He hates himself for peeling her off and setting her down on her feet, but it's the only safe thing to do.

The girl beams up at him, all smiles. Her ponytail is messy, like it was done in the morning and she's been doing somersaults ever since. Maybe she has. The thought makes him smile.

"Well, well, well."

He looks up to see Helen, standing in her living room with her arms crossed, an eyebrow raised. "Look who's decided to visit."

Elli, completely missing Helen's tone, jumps up and down. "I know! Igor's here!"

Igor steps closer to Helen. He can't help himself. She is also wearing a sloppy ponytail, and sweatpants. She is warmth and comfort and adorable messiness.

"Come on in," Helen says, with a tilt of her head.

Igor obeys.

He follows his girls inside, where he now sees that they've set up some kind of weight-lifting obstacle course. It's sort of like a typical circuit training circuit, but they've added some interesting elements. Next to the chest press station is a stack of couch cushions. He is not sure what they could possibly be for. There is also a mini trampoline, and a throw pillow, set against a wall.

"Igor watch this!" Elli runs to the throw pillow and presses her head into it, lifting her legs up into the air, slamming her feet into the wall. "I can do a headstand!"

"Nice!" He turns to Helen, smiling. "Quite a cool setup you got here."

She shrugs. "We keep busy."

Igor reaches his hands for her, wanting to pull her close, or at least touch her shoulders. He forces his traitorous arms back down by his sides, where they belong. "I really can't thank you enough for this, Helen. Seriously. I owe you."

Her face softens as she looks at the girl, who is still holding her headstand. "It's alright. It's been a lot of fun, actually."

"I'm glad."

"Elli, it's time to get ready for bed, ok? Can you say goodnight to Igor?"

Elli flips back down, sitting cross-legged on the ground. Her face shows confusion and hurt. "But he just got here. I want to play with Igor."

"But you have school in the morning. You need your rest."

"I can't sleep!"

Igor kneels down so he's more or less on the same level as Elli. "Hey, no worries. I'll see you later this week, ok?"

"Really?"

He smiles. "Really."

"Ok then." She jumps up and runs down the hallway, presumably to a bedroom where she will sleep, safe and sound.

"You shouldn't say things like that if you don't mean them," chastises Helen.

Igor is annoyed. "I do mean it. I'm back in town now. I've got some work to do here. As long as it's fine with you, I'd like to see Elli. And you."

He feels his face flush, and he wonders if he's red enough to camouflage his tattoo.

She gives a small smile in return, and Igor feels lighter than he has in days. Maybe there's hope.

"Are you hungry?"

He nods. He doesn't want to tell her exactly how hungry he is. It might scare her.

"Come in the kitchen. I'll fix you a sandwich."

She does indeed fix him a sandwich, whole wheat bread with cheddar, tomatoes and mayonnaise. He wolfs it down in mere seconds.

Helen, having watched his speed-eating, hands him a glass of water from the tap. "Don't choke yourself."

“Thanks.” He gulps it down. Refreshed, he proceeds. “So, you got her enrolled in school, huh? How’d you manage that?”

“I said she was my niece, and that her parents are infected, and I’m her guardian. They didn’t ask too many questions. You know how it is nowadays.”

Igor did know. As infection rates continued to grow, school attendance rates declined, as infected parents pulled their kids out of school and went into hiding, or the kids themselves got infected and were no longer allowed to attend. An uninfected, bright child meant money for the district, and improved test scores.

“How’s she doing?”

Helen waggles her head back and forth, considering. “It took some time to get her adjusted to having a real schedule and listening to her teachers and all that. But now she really seems to like it. She’s got a lot of friends.”

Igor’s heart spreads warmth through his veins. He is so glad to hear it.

“Is she... is she happy?”

Helen nods. “I think so. We decorated the spare room so it’s her room now. I think she misses her parents, and she’s obviously got some scars from all she’s been through. She misses you.” She looks at Igor pointedly, and his stomach churns with shame. “But yeah, I’d say she’s pretty happy.”

“And how are you? How has all this been?”

She looks at Igor, exasperated. “Igor, why are you here?”

He frowns. “I told you. I have business in town. I’m going to live here now.”

“Can you elaborate? What kind of business are you talking about?”

“I’m afraid I can’t talk about it. The less you know, the better.”

“Oh my god! Are you getting involved in something illegal?

Black market stuff? Because I don't—"

He waves a hand. "No, no, nothing like that. It's just confidential, that's all. Not illegal. Not anything bad. In fact, if you did know what I was doing, you'd probably be pleased."

She rolls her eyes, but Igor can tell she's not really mad.

"I've missed you," he blurts, without thinking.

She blinks at him, speechless.

"I mean—" He can't think of anything to add to that, so he shuts his mouth.

She laughs. It's a sudden burst of laughter, like machine gun fire. "You don't need to do that. You don't even like me, Igor."

Igor is flabbergasted. How could she ever think something so idiotic? "What are you talking about? What do you mean, I don't like you?"

"Every time I came to your house, you acted like I was a cockroach. You would never talk to me about anything, no matter how hard I tried. You cringed that time I tried to shake your hand. You don't trust me at all, not enough to tell me what's going on with you, not enough to—" she breaks off, shaking her head.

Igor stares at her for a long moment, considering his next words. When he speaks, his voice is tight, more emotional than he would like it to be.

"You say I cringed when you offered to shake my hand. That's because you so clearly didn't want to offer it. You always acted like I was some kind of scary monster, ready to eat you. And I get it. I do. I'm a scary looking guy. But the way you cowered from me... that was rough."

They look at each other now, making eye contact for the first time that evening. Her eyes are so dark, almost black. He can hardly see her pupils. And in that moment, he realizes something new. Maybe she hadn't been afraid he'd eat her. Maybe she'd been afraid of something else.

He reaches out a hand. "Hello, Helen. I'm Igor. Nice to meet you."

She grins at him and shakes his hand. "Nice to meet you, too."

The handshake is over. It was over many seconds ago. But they do not release hands. Igor pulls her hand closer to him, using both hands. He runs his fingers over her skin, which is soft and dark and oh so touchable. He entwines his fingers with hers.

His heart sprints. This is a dangerous game he's playing. She is not infected. But it's ok. As long as they don't kiss.

He scoots his chair a bit closer, wanting to touch more of her, to feel the skin on her arms, her stomach. But she is faster and hops up from her chair and onto his. She sits on his lap, legs straddling him, facing him. The parting of her thighs is all it takes to undo Igor, and he reaches his hands up to her face.

She leans down, bringing her lips closer.

"Wait," he pulls back. "We can't."

She grins at him, which is unexpected. "I know, silly." And she puts her hands back on his face. She leans closer. Closer. She trails her nose along Igor's exposed neck, a tickling sensation that drives him crazy, in a good way.

He reaches his hands around her, feels the small bit of exposed skin above her sweatpants, on her lower back. He trails his fingers along it, moving them up and down.

She is tickling his ear with her nose now and he smiles. He dips his fingers into the waistband of her sweats, just a tiny bit. Keeping one hand on the small of her back, he moves his other hand around to the front. He pulls the elastic away from her skin, slightly.

"Is this ok?" He murmurs, hoping to god the answer is yes.

She smiles in return, nodding into his neck. "Only if this is."

And she reaches down and unbuttons his fly. They realize at the same time that this is not the most comfortable position for the activities they have planned, and they laugh.

"Is there someplace else we can go?"

She stands up and grabs his hand, leading him away from the kitchen table.

"Whoa, wait, what about Elli?" Igor is suddenly worried about the girl waking up and finding him there, in the condo. Would it bother her? Would it be setting a bad example, or whatever?

She shrugs and grins. "I don't think she'd be mad to see you in the morning."

Igor grins in response. They go into Helen's room and shut the door behind them.

Igor lays in the quiet darkness of Helen's room, his feet dangling off the end of the bed, a sheet draped over most of his body. Next to him is Helen. Soft, warm Helen, curled up against him, her lovely head nestled where his chest meets his shoulder, her soft, sleeping breath caressing his skin. He uses his free hand to smooth her hair out of her face. The heat of her floods him with endorphins, and he sinks into the first cuddle he's had in ages.

He can't sleep, of course. He has to stay awake, stay vigilant. What if he has a feasting dream, and wakes up with Helen's bicep in his mouth? What if he wakes up in the morning, hungry, and smells her next to him and loses control? What if he drools in his sleep and contaminates her pillow or, worse, her? No. It's better to stay up, to enjoy this moment, to cherish it while it lasts. While he is firmly in control of himself.

He is damn tired though, so relaxed and happy.

He remembers the time he took a tour to see the Statue of

Liberty, but he'd been out all night partying the night before, and was so very tired. He had been sure he'd fall asleep on the ferry. He'd stood and walked around, breathing in the cold air, pinching himself to stay on his feet. Maybe he should get up, move around, get out of bed, go sleep on the couch.

He will. He will get up and do that. But first, he will close his eyes, for just a second.

He sits up in bed, panicked. Where is she? Is she ok? Did he drool on her? It's not quite light yet, but light enough to see the outline of Helen, rolled over on her side, facing away from him. He can't see her face. He needs to know that it's safe and unbitten.

Gently, he puts a hand on her shoulder and rolls her toward him a bit. She clenches her eyes, brows furrowed against this irritating turn of events. She obviously doesn't like to be messed with when she sleeps. Igor makes a note of that. The important thing, though, is that she is fine, perfectly fine.

He removes the pillowcase from his pillow. He inspects it for moisture and finds it dry. He will put it in the washing machine, just in case. He can't be too careful. Quietly, he pads out of Helen's room, into the hallway, glad for the silencing effect of the soft white carpet.

"Hi Igor!"

Igor jumps, startled, but it's only Elli of course, leaving her bedroom, dressed in a fluffy pink robe and matching slippers. She walks to the kitchen with businesslike efficiency, opens the refrigerator, and pulls out a half gallon of milk.

"Do you want some cereal?"

"No thanks," says Igor. He is still waking up, and the stress of the morning has dimmed his appetite. He will get something to eat later. He has to leave, now, right away. He glances at the clock. He can make it, but he needs to get a move on.

He wonders if, by some miracle, his motorcycle is still in its place at his old trailer, parked in the carport. He misses his bike. He briefly considers going to check but realizes how stupid that would be. He's been checking the AWOL cannibal lists regularly, any time he can get computer access, and he is definitely still on there. Since Helen didn't report him missing, it must have been one of the guards or one of his neighbors, which makes him angry. Meddling sons of bitches.

It occurs to him that he hasn't asked Helen about how she handled his disappearance at work, and that this oversight was rude and inconsiderate. He hopes she didn't get into any trouble over him.

He is distracted by Elli, who is now lugging a giant paper mache sculpture of some kind into the kitchen.

"What do you have there?" He nods at the thing.

Crestfallen, she stops in her tracks and looks up at him with hurt, slightly panicked eyes. "It's Ramses the Second. It's for school. You can't tell who it is?"

Igor can't even tell *what* it is, much less identify it as a specific person. He smacks his head theatrically. "Oh, right. I forgot to put my contact lenses in, so I can't see very well."

"You wear contact lenses?"

Dammit. Igor forgot that she'd lived with him and had never seen any kind of contact lens accoutrement during that time.

"Yeah, just got them recently. Anyway, it's great. You're gonna do a great job."

She is looking at her sculpture, fretting.

Igor kneels down to get a better look at it. "Oh, yep. Close up,

I can see it's Ramses, for sure."

She smiles now. "Ok."

"Alright then. I gotta go. But we'll talk later, ok?"

Elli flaps her hands in a stressed out dance. "But you can't leave! You just got here."

He is still squatting down at her level. "I know. But there's some important stuff I have to do. Really important stuff. And if I don't do it, a lot of people might get hurt. You understand?"

She nods, but her face is not a happy one.

"Another thing, Elli. Has there been anyone hanging around here who you don't trust? Someone acting weird?" He does not want to ask flat out if she's seen anybody from Moonlight Run, doesn't want to put that fear in her mind, especially not before she has to do a doomed school presentation with that terrible Ramses II sculpture.

She frowns at him, looking confused. "No. Why?"

He straightens up, affecting a businesslike tone. "No reason. I guess I'm just looking out for you."

This seems to make the girl happy, and she grins at him. "So, are you coming for dinner tonight?"

Igor sighs and shakes his head. "I wish I could, but remember that important stuff I was talking about? I'm not sure how long it's gonna take me. But I'll come back as soon as I can, alright?"

"Alright." She says it in that sing-song way of disappointed kids everywhere. It's cute, and Igor smiles.

Unprompted, she hugs Igor, and he is gratified to notice that he feels no urge to bite her. None at all. And for the first time, he hugs her back, tight.

CHAPTER EIGHTEEN

In order to prevent infections, cannibals who are convicted of crimes are not kept in the regular county jail. Instead, they are kept in privately run camps, typically financed and supervised by churches and other charities with a stake in rehabilitating the souls of the evil and the sick. These are not nice places. For the most part, they operate free of government intrusion, leaving the infected to the mercy of whoever signs up to work with them.

When Igor called the county cannibal jail, pretending to be Jud's brother, Zeke, and asked to speak to Jud, he'd learned that Jud was to be released the next day, having served his ninety-day sentence for possession of contraband. Igor had arranged to meet him today at Sparrowbeak Pub, a known cannibal hangout, where they were unlikely to be bothered. The pub used to serve actual beer, but since some recent crackdowns, they've been forced to confine their beverage offerings to lemonade and soda. Still, the atmosphere is cool, and it's nice to hang out in a normal, social place with other infected people.

Igor arrives a bit late, owing to a frustratingly late bus. He really needs to get his motorcycle back, or maybe even a car. He thinks of Elli and Helen. Maybe a nice, safe, SUV.

Jud looks alright for someone who has been locked up for three months. A bit thinner and paler than he used to be, but in generally good spirits. He is holding a ragged paperback book, which Igor sees is *The Lion, the Witch, and the Wardrobe,* by C.S. Lewis. He vaguely remembers reading it as a child and not thinking much of it.

"Igor. Good to see you, man."

And he does look glad to see him. Igor smiles, but he can feel that it is a wan smile. "God, Jud, I'm so goddamn sorry about all this." He says it as he's sitting down at their table. He needs to get his apology out, before anything else is said or done.

"Hey," Jud looks stern now. "None of that. I was my own fault. You asked for groceries, and I brought you some jerky and shit 'cause I know you like it. I forgot about that dumbass guard at your place, with the piece of balsa wood jammed up his tender little asshole. I wasn't thinking. This isn't on you, man."

Igor will not cry in front of Jud and the server and the guys playing pool in the corner. He absolutely will not.

"But still. You could have visited me in lockup. Or wrote me a letter. Or sent me some money or some shit. Jesus, I couldn't buy shit to eat, and I think I'm never gonna be able to look at a peanut butter and jelly sandwich again." He cringes, looking truly disgusted.

"I'm sorry, Jud. I feel like shit about that. Thing is, I've been out of state."

"What do you mean, out of state?"

Igor launches into the story, while Jud sips his root beer, exclaiming from time to time, or shaking his head, or cursing. He is a good audience. When Igor finishes, Jud shakes his head.

"Damn, dude. That's one crazy, fucked up story. But why did you come back here? You know MACT and Karl and all those fuckers are gonna be after you."

"I know. But I had to check on Elli and Helen. And you."

Jud nods, understanding.

"Also, I have a plan. I was thinking you might want to help me out."

Jud folds his hands in front of him on the table and looks at Igor levelly. "I hope you don't think I'm gonna be your grocery boy again."

Igor laughs, despite the sick guilt in his gut.

"No. Not groceries."

"Well then count me in."

An hour later, Igor and Jud leave the bar. They stand outside, in the exhaust-perfumed air, two guys ready to head home.

"So, where are you planning on staying?"

Igor sighs. He still hasn't figured that part out yet. He can't go back to his trailer, obviously. "Probably a hotel somewhere. I have cash."

Jud shakes his head. "A lot of hotels have mandatory reporting now. Not all of them, but still, not a risk you want to take."

"Shit."

"Well, I'd offer to let you stay with me, but you know... the guards."

Igor does know. The guards at Jud's place are zealous in their duties, and they will probably remember Igor. Once again, Igor curses his fucking face tattoo.

Instead, Jud hands Igor a book. "Here. I think you actually need this more than I do." Igor looks at it. *The Lion, the Witch and the Wardrobe.*

"No thanks, dude. I read this one already."

"Open it up, idiot."

Igor opens it up.

There are highlights all over the pages. Not phrases and sentences and paragraphs, as you might expect, but single letters.

"What the hell is all this?"

"It's a code, dumbass. You gotta decipher it. Once you do, it'll tell you where to go."

"But... what..."

Jud waves a hand at Igor. "I got it from jail. It's a guidebook to underground cannibal hostels and services. Doctors who treat the infected. Detectives who can find your missing kids. Places to rent violent movies. You know, stuff like that. I met a lot of interesting guys in there, Igor. You'd be surprised. There's a lot of us who don't like the way things are going, the new laws and rules that are coming out all the time."

"Wow, so it's like... a guide to a whole network of assistance. That's awesome." And it is. Igor is surprised he's never encountered this kind of thing before. Then again, before this, he was determined to stay the strait and narrow, and keep out of trouble. Things have changed, as of late.

"It is. Anyway, I brought the guide today, because... I don't know. I had a hunch you might need it."

Igor pulls Jud in for a hug. "You're a damn good friend, you know that?"

"Yes, I do," Jud says, pulling back, catching his breath.

"So, can you just tell me what it says?"

"Nope."

"Dude, just tell me the code, so I can figure it out."

But Jud is already walking away.

"Jud! Tell me the code!"

Jud turns around, grinning. "Hey, I did three months in jail so you could have some bacon. Lost that job offer my sister was gonna hook me up with, too. You gotta suffer a little bit for that."

"Jud!"

But Jud is already to his car, opening the door, getting inside.

Igor almost chases after him, but stops. He realizes all at once that Jud can't decipher the code. That's probably why he brought it today; hoping that Igor would help him with it, but now he's decided it's more fun to torture Igor.

Igor lets Jud go with his dignity intact, not willing to point out his friend's lack of code breaking skill. It's the least he can do.

Igor is no Stephen Hawking, but he is very, very good at cryptograms and word puzzles of all kinds, and it takes him less than ten minutes to break the code.

The name of the headquarters is Blackout Island, which is odd, given that the location is not an island, and indeed, is not even near a body of water. Perhaps the name was chosen to throw people off their trail. If so, Igor congratulates the namer. No one will look for an island inland.

The directions are vague, and a little bit creepy, including such gems as "take a left when you see the tree with a face in the bark" and "if you see a red chicken coop, you've gone too far." Still, it's the best chance Igor has to find a safe place where he can get some help. So he sets out on foot. If he starts now, he might be able to make it by tomorrow morning.

CHAPTER NINETEEN

Igor is standing at the edge of a junkyard. Rows and rows of badly used cars spread before him, rusting and dirty, eerily quiet. He double checks *The Lion, the Witch and the Wardrobe*. He is sure his interpretation of the code is correct.

Blackout Island is, apparently, located in an abandoned junkyard.

"Hello?"

His voice is absorbed by the wind, and there's nobody around to hear him, anyway. Unsure what else to do, he enters the rows and wanders among the cars and trucks. He peers into filthy windows, knocks on doors.

"Anybody here?"

Should he turn around and go back? This seems to be a dead end. But there's no place for him to go. He keeps looking.

He approaches a baby blue Volkswagen Beetle. It's quite a bit cleaner than the other cars, which is what draws his attention. The windows are clean, the exterior is dent free, if a little chipped in places. He peers inside and sees a small sticky note on the steering wheel.

"PUSH ME."

Igor tries the door and finds that it is unlocked. The interior smells like food, like greasy french fries, and indeed, he spies two McDonald's bags on the floor on the passenger side. This car has been used, and recently.

Igor's heart picks up the pace. He looks around. Obviously nobody drove the car anywhere; it's blocked in on all sides by other, less fortunate looking cars. But somebody has been here, all the same. Who? Where are they now?

Igor crams himself in the small seat, immediately pushing the seat all the way back to better accommodate his legs. He gently closes the door behind him, though it makes him feel slightly claustrophobic. Obeying the note, he honks the horn. "Dixieland" bursts out, loud and startling in the silence. He wrinkles his forehead. "Dixieland" in a German hippie car. Huh.

The ground beneath him shakes and rumbles.

"The fuck?"

Is it an earthquake? A sinkhole?

There is a sliding sound beneath him, like heavy machinery, or like a garbage truck lifting a garbage can high in the air. The car's nose tilts down, the rear of the car lifting up. The ground gives way in front of him, splitting apart like saloon doors. Igor only has a moment to take in the sinister black tunnel before he is inside it, rolling down into the darkness.

He thinks of the Chilean miners, stuck underground for weeks, trapped. Igor is not a particularly fearful person, but he does not want to go underground. He absolutely does not. Nothing good happens in an underground lair. He wants to get out of the car, claw his way back to the surface, but the tunnel is narrow, barely big enough for the car, and there is no way for him to open the door even a few inches, much less wriggle out of it.

He bangs on the dashboard. "HEY! LET ME OUT. HEY!"

Of course, there is no answer. There is only the dark, interminable drive into the abyss.

Except it is not interminable. It terminates, suddenly and alarmingly, in a large cavern, well-lit by electric torches. There are two guys there, standing guard at a large, wooden, medieval-looking door. They are in their twenties, strong-looking guys wearing camo fatigues. Igor wonders if they are actually military, or if they are just dressed up like that for effect. Either way, they are sufficiently intimidating that Igor decides to speak to them respectfully.

The men approach the car. One of them opens Igor's door for him and asks him to step out of the car.

Igor steps out of the car. "What is this? What's going on here? I—"

"All questions will be answered once you get inside," says Guard Number One. He sounds bored, like he has to give this speech several times a day. Hell, maybe he does. But for Igor, this is all very unsettling, and he wishes this guy would give him a little something to put him at ease.

Guard Number Two asks to see Igor's ID. He fishes in his wallet and provides it. Guard Number Two uses a smart phone to take a picture of the card and then writes something down on a clipboard that hangs on a hook on the wall.

These procedures handled, the guards open the door, and gesture that Igor should enter.

And when he does, he is amazed.

Through the door, there is another world. Gone are the dirt floors and antiquated lanterns. Inside is a land of polished white tiles, energy-efficient lighting, and gentle classical music playing over a speaker. Igor recognizes the piece as part of "The Four

Seasons," by Vivaldi. Spring. Nice.

There is a woman seated behind a pale beige desk, her dark hair pulled back in a neat bun. The plaque on her desk names her as Zora. She looks up from her desk with a polite smile, which jumps off her face when she takes in Igor's face and body. Her jaw drops briefly. Then the professional smile is back, but it's now tainted with a little panic.

"Good afternoon, welcome to Blackout Island. How can I help you today?"

"Well, Zora, frankly, I'm not sure."

"Fine, one moment."

Zora looks at her computer and types.

"Igor Fenenko, infected, assigned to Containment Center A, gone AWOL..." Zora lists these intimate facts off as if she's reading a sandwich menu.

"Where are you getting that?"

She looks up at him with quizzical eyebrows. "They snapped your ID out front, like two seconds ago. Remember?"

Igor nods. This place is obviously very serious about their security, a fact he should have registered as soon as he learned that it was located in an underground lair.

"You might be interested in our relocation program. Are you in need of detox services?"

He shakes his head, cringing. Detox is the worst part of rehab, without question. There is something about human meat that transports you beyond the ordinary cares of the world, beyond such trivial things as bodily pain. You're wild with it, crazy with invincibility. Nothing can hurt you, nothing can stop you.

When you quit eating human, the first week is fine. You're hungry, but it's nothing you can't handle. It's like when you have a craving for a really specific food, but you can only get that food in Zurich or whatever.

Week two is when shit gets real. The hunger overtakes you. It completely ravages your senses. You can't do anything but crave human meat, and you'll do anything to get it. This is when the infected are at their most dangerous. This is when you go feral.

Rehab centers put you under strict lockdown during week two. Each cannibal is placed in his or her own cell, fed through a slot in the door, and denied all human contact until the danger has passed. During Igor's own week two, they'd had to put him in a literal strait jacket, because in his adrenaline-fueled, wild state, he'd managed to bend the bars of his cell, nearly escaping.

The pain he'd felt in his body during week two was... unimaginable.

"You have a detox center here?"

Zora smiles and nods, unaccountably cheerful. "Of course, for those who need it. But it's nothing like what you've experienced in those horrible government centers."

"Really?"

"Yes. Here we are focused on 'kind detox.' Week one is spent in a group therapy center, where you live and work with your fellow detoxers. Week two, which, as you know, is the most difficult time, is spent in a state of complete and utter relaxation. It's really more like a day spa than anything else."

"But... how?" It would not be possible to relax during week two. The government center had administered Valium to him during his detox, and it did exactly nothing.

A new woman has entered the room now. She is short and curvy, with a lovely fluffy afro clouding around her face. She extends a hand to Igor. She has to reach up to do so. Looking into his face, she registers brief surprise, but not terror.

"Igor Fenenko, pleased to meet you. I'm Joy Campbell."

He shakes her hand. "Nice to meet you."

"I've just finished reading your file. I'm assuming you've come to us because you need a place to stay?"

"Yes."

"Well, alright then. Come on in and let me show you around."

He follows her through a white painted door and into a corridor.

"So, first, a little about myself. My father was Earl Campbell, and when he was alive, this all belonged to him."

"Wait? The Earl Campbell? The actor?"

"Exactly," she replies. "In his later years, things started to take their toll, and he got real paranoid. He had this place built in secret. He was convinced that there would be an upcoming pandemic and that he would need a place to hide with all his family and friends until it was under control." She stops walking and turns to Igor, shrugging. "Turns out, he wasn't wrong."

Igor chuckles a little. He still can't believe he is in Earl Campbell's underground lair, with Earl Campbell's daughter. The man was an acting legend, one of the greatest to ever act in movies. His death had caused widespread, international mourning. Earl Campbell. Damn.

"So, as the manager of his estate, it's up to me how we use this place. So I've turned it into Blackout Island—the one-stop shop for all your cannibal needs." She grins as she recites her slogan.

"What kind of needs?"

They are walking again, down the bland, well-lit corridor. She gestures to a door with the number 6 on it. "This is the Employment Office. Here we have job listings from companies that don't mind hiring the infected. Typically, these companies will have a confidentiality clause, meaning you can't reveal to anyone at work that you're infected. Sort of a 'don't ask don't tell" thing."

She shrugs. "But what are you gonna do?"

They walk to door number 7. "This is the Family Reunification Center. Here you can list any friends or relatives you might have lost through raids or split-living assignments, things like that. Mostly, it's parents looking for their kids and kids looking for their parents. It's hard, hard work, but we do a lot of good here."

Igor thinks of Elli. He wonders if someone has listed her in there. Maybe her parents are here looking for her, right now. He will check on that later.

"At the end of this corridor is an elevator. That takes you down to the residences. We have sixteen dorm rooms that can house up to thirty-two people. The floor below houses thirty-two more."

Igor sees the elevator in question, an ordinary steel contraption with the usual buttons located to the side. "And who lives here?"

"Mostly people like you, who have escaped from their Containment Centers for whatever reason. Some of them are fleeing unjust persecution. For instance, there's a man staying here who was accused of killing dogs in his neighborhood. It wasn't him; there was never any evidence that it was him; but the neighbors all assumed it had to be one of the cannibals in the local Containment Center, and he just happened to be walking by when an angry mob accosted him. He was badly beaten. The police, of course, did nothing. So now, here he is."

"And how is all this funded?"

"My dad's estate. There's more there than we could ever spend, so I might as well put it to some good, right?"

Igor smiles at her, liking her immensely. "Right."

"Now, according to your chart, you don't need detox services, is that right?"

"How do you have my chart? What chart?"

She laughs. "You're gonna need to get used to that Igor. Information travels fast around here. It has to. That's how we keep ourselves safe. Our network used your ID to do a quick search for you. We got your rehab records, your criminal records, and social media profiles. I checked them over before I came out to meet you."

Igor is unsettled by this egregious violation of his privacy. "I'm not sure I like that."

She spins and glares at him. "Well if you don't like it, you can leave. I'm not here letting in any old person who claims to be infected, needing help. We can't take risks like that. What if the government found out what we were doing here, hiding fugitives? What if they found out that we are helping reunite children with their infected parents? Huh? We'd be shut down and I'd go to prison. So, yeah, we're nosy as fuck. But that's how we keep this place running."

Igor is taken aback by her sudden anger. "I'm sorry. I understand. This is just... this is new for me."

Joy Campbell seems placated. "Alright then. What was I saying? Right. Our Detox Center is down the way. The Week Two Center is the room at the back there."

"Zora was saying something about how you do a 'kind detox?' So you have a way to keep them calm when they go feral?"

"Yes, we do, Igor. In fact, our pharmacologist has developed a very sophisticated sedative that completely controls the week-two frenzies."

"You have a pharmacologist?" Igor feels a rush of happiness and relief so intense he wants to jump and fist pump.

"Of course. We have a full medical center, located—"

"Ok, cool. Listen, I'm gonna need access to your lab."

Ms. Campbell tilts her head, looking at Igor like he's insane.

"Are you insane? We don't let just anybody waltz into the lab and start messing around. There's important stuff going on in there."

"As important as a cure for the virus?"

She frowns. "A cure?"

"That's right," Igor nods solemnly. "Ms. Campbell, for the past few months, my colleagues and I have been working on a cure. We recently made a major breakthrough, but then we had a setback when our lab was burned down by the Cannibal Rights Association."

Joy stares at him for a long minute. "Are you for real?"

"Yes. And I can prove it."

She spins and strides toward the elevator. "Come into my office. Let's talk."

Igor doesn't need telling twice. He follows her into the elevator, and down to her office. And as they talk, Igor animatedly explaining his research and methods, Joy Campbell growing more and more enthusiastic as he speaks, Igor doesn't even care about the fact that he is contained in an underground lair. His breathing is deep and full, and his body is relaxed. He does not think of Chilean miners at all.

He is much too excited.

There is a theory, mostly espoused by crackpots, that the virus is the next chain in human evolution, and that the virus arose as a means of population control. This theory flies in the face of what we know about evolution, but the notion does have its adherents.

Igor's suitemate is one of them.

His name is Xander, and he is one of three staff scientists living in Blackout Island. At one time, he'd worked for Karl, doing research for the Cannibal Rights Association, but had escaped when he discovered the full scope of Karl's maniacal plans.

Now he lives here, in seclusion. While he does not believe in the inherent superiority of cannibals, and that they should control the world, he has not abandoned the idea that the virus is an evolutionary adaptation. His research is focused on viral impacts on human abilities—for instance, the heightened sense of smell that comes on during the virus's incubation period and the extreme strength that accompanies the week-two frenzies.

Igor and Xander live in cautious civility. Igor images that Xander is somewhat threatened by Igor's claim that he can make a cure for the disease, and Igor understands this. After all, if Igor is successful, Xander will be out of a job. Igor feels slightly bad about that, but not bad enough to abandon his plans. And so the two men are civil, politely stepping around each other in their small kitchen, handing the remote control to each other to trade TV choices, jokily bemoaning the lack of windows in their underground apartment. But they are not besties.

Food is provided to them on a weekly basis. A courier brings a big cardboard box filled with canned goods, cereal, peanut butter and the like. Not the best food in the world, but it's fine. The apartment is nothing luxurious, but it has phone, cable, internet, and two perfectly serviceable bedrooms. The walls are painted white, and the lights are somewhat dim. There is a shared bathroom with a shower stall and toilet. It's all fine.

Now that Igor is settled in and Ms. Campbell has set him up in his own laboratory, he needs an assistant. Someone to get him the supplies he needs from the outside world. Someone to wash slides and test tubes, take notes, feed the rats, get tissue samples, and all that. Joy has offered to send one of her guys to come assist him, but Igor won't hear of it. He is not about to let some stranger into his lab. He needs someone he knows, someone he can trust.

He needs Jud.

In his former life, Jud had been a surgical tech. He wasn't a doctor, but he had enough knowledge to swab a cheek to get a tissue sample, to sterilize equipment, to take good notes. Also, he might still have contacts from before.

Igor picks up the phone.

CHAPTER TWENTY

The problem is, Jud isn't answering his phone.

At first, Igor is not concerned. He imagines that Jud has stepped out to get groceries, or visit his sister, or maybe he's drunk and watching *The Three Musketeers* for the seven-hundredth time.

A day passes, and still Jud isn't answering. Igor sends an email, to which he receives no reply.

Two days.

Three.

Now Igor is concerned. Jud doesn't have a job, or an active social life. He has few hobbies. If he's not answering his phone or email, there must be something wrong. Igor doesn't want to think about what, but he has to. After all, there's no one else to help his friend.

Just as his worry is turning to panic, and he's considering drastic measures, like leaving Blackout Island and searching for his friend, his email pings. He checks it, honestly expecting spam, but is pleasantly surprised to see that it's from Jud.

Relief allows Igor to collapse into a chair and exhale. Thank god. He really didn't want to have to risk his life again. He clicks on it, and sees no text, just a link to a video. Curious, he plays it.

It's Jud, playing the saxophone. It's a soulful, 1980s soft-porn sounding tune, and he plays it with his eyes closed, leaning back and forward, rocking to the music. Igor can't remember Jud ever mentioning that he played the sax, but he plays well, so it's obviously not a new hobby.

Suddenly, in the middle of a long note, Jud drops the instrument to the ground. Igor flinches instinctively, worrying about dents and damage. Jud stares at the camera for an interminable minute, and Igor is transfixed.

Jud's eyes are bloodshot, staring straight ahead. He is standing still, but his mouth is working, tongue lolling grossly in his mouth, poking out his cheeks, flicking out and licking his lips. Igor sits forward, as if he can reach out and touch his friend, do something.

Finally, Jud speaks. His voice is higher and tighter than usual. "That song was for you, Buddy. Bet you didn't know I had it in me, huh?"

Jud walks toward the camera, peering into the lens. "I'm sorry I didn't return your calls. I've been real busy. See, the thing is, I've come around to another way of thinking. Things are changing for me, Igor. Everything's changing all the time. And the fucking government, they aren't helping us out. The teachers and the lawyers aren't helping us out. None of it makes any sense, until now."

Igor massages his temples. This is bad. He recognizes this kind of talk, the crazed, hyper look in his eyes.

Jud reaches into the pocket inside his jacket and retrieves a human earlobe. He holds it in his hand, considering, it. He smiles at the camera.

Despite himself, Igor salivates. Earlobes are the bubble gum of the cannibal community, a chewy treat that lasts forever and satisfies cravings between meals. It does not, however, freshen the breath.

"Igor, we've been thinking about this all wrong. You and me and all of us who were trying to do it their way. But that shit is toxic. We can't do it anymore. It's not sustainable."

Igor drops his head. It's hard for him to see Jud like this. He remembers Jud sending Igor to Containment Center C because he was afraid of relapsing. He remembers all the times Jud called Igor in the middle of the night because he was craving and was having trouble staying the course, and Igor would say something lame about getting some sleep and having a beer and taking his mind off things, to get him off the phone. All these signs that trouble was afoot, and Igor did nothing to help him.

And now Jud has relapsed.

Well, there's no getting around it. Igor is going to have to leave Blackout Island to help his friend. Yes, he will be putting himself in danger. Yes, it will slow down his research. Yes, it is probably a very, very stupid idea. But what choice does he have?

Oddly, and somewhat infuriatingly, Igor remembers something that Karl used to say, back when he was still abstaining, back when he was a role model for the recently rehabbed. "You're not responsible for anyone else's choices. We can only control our own actions. So when people around you are relapsing, you can't take it personal, you can't get involved. That's their journey."

Except that's not right, is it? We each have our own journey, sure, but we're all on the same damn road. And if somebody's car is broken down, yeah, that's the car owner's problem, but that goddamn car is blocking the road for everyone else. It's a nuisance at best, and a hazard at worst.

Jud's car is broken down. And Igor might be the only one with a set of jumper cables.

Goddamnit. Igor hates the saxophone.

Another email arrives in his inbox. It's from Helen, and the subject is "What the fuck Igor?"

Immediately, his heart accelerates. That is not a good subject line. Taking a deep breath, he opens it and reads.

When you left without saying goodbye, I made excuses for you. I figured you probably had something important to do, or maybe an emergency came up. I figured you'd come back later, or at least call. But it's been over a week now, Igor, and I am done making excuses for you.

Maybe you think I'm the type of woman who you can treat however you like, show up and fool around and then disappear, and I'll just sit around waiting for you, like a dog. If that is the impression you have of me, I am here to dispel that notion. I am not that type of woman, Igor, and I will not allow you to treat me like it.

Elli and I will be fine without you. Don't bother me again.

Igor's jaw works, eyes bugging out at the screen. He has fucked up. He has fucked up so bad. She is never going to forgive him; she basically said so right there in the email. Why didn't he say goodbye? Why didn't he call? Why hasn't he messaged her all this time, if for no other reason than to let her know he is alright?

He slams his hands on the desk, shaking the monitor. Because he's been busy trying to save the goddamn world, that's why! Because he's been breaking codes and finding secret cannibal lairs and doing important scientific research and trying to help his relapsed friend. He's had his hands pretty damn full. He types.

Helen -

I'm sorry if I haven't been giving you enough attention, it's just that I've been busy trying to save the world, and all that, no big deal.

He stops. He breathes. He is being a dick, and he absolutely cannot send this email. She's probably been worried about him, that's all. The thought fills him with unexpected warmth and tenderness.

But what is he supposed to say to her?

He rereads Helen's email, looking for clues, but comes up with nothing. It seems pretty clear that she never wants to speak to him again. His head throbs and his palms are sweaty on the desk. He feels like he's going to vomit.

It goes against his every instinct, but he is going to respect Helen's wishes. He is going to leave her alone.

Obviously, Igor cannot go to Jud's trailer, but that's ok. He doubts Jud is hanging out there much, now that he's relapsed. It would be too dangerous to feast with all the guards around, especially since his compound is one of the many compounds who use human-flesh-sniffing dogs.

Igor watches the video of Jud playing the saxophone again. In it, Jud is standing on plain, gray concrete, in front of a concrete wall, so that isn't helpful. It could be anywhere. But, at the end, when Jud approaches the phone to turn it off, he picks the phone up and there is a momentary flash of something Igor recognizes. It's a statue of Langston Hughes, or part of it anyway. He recognizes it because he has seen it many times, at Langston Hughes Memorial Park. It's one of the places Igor used to go to collect wildflowers and leaf specimens.

Parks are not a great place for cannibals to hang out because they are not very secluded and any of their activities might be happened upon at any time. And Igor has no proof that Jud stuck around after the video, or that he has any plans to go back. Still, it's the best lead he has at the moment, and so he will go.

There is a knock at the door. Frustrated at the interruption, and angry about this shitty situation, and still hurting over Helen's email, Igor stands up abruptly, knocking over his chair. He flings the door open to see a frightened teenaged porter gawking up at him.

"WHAT?"

There is a moment of horror as Igor realizes that the boy has wet himself, a small puddle of urine collecting around his shoes.

Embarrassed for the boy, but also embarrassed that he has let himself get so worked up, he politely ignores the pee and fixes his face into a calmer, more pleasant expression. "I'm sorry. I just got some bad news. How can I help you?"

The boy will not meet Igor's eyes, and Igor feels like shit.

"Can I get you a tow... something to eat? Like, a cookie?"

The boy shakes his head, still looking down. "I'm supposed to tell you that your delivery has arrived, and it's been brought to your lab."

"Delivery?"

The porter nods. "The plants you told Ms. Campbell you needed. She got a bunch for you."

Igor's chest clenches with excitement. Already? Campbell doesn't fuck around. Igor is impressed. He figured he'd have to get outside help to get the necessary specimens, but he was obviously mistaken.

He thanks the boy and closes the door. He is glad about the plants, but before he can get started, he has to help Jud. The cure can wait another day. Who knows what trouble Jud might get into in the meantime? His friend is his priority right now.

He packs some of the Blackout-Island-issued clothes and hygiene items into a plastic garbage bag. He wishes he had a suitcase or at least a backpack, but he will make do with what is on hand. He frowns a little as he holds up the pants. They are four inches too short and look silly on him. Still, it's better than nothing, and he can't exactly complain, since they were free. He misses his specially tailored Esteban Zappa wardrobe and realizes that he has been ruined for ill-fitting clothes forever.

There is another knock. He practices a friendly grin, stretching his mouth a few times before opening the door.

Standing there is Ms. Campbell herself, looking at the floor, perplexed. "Did you spill something?"

Igor looks down at the puddle of urine. Right. He supposes he'd better get that cleaned up.

"Hello Ms. Campbell. How are you?"

She looks up at him and grins. "Did you hear the good news? We got the specimens you requested. They're in the lab, ready and waiting." She bounces a little on her feet.

"I did hear, and that's fantastic. I can't wait to get started." He smiles down at her, finding her enthusiasm charming.

"Great! Why don't you come with me now, and I'll make sure they're right for your needs."

Igor shifts his weight, awkward. "Well, unfortunately, I can't go with you right now. I've got a... thing I need to do."

Ms. Campbell is no longer grinning. "What?"

"I have a thing I need to do right now."

Her face relaxes and she chuckles, gesturing toward the bathroom. "Oh, I see. Ok, go do your business and then we'll head down."

"No, no. I mean, I need to leave the compound. I have this friend, you see. He's got himself into some trouble, and I need to help him."

Her head tilts to the side, and her face is full of murder. "Are you shitting me right now?"

Igor steps back instinctively, a little freaked out by her sudden anger. "Well, no. Don't worry though, I'll be back soon. I just need to check on him. I'll be gone a day. Three days tops."

There is a long pause while Ms. Campbell stares at him. His skin burns hot under her gaze.

"Do you have any idea how much it costs to get medical grade, organic, uncontaminated deadly blackhorn, in such a large quantity?"

"I—I'm sure it's a lot, and of course, I appreciate that, but—"

"And who is going to take care of the plants while you're on your wild goose chase? Huh? Am I supposed to take someone off gardening duty to tend to them, so the whole island suffers?"

Igor presses his hands down, trying to calm the situation. "I think you're being a bit dramatic, Ms. Campbell. I'm only talking about—"

"Oh, I'm being dramatic? An enormous amount has been spent on you. Not only on these plants, but on setting up your lab, furnishing your apartment, getting you clothes, feeding you. And I was happy to do it. But all this has been provided to you because you are doing a job for us. An extremely important job."

Igor is getting annoyed. He crosses his arms over his chest. "So what? Now I'm your slave? I can't go anywhere without your say so?"

"This isn't just about you, Igor. We and the work we do here is confidential. You are here because you're in hiding from the government. What if you get caught while you're out on your little Captain Save a Ho mission? What will you say to the cops about where you've been? And, more importantly, what will happen to your research?"

Igor rolls his eyes. Captain Save a Ho? Really?

"I'm not going to do anything unnecessarily risky. Like I said, we're not talking about a long trip. I'll be back before you know it."

She presses her lips together and shakes her head. "I'm sorry, Igor. But I can't allow it."

"Well you can't keep me here. What are you gonna do? Lock me in the lab? Take away my phone and my computer?"

After he says it, he flinches, because if that's not what she was planning on doing, he has given her a blueprint for how to capture him.

She sighs. "No, Igor. Contrary to how you're making it sound, I'm not a monster. But if you leave here right now, I'm afraid you can never come back. You will be banned from Blackout Island, and from receiving any assistance from us in the future."

At first, Igor is tempted to take this punishment. But the fact of the matter is, his chances of finding another safe place where all his needs are met and he can do his research are slim. How many places like this can there be in the world? And his research is very important.

For a moment he experiences a flash of hatred for Jud, and his fucking weakness and lack of self-control. If he'd just managed to keep his shit together, Igor wouldn't be in this situation.

The feeling dissipates as soon as it is felt.

He sighs. "How about we make a deal?"

"I'm listening."

"I'll stay here and get my research started. There are a few more things I'll need before I can do a full experimental run, but I can get a good start with what you've provided me. So how about this? I'll get set up, get things going, and then I'll head out in a few days. I'll check on my friend, get the rest of the supplies I need, and then come back."

"But that doesn't solve the problem. You could still be caught. It's not a risk I'm willing to take, not until you're finished with your work. This is a cure we're talking about, Igor, not some stupid plan to build a better tomato."

"I'll use this time to fill Xander in on my research and hypothesis. If I don't come back, he'll be able to carry on without me. He'll be your backup."

"And what about the safety of the island?" She looks up at him, obviously exhausted and tired of fighting with him. "What if you talk?"

He looks at her squarely in the eyes. "I guess you'll have to trust me."

She runs a hand through her hair and exhales. "If you make me regret this, Igor, I swear to god I will hunt you down and eat your face."

This heinous threat coming from sweet, short, Ms. Campbell makes him laugh. "Fair enough."

He extends his hand to her, and with reluctant smile, she shakes it.

CHAPTER TWENTY-ONE

Igor had expected to encounter lots of difficulties and hassles in his search for Jud, but as it turned out, Jud was very easy to find. Mostly because he is running around Langston Hughes Park with no shirt on, painted bright blue.

It's been over a week since Igor received the troubling saxophone video, and things have obviously taken a turn for the worse. Not only is Jud blue now, he is also crazy-eyed, snarling, and his hand is tied to a tree. There is a note pinned to the tree above him.

Igor comes closer. "Jud? Hey buddy. What... what's going on here?"

Jud looks up at Igor, recognizing him. "Igor. I'm glad you're here. I'm glad you're ready to be a part of this."

"A part of what, man?" Igor is cautious.

"The new world. The one Karl has promised us."

"You've been talking to Karl?" Igor crouches down lower, elbows on his knees, looking into Jud's face.

There are a few people in the park today, not many, but they are all politely ignoring the tied up blue man. They probably assume he's an unfortunate, insane homeless person, and they don't want to get involved. Igor scans around to make sure nobody is listening, just in case.

"He came and visited me at my trailer," Jud explains. He is clutching something in his free hand, and Igor sees that it is a tube of lipstick. "Electric Eel" is emblazoned on the side. He supposes that's how he painted himself blue. There is also an assortment of empty water bottles on the ground next to him. Igor wonders how long he's been here. "He had a lot of interesting things to say."

There is a buzz overhead, and both men look up. It's a small airplane.

"You see that plane?" Jud nods at the sky. "It's not gonna land. It's not that kind of plane. It's sent by the government to spy on us. You know that, right? I mean, you're not some sheep who believes everything it's told, right?"

Jud is talking in a jittery, quick way that makes Igor feel sick and panicked. It takes him a moment to realizes why. It's because he sounds like Igor's dad when he was high on crank. And now Igor can see what's happening.

Jud tried to quit cold turkey, and now he's on Week Two.

Igor reaches for the note that is tacked to the tree. He reads it. "WEEK TWO FRENZIES. DO NOT TOUCH."

Igor shakes his head. This was Jud's plan? To tie himself up until the frenzies passed, and then get someone to untie him? What if the cops had come? What if nobody agreed to untie him when the crazy passed? This must have been the stupidest plan ever hatched.

"Jud, I'm gonna help you, but I need you to promise me that you're not gonna bite me. Ok?"

Jud makes no such promise. Instead he points at Igor and says, "Run and you'll live, at least a while."

"Umm—"

Jud's voice takes on a terrible, embarrassingly bad Scottish accent. "And dying in your bed many years from now, would you be willing to trade all the days from this day to that, for one chance, just one chance to come back here and tell our enemies that they may take our lives, but they'll never take our freedom?"

"Ok. So that's what we're doing? Braveheart?"

"ALBA GU BRA! ALBA GU BRA! ALBA GU BRA!"

"Ok man, settle down." Igor drops to his knees. Jud's hand is tied with a small rope to the tree, which is not so much a tree as a little sapling. Big enough to keep Jud in place, but not so big it was hard to make a knot around it. The knot was a complicated one. Igor can't imagine that Jud had tied it himself, one-handed.

"Who tied you to this tree, Jud?"

Jud doesn't answer. He is staring at Igor's bicep, which is not far away from Jud's head.

Instinctively, Igor pulls back. "Hey. Remember what we talked about? No biting."

Igor knows it is futile to try to reason with someone in the grip of the Week Twos. There is no reasoning with them when they're like this. Still, he feels he owes it to his friend to try to do things the nice way.

Igor takes a knife from his plastic garbage bag and begins working on the knot. "How long have you been tied up, Jud?"

"Since this morning."

That's good. He hasn't been like this for very long. That also explains why the cops haven't come yet. It's only ten am.

"Alright, Mr. Wallace," Igor loosens the rope. "You're coming with me."

Jud springs up from the ground and launches himself at Igor. His teeth sink into Igor's arm, gnawing and hard.

"AAA!"

Igor uses the arm that is not currently food and punches Jud on the top of his skull, like he's playing the world's least fun game of whack-a-mole. Unfortunately, this makes Jud's teeth sink in deeper, and Igor shouts accordingly.

"Goddammit!"

Igor sweeps Jud's leg, and that does the trick. Jud falls to the ground, face covered in blood, a hunk of skin held loosely between his lips. He slurps it into his mouth like a wet noodle, swallowing it down in one gulp.

"Alright, that's it."

Igor drops his weight onto Jud's torso, pinning him down. With one free hand, he roots around in his plastic bag for a sock. Jud is pounding on Igor's arms, but he is not strong enough to really affect any change in his circumstances.

Igor shoves the sock into Jud's mouth, holding Jud's nose closed to force his mouth open. Sock inserted, Igor holds it in place with his hand, looking around for something to keep it in place. If only he'd thought to bring duct tape!

He sees the rope on the ground, thin and available. It's not perfect, but it'll do.

Jud is not a tiny man, but he is much smaller than Igor, and Igor is able to handle him as if he were a large, tantrum-throwing child. He turns him and pins him, turns him and pins him, until he has the length of rope tied around Jud's head. The sock is in place, for now.

There are sirens in the distance.

"Shit."

He supposes one of the disinterested park goers must have become interested once they heard the screams and saw the fighting and such.

"We gotta get out of here."

Igor picks Jud up, throws him over his shoulder like a sack of potatoes, and runs away from the park as fast as he can.

Igor is superhero strong, so carrying Jud is not much of a challenge for him. However, running fast is another issue, and Igor now regrets neglecting a cardio routine. He remembers "The Tortoise and the Hare," tells himself that slow and steady wins the race. He'll be fine, as long as he sticks with it and keeps going.

But then he remembers that the only reason the tortoise won was because the hare was an arrogant shitbag who decided to take a nap instead of competing. The kind of arrogant shitbag who was so full of himself he didn't bother putting in the work when it was required, who underestimated the dangers posed to him by slower creatures.

The kind of arrogant shitbag who only lifts and never does cardio.

Jud is squirming and beating ineffectually on Igor's back, which is annoying and slightly painful. He considers delivering a quick blow to his friend's head, just to make him still for one goddamned minute, but of course he doesn't do that.

The junkyard that disguises the entrance to Blackout Island is located a couple miles outside town, on a country backroad. Igor is glad for this. Once he is out of town, he won't have to hurry so much since the odds of him being seen carrying a panicked struggling person are slim.

"Hey, Jud. We'll be there soon. Another hour or so I'm guessing. I wanna thank you for giving me that book, by the way. I think you'll like the Island. The folks there are pretty nice. A little intense about security, but you can't really blame them."

"Mmmm ffffft."

"Right. And they've got a great detox center there, I heard all about it. They can actually put you to sleep during the Week Twos and you wake up all refreshed and ready to go. Hell of a lot more pleasant than what we went through at The Center."

Igor shudders, remembering the terrible panic and nightmarish physical pain that accompanied week two. It had been one of the worst experiences of his life. He actually kind of envies Jud for the soft, cushy rehab he is about to go through.

The buildings are out of sight now, and Igor slows his pace, taking deep breaths, relaxing a bit. Jud is still obviously unhappy about his abduction, but he isn't hitting Igor so much. Maybe he's becoming resigned to his fate. Or maybe there's some small part of his brain that is clinging to rationality, telling him that this is what's best. Regardless, Igor is glad for the reprieve.

By the time they reach the junkyard, Igor is exhausted, and Jud is quiet. Igor thinks about removing the gag, allowing his friend to have some semblance of dignity, but decides against it. It's Week Two. Quiet doesn't mean safe.

He inspects the bite on his arm. It's not as bad as it might be. There is a chunk of skin missing, and it's very bloody, but it doesn't appear that Jud got any veins or arteries, and the bleeding has already stopped. It stings like a motherfucker, but he imagines that once the medics clean it up, it won't give him much trouble.

He thinks of Helen, and how she'd stroked his biceps that night, admiring them, impressed. In fact, his arms had really seemed to excite her. He is embarrassed to remember how good that made him feel, having her look at his diseased, dangerous body that way.

Now his arm, like his relationship with Helen, is all mangled and fucked up.

He doesn't have the time or energy to dwell on this. There is work to be done, and people to save.

He shoves Jud into the car and beeps the horn. It's time to get his friend some help.

Igor doesn't like to think about his own Week Two Frenzies, but Jud's relapse and subsequent trouble have made him remember.

The first week of rehab had been difficult. He imagines it was not much different than a heavy smoker quitting cold turkey. He'd been irritable and grumpy and felt slightly sick, with headaches, fatigue, and a general sense of crappiness.

Then week two rolled around. He knew, in theory, that week two was going to be bad. He'd seen the videos. He'd heard the stories. But he assumed that as a large, strong man, he would be better able to tolerate the physical pain and torment that other, smaller people suffered.

In fact, the opposite was true.

As a large man, he had a large requirement for calories and a body that was crying out for huge quantities of human meat. The strict vegan, sugar-free, gluten-free diet he was provided with at the rehab center cafeteria was not cutting it. He never felt full, he constantly felt on the edge of a blood-sugar meltdown.

That was how it started. Then came the cramping, the diarrhea, the loss of mental faculties, the inability to feel compassion, empathy, or basic human decency. He'd actually assaulted a nurse during a toothpaste dispute, and the nurse had called for backup, and Igor had been forcibly restrained for the remainder of the week.

To make matters worse, the owners of this particular rehab facility were stridently religious and believed that the virus was God's way of testing humanity. If you were infected, that was God's way of testing you. A strong, Godly person with good morals and strength of character would rebuke the evil in their souls, could ignore the siren's song of human meat.

Weak, sinful, gluttonous people would give in to temptation, and would commit the sordid act of cannibalism. These sinners were destined for Hell unless they turned their lives around an chose a new, religion-filled path.

Because Igor and the other men in rehab at The Alliance Clinic had allowed their moral shortcomings to lead them astray, they were in need of punishment. It was the only way to cleanse and purify their souls. That is why, during the Week Two Frenzies, the patients were not allowed to miss out on any of the fun.

In an unassisted detox, a cannibal's body would typically pass out from pain and exhaustion, usually around day two or three. This unconscious state would last a few hours, the person would wake, suffer for a few hours, and then go unconscious again. It was the body's only way of coping with the acute pain and psychological breakdown that always accompanied the second week of fasting.

The good people at The Alliance Clinic had discovered a way to stop this loss of consciousness; namely, they provided their patients with medium doses of amphetamines, to keep them wide awake during the daytime hours. There would be no such self-indulgent napping on their watch. After all, the discomfort of the Week Two Frenzies was God's way of meting out punishment to the dirty cannibals. God must punish the ones he loves. If the Clinic didn't ensure that their patients experienced God's Love to the fullest, then they were not doing their duties.

And so, Igor had experienced more than the usual amount of pain during his Week Twos. Just the thought of those horrible days is enough to make his toes curl and his mouth dry. If nothing else, it is a powerful incentive to stay off the people meat. He never wants to feel like that, ever again.

He watches as the medics take Jud away. There are four of them carrying him while he struggles and wriggles on a stretcher, straining against the black straps that hold him down.

Igor sits down on the floor, back against the wall. He is still in the lobby; the medics had come to meet them there. The bright lights are giving him a headache, and his arm hurts badly where it was bitten.

It takes him a minute to stand up. He's not sure when he's ever been so physically exhausted. Still, there's no time to waste. Not only is his arm likely to get infected if it doesn't get it cleaned, but he has been gone from his research long enough. Time to get back to work.

CHAPTER TWENTY-TWO

Xander's mustache has grown from an ordinary seventies-dad 'stache to a full-on Grover Cleveland. As far as Igor can tell, this has been his only accomplishment since his arrival. He talks about his research continually but never makes any progress, for reasons that are, according to him, not his fault.

Igor is extraordinarily glad to be back in his lab, beyond grateful that his research was not left in the hands of his carnival-faced suitemate. He shudders to think what might have gone wrong if Xander had taken the reigns for any real length of time.

Igor has been checking up on Jud every day, just to make sure he's alright. And every time, he is very much alright. In fact, to Igor's eyes, it looks like Jud is enjoying a nice long siesta, propped up on pillows, unconscious in bed, classical music tinkling in on a discreetly placed speaker.

He is glad his friend is being treated well, but he is also jealous. What were those sadistic fucks at Alliance Clinic thinking, keeping their patients awake through the withdrawals? This, this extended nap that Jud was experiencing—that could have been Igor's experience too. That could have been everybody's experience.

He has a mind to get revenge on those fuckers after all this is over, and he's found the cure. He will use his cure money to buy the clinic and turn it into a Satanic Temple. He imagines a particularly zealous nurse clutching her pearls and sobbing as a naked man holding a pitchfork chases her out of the building. It will be glorious.

Igor looks up, sensing that someone is in his lab. He is right. It's Xander.

"Igor, your friend just woke up. The frenzies are over. You wanna come up and see him?"

Igor drops his notepad and rushes toward the door.

Jud is looking like his old self again. A bit groggy, a bit pale, but lucid, cleaner, and free of blue paint.

They are sitting together in the communal living room area in Jud's new suite. After release from the Week Two Room, patients are discharged to their regular living quarters, where they receive ongoing therapy and medical care. In a few weeks, Jud will be expected to assume a job and contribute, but for now, his only focus is on getting well.

The layout of the suite is identical to Igor's, but the decor is much different. Jud's suitemate has turned the place into quite the man-cave, complete with a framed sports jersey, a foosball table, a mini beer cooler, and a gigantic bong on the coffee table—the bro version of a floral centerpiece. There is also a heavy, hardbound copy of Karl Marx's *Das Kapital.*

Igor is curious about this suitemate. He hopes to meet him sometime.

"So, what happened?"

Igor leans forward onto his knees, not looking directly at Jud, who is sitting next to him on the couch. He doesn't want to appear judgey, or like he's interrogating his friend. He's just here to listen.

Jud sighs and sits back on the couch. "I don't know man. Karl came by my place. At first I was all pissed off at him, for all the Moonlight Run shit, but, I don't know, we got to talking. And he had some fingers with him. Like, I don't know whose, or where he got them, but he took one out and started eating it, and before I knew it... Jesus I'm weak."

Igor looks at Jud now. His eyes are closed and he's pressing on his forehead, like he's dealing with a massive headache. Every ounce of annoyance Igor has been feeling toward him melts away in this moment. Because the fact of the matter is, Jud isn't evil. He's not a dick. He's just sick.

Igor pats him on the shoulder, rubbing it a little. "Hey, man. It's ok. Hell, I might have relapsed too, with the meat right in front of me like that. Could happen to anyone."

"Yeah, but it didn't happen to you, did it? That's why I asked you to go down to Moonlight Run and deal with those guys. I knew that—" Jud shakes his head and doesn't finish the sentence.

"But why did Karl come looking for you anyway? It wasn't just to get you feasting again, was it?"

Jud shakes his head. "Of course not. You know good and well what he wanted. He wanted my help finding you. He said I only knew half the story, that you were up to some dangerous shit, that you were a threat to cannibals everywhere. Stuff like that."

Igor's stomach wobbles. "What did you tell him?"

Jud smiles a little. "Don't look so freaked out. You know I didn't rat you out. I gave him the runaround, said I wasn't sure where you might be. Which, technically speaking, was true."

Igor exhales. "Good. Good."

"The thing is, Igor... I don't think he's gonna stop looking for you. I think you've really got him in a panic, and he's not gonna just forget about it and go home."

"I know." Igor glares at the table in front of him. He is stressed out, and wants to light up the bong, but knows it would be bad form to steal some stranger's weed. Even though it would be really awesome right about now.

"So? What's the plan?"

Igor quits his bong-glaring and looks at Jud. "To come up with a cure, as fast as possible."

"How can I help?"

Igor grins at his friend. "I was afraid you'd never ask."

Igor shakes his head, smiling a little to himself as he carefully fertilizes his plants by hand. He remembers when he thought botany was the science of hobbyists and Victorian ladies, not worthy of his time. Now look at him! He is eternally grateful that he took up this particular "hobby" when he got out of rehab.

He has a theory that he can create a more potent serum by using the seeds of the deadly blackhorn, rather than the leaves, and so he is forcing a pollination, using tweezers, blacklights, and a lot of patience. He does not want to wait for them to pollinate naturally. Time is of the essence.

The telephone rings. He ignores it, at first, but then remembers that Jud is out getting some cheek swabs for Igor today and might have run into trouble. God, what a headache that would be.

He sets down his tools and answers it.

"Hello?"

"Igor?"

It's Helen. Her voice is soft and clear in this fuzzy dark cave.

The sound makes his insides leap with joy and then immediately clench in distress.

Igor's chin trembles. He had given her this number in an email, telling her to delete the email immediately and commit the number to memory. Of course, that was before she'd told him she never wanted to hear from him again. Why is she calling him now?

"Igor?"

He realizes he has not spoken yet, but can't force himself to say anything. He is speechless.

He thinks of tiny little Elli, with her messy hair and her tiny arms wrapped around his neck. Does Elli miss him? Does she know that Helen dumped him? Does Helen ever talk about him? Do they even think about him at all?

His eyes are watering. He is breathing heavily. He realizes he is about to lose it.

He hangs up the phone.

He presses his fingertips between his eyebrows and takes several deep, calming breaths. That was a close call.

Jud is in the doorway, jeans hanging off his skinny frame, hands in his pockets.

"You ok, man?"

Jud shrugs. "Yeah. Fine. I thought you went into town."

"Haven't left yet. Had a quick session with Dr. Bennett. I was just stopping by to see if there's anything else I can get you while I'm out."

Igor mentally goes over his inventory, thinking of things he might need, but it's hard to focus on anything other than Helen and Elli and the mysterious telephone call.

"Actually, there is. Would you mind going to this address and checking up on the people living there?" Igor tears a page from his notebook and writes Helen's address on it. "I'm probably being paranoid, but..."

Jud frowns at the paper. "Who is this?"

Igor shrugs. "Her name is Helen, and there's a little girl there, too, named Elli. I got a phone call from Helen today, and I just... I just want to make sure she's ok, that's all."

"Did she say something was wrong?"

Igor sighs in frustration. "Can you please just check?"

Jud raises his eyebrows, but nods. "Alright. Anything else?"

Igor smiles, lightening the mood. "Yeah. Don't tie yourself to any trees while you're out there."

Jud rolls his eyes and turns toward the door. "Fuck you."

"Not without that pretty blue lipstick."

CHAPTER TWENTY-THREE

Penicillin is created from a mold that releases a compound that inhibits the growth of bacteria. The story goes, that Alexander Fleming made this discovery by accident when an open window and an unsealed Petri dish caused a bacteria sample to become contaminated with the magical mold, forming a bacteria-free zone and heralding a new era in medicine.

Igor cannot help but smile at the similarities in their discovery, with the deadly blackhorn. Does the fortuitousness of the event have some deeper meaning, some magical factor that might help ensure success? He is not one to believe in magic, or portents, but he can't help but hope that it's so.

The pollinated plants are progressing beautifully. In a short period of time, he will have several batches of fresh, potent seeds, from which he will make his first serum.

He peers into the rat cage, frowning a little. He wishes there were some other way to test his research, but unfortunately, there isn't. In the meantime, the least he can do is treat the rats well.

He grabs a piece of string cheese from his mini-fridge and breaks it into small pieces, dropping them into the cage, one by one. He refuses to watch them eat their snacks, can't bear to witness their dainty little paws and wiggling noses. Once, he noticed a particularly fussy rat sniffing at a suspicious snack for an inordinately long time. Igor had put his face up to the cage and tickled the glass with a gentle finger.

"Hey there, Sniffles, it's ok. Eat up!"

He'd clasped his hand to his mouth in horror. He'd broken his number one rule for medical lab work. DO NOT NAME THE RATS.

Now he feeds them treats, but he tries not to look at them.

His phone rings. He answers it.

"They're gone."

Igor has not said hello yet, and it takes him a second to orient himself to the voice on the other line.

"Jud? What do you mean they're gone?"

"Whoever it is you wanted me to check on at that address. They're gone."

Igor's muscles clench, and his breathing accelerates. There is a snap, and he looks down and notices that he has snapped a ruler in half. He hadn't even realized he was holding one. His palm is bleeding a little where the metal dug into his palm.

He needs to get a grip.

"You mean, like, they stepped out to go to the store? Or for ice cream?"

Igor knows that they did not step out to go to the store, or for ice cream. Or else Jud would not be calling now, talking in that strained voice.

"No, man. The place is trashed. There's broken glass in the kitchen, like someone was throwing it around. And the oven is still on. Looks like they were cooking a pizza."

"Oh shit, Jud. What the fuck?"

"Yeah, I don't know man. It doesn't look good. I turned the oven off, by the way. The pizza is just a lump of coal at this point."

Igor does not give a shit about the pizza. He does not give a shit about ovens, or glass, or Jud, or his research. His girls have been snatched, and he's pretty fucking sure he knows by whom.

He hangs up the phone. He does not hesitate. He does not speak to anyone. If Ms. Campbell has a problem with him leaving, she can fuck off and die. He will snap her like a tiny-ass twig if she dares get in his way.

The last thing Igor does before leaving is leave a note for Xander, explaining where he is with his research and experiments, quickly outlining the next steps. It's not as thorough as he'd like it to be, but he supposes it will have to do. There is no time to waste.

Enough is enough. Igor has vengeance to wreak.

Fortunately, Igor is still in possession of most of the money from Esteban Zappa's coins. The money serves him well on his journey to Karl's new compound, smoothing ruffled feathers and nudging information from reluctant sources. His rather intimidating presence didn't hurt, either.

When he discovers the location of The Shadow Lake Kin's compound, he is unbelievably pissed. The location is Shadow Lake, in Idaho. It is located in Shadow Lake. Those fucking arrogant rich assholes aren't even trying to hide. They are basically shouting FUCK YOU to Igor and everyone like him. This only fuels Igor's hate.

The journey to Idaho is quick and uneventful. Igor keeps to himself, glares straight ahead without blinking, like a movie psychopath. Nobody speaks to him, and then he arrives.

The compound is secluded indeed. There is a quaint, unpaved road snaking through the hills, which leads to a dark, looming edifice that reminds Igor of giants and medieval castles. It is made of some kind of stone and spreads all across the top of the highest hill. It is intimidating, and he swallows as he beholds it in all its sinister glory.

Of course, Igor has not come unprepared. The work that he and Esteban Zappa and Jesse had done, creating a virus that could take out every goddamn cannibal in the place, had not been for naught. In addition to his work on the cure, he'd also secretly continued his work on the plague.

Of course, he does not want to use it, because in order to do so he will kill himself in the process. But it is an option, and he is glad he has it, for protection.

The walk to the hilltop is long and slow. Angry as he is, desperate as he is to save his girls, each step is interminable. The road is never ending. He will be walking on this goddamn path as long as he lives, and he will die on this hill.

But as he gets closer, his panic and fury fuse into an icy calm. It is not the icy calm of a scientist working in his lab. It is not the icy calm of an athlete before a big match. No. It is the icy calm of young Igor, right before he crushed his father into the floor.

He has arrived.

The building is enormous and gray, with glowing blue windows that peer out like evil eyes. Igor cannot imagine that they open or let in any light, but he doesn't know what purpose they might serve otherwise. The door is some sort of high-tech marvel, shiny, and lacking in anything resembling a doorknob or a doorbell. He was surprised that there was no gate to protect the property; but now he understands. There is no way to get inside this giant stone monstrosity unless you are invited in. There is no need for additional security measures.

This presents Igor with a problem. A fence, he could manage. Fences can be hopped or knocked down. Security guards would have been alright, too. Security guards can be bribed, tricked, or beaten. But this fucking slab of stone and metal is another thing entirely. You can't outsmart a rock.

He looks up at the windows again. Can he climb something and get in through one? Can he break one open? The lights are bright, and it takes him some time to realized that they aren't windows at all. Rather, they are some sort of cameras, watching his every move.

That suits Igor just fine.

He gets into his backpack and takes out a piece of paper. He writes. When he is finished, he uses some duct tape to affix it to the compound door, feeling a bit like Martin Luther laying down the gauntlet on the church stairs, making his demands. He is every bit as righteous, if not more so.

Having done his part, he backs away from the door. He looks directly up at the camera/security lights and waves. He points to the door. He mimes "call me." And then he walks away.

Igor is sleeping under a tree, his back propped against the heavy bark, arms folded in his lap. His backpack sits next to him, awaiting his awakening. He is startled when said backpack is kicked into his thigh with a harsh violence that seems out of proportion to any imagined offense he might be giving.

His eyes fly open, and he stares into the face of a grim man wearing camo-fatigues. The man is holding a gun, a Knight's SR-25. Igor is not himself a gun enthusiast, but his father had been, and he knows his way around a gun shop. The gun in question is a semi-automatic hunting rifle, designed to shoot accurately over long distances. It is not a close-combat weapon, and from the way the man carries it, awkwardly, out in front, with both hands, he gathers that it is mostly for show. Still, it will hurt him if used, so Igor proceeds with caution.

"Hey. Are you from the compound?"

"Get up," says the man. His face has no expression, his dark eyes unmoving.

"What's your name?" Igor asks, standing, hauling his backpack up with him.

"I'm supposed to bring you to the big house, to talk to the boss. Come along with me."

Of course, this is exactly what Igor wants, and so he follows the guard with no arguments.

"The boss. His name is Karl, right?"

The guard says nothing, continuing to walk.

"I'm here looking for two specific people. A woman and a little girl. They would have been brought here—"

"Shut up." The guard says it calmly, in an almost bored tone.

"I'm just trying to—"

"I said shut up!" The guard has whirled around and is glaring at Igor now, furious.

Igor sighs. It was worth a shot.

They approach the formidable stone building, and the guard runs his hand over the smooth metal door. He finds the spot he's looking for and holds his hand to it for a moment. A glowing red handprint lights up against the silver, shocking in its intensity.

So that's how they get in. It's some kind of handprint sensor.

The door retracts into the wall, lifting up into it like a garage door. Following the guard, he steps inside the lair.

He would like to take his time and absorb everything he's seeing, but his guard is walking double time, and Igor doesn't want to be left behind. Still, he takes in as much as he can.

The first room has an ultra-modern cave vibe. Lots of gray stone, with a glowing neon fountain in the center of the floor. Guards are posted around the room, and they nod to Igor's escort.

Through the cave, they enter an open space the size of a fancy ballroom. The ceiling is all window, and light pours in over exotic plants and plush furniture. People mill around, talking and eating.

Eating. Igor smells the human meat almost instantly, and his knees go weak. He hadn't realized how hungry he was until that smell assaulted him. He drops to the floor, panting.

The guard watches him, curious.

Igor is going to snatch some of the meat from one of their plates. He doesn't give a fuck. He needs it. Just a few bites, and he'll be ok again.

The guard uses the butt of his rifle to smack Igor in the arm. This gets his attention but infuriates him.

"Hey!"

"Hungry, huh?" The guard smirks, and his mocking face only makes Igor madder.

"The fuck is wrong with you?" Igor stands up. He is taller than the guard, and much more muscular, but thc guard is armed. Other guards see the commotion and creep closer.

Igor holds up his hands. "Alright. Alright."

"If you're done drooling over other people's food, can we go now?"

Igor glares at the guard. He will remember this man, later.

They pass through the atrium and into a hallway. There is an elevator at the end of it, and Igor and the guard get in. "Kiss" by

Prince is playing, and Igor shakes his head at the incongruity of it.

When the reach the top floor, there is a soft ding. Of course, Karl lives in the penthouse. Of course he resides at the top of it all, passing orders down to his minions below. It's just so... typical.

The elevator door opens, and there is Karl. He smiles a tired smile.

"Igor. We have to stop meeting like this. Come on in."

Igor steps inside.

Karl looks different. He's cut his hair, for one thing, which gives his face an entirely new personality. No longer is he the magnetic Apache warrior. Now he's more like a slick Mafia baller. He's even wearing a suit.

Igor supposes this new look is because of his new friends, and he is sorry for it. It doesn't suit Karl.

The penthouse is all open-concept, airy and light, which is a remarkable feat considering the building that houses it is so dark and sinister. A chlorine-scented breeze caresses Igor. His eyes follow it out the open door, to a balcony with a swim-up bar and unnaturally clean outdoor furniture.

Nobody is here but Karl and Igor.

"Sit down." Karl gestures to a gray suede armchair.

Igor sits.

"I need to see Helen and Elli."

Karl says nothing, just sits down opposite him, in his own matching chair. A teak table separates them, and Igor wants to stomp it to pieces.

God, he's hungry.

A thought occurs to him.

What if he kills Karl? Right now? It wouldn't be too difficult. He's sickly from the Crohn's and he looks like he's put on some weight, likely because of his rich new diet and cushy living situation. He's soft. His muscles are fatty. Tender.

All of Igor's problems would be solved at once.

Karl raises an eyebrow. "You want something to eat, Igor?"

Igor shakes his head, clearing it a little. "I want Helen and Elli."

"You look pretty hungry," he smiles. "I could get you something from the fridge. Apple? Carrot? Maybe... something a little more satisfying?"

It's like the motherfucker wants Igor to eat him.

He leans forward, his voice growly. "I told you what I want, you bastard. Now tell me where they are before I mash your fucking face in."

Karl rolls his eyes. "Calm down, Igor. It was just an offer. Now, about the ladies. I'm afraid I can't let you see them. They've just joined the program, you see, and during the first month, they're forbidden contact with outsiders."

"What the hell are you talking about? What program? There's no way they came here on purpose, to join you. They're not even infected."

Karl shrugs. "What can I say? I can be very persuasive."

Igor stands up and knocks over the teak table, scattering a few pretentious, artsy magazines onto the floor. "Yeah? Well I can be pretty persuasive too, motherfucker. Now you tell me where they are or I swear to God, I'll destroy this whole place."

Karl has not moved from his spot. He stares at Igor calmly.

"Are you finished?"

Igor glares at Karl. His pulse is thundering. His muscles are poised, ready for action.

"If you can calm down and speak rationally, maybe we can work something out. If not, then I'll call security and have them deal with you. Your choice, Igor."

Igor's brain starts functioning again. His girls need him to keep it together. If Karl is willing to negotiate, he needs to be willing to hear him out.

He sits.

"Good. Thank you. Now. As I said, they are unable to see outsiders for the duration of the month. However, they aren't in some nasty solitary confinement. They have plenty of company. From insiders."

Igor watches Karl closely. What is he getting at?

"So, I'm afraid you can't see them. Unless, of course, you're willing to come to work for me. My employees are all insiders, Igor. If you sign this contract, I'll take you down to see them at once."

Karl gets up and leaves the room. He comes back with a stack of papers. "This is an offer of employment. You'll live and work here, doing scientific research. All your needs will be provided for. Helen and Elli will be safe with you. I'm sure I could even arrange for you all to live together in a family-style suite. You would have work—good, meaningful work. Everything you've ever wanted, really." Karl shrugs. "You just have to swear your loyalty to us and our cause."

"By 'cause' you mean taking over the world and enslaving the uninfected."

Karl sighs. "You always put such a negative spin on things. It's boring, Igor. Can't you try to see the positive, for once? We're talking about a world where our kind are given the freedom to control their own lives. Where we are no longer oppressed, no longer outcasts. Where we can live the natural lives we are intended to live."

Igor shakes his head. "We've been over all this before, Karl. You know I can't agree to that."

A sudden realization kicks Igor in the face. He jumps in his seat. "Helen! Elli! Did you infect them? Are they still..." He breaks off. He can't bear to think of his girls, sick, changed, wild in the Week Two Frenzies.

Karl holds up a placating hand. "Relax. They're fine. As of now, they're still uninfected. We aren't in the business of forcing people to accept the virus."

Igor exhales and sits back.

"That being said, if you don't join us and agree to give them your protection, well..."

Igor feels his eyes widen with crazy. "What?"

"Well, then, they'll be sent out to pasture."

Igor is sweating now. He runs a hand over his head. "Pasture. What the hell does that mean?"

"It's exactly what it sounds like. They'll be sent into our free-range human pasture, where they will be fattened and eventually eaten."

"You son of a bitch." Igor feels the skull of the ninja beneath his boot, smells the smoke in the air. It would be so easy to do it again.

Karl grins. "Elli is such a neat little kid, isn't she? You know, I think she'll fit in great with the group. You know we have a kid's program here, right? School, soccer, the whole deal. She could really make a life for herself with us. Or with you and us. Depends on what you decide, of course." He tilts his head and spreads his hands, like a smarmy magician.

"So that's your angle? You kidnap the two people I care the most about and try to blackmail me with them? Either I join you, or you eat Helen and Elli."

Karl nods agreeably. "Yes, exactly."

"Goddammit, you're evil." Igor is almost impressed.

"I'm not evil, Igor." Karl leans forward, serious. "I just know what I want and how to get it. You're a talented scientist, one of the smartest I know. If you're working against us, we're gonna have a hard time of it. I know that. My partners know that. And so I'm doing what I have to do to bring you around to our side."

He sits back and crosses and ankle over one black-suited knee. "You're my brother. I don't want us to fight. Besides, it's not like there's nothing in this for you. You get financial security, meaningful work, community. Do you really want to go back to living in one of those government issued trailers? Guards bugging you night and day? Inspectors coming in and bitching at you for eating fried chicken? What kind of life is that?"

"You know that notice you pinned to the door, letting me know you were here? You straight up called me out, listed your demands, made me take notice. That letter was full of such passion, such eloquence. Such clarity of thought. That's exactly the kind of thinking we need on our team. Driven, focused."

Igor sits and thinks for a long time. Karl allows him this silence.

Finally, he looks Karl in the eye. "Give me that contract."

Karl smiles, a real, genuine smile, with no mockery in it. "Of course."

Igor takes the papers and reads.

At first, it looks like an ordinary employment agreement. Work hours, salary, duties, benefits, things like that. Then it veers into creepy territory. Non-disclosure agreements. Division of human meats. Hunting and farming regulations. Laws and bylaws of the community.

It all makes him sick to his stomach.

He could do it. He could sign it right now, be taken to Helen and Elli. He could have everything Karl is promising him. He could have his brother back. But at what cost? His freedom. His dignity. His goddamn soul. He cannot work toward the goal that Karl wants. He cannot contribute so such a fucked-up cause.

He thinks of Helen and Elli. They aren't stupid. They'll accept the virus, if for no other reason than to stay alive. Together, they'll manage without him for a while. The cure is almost ready. Or at least, he thinks it is, if this batch of serum works. And once he has developed a cure, he will rescue his girls for good, and everyone else in this godforsaken compound. He will rescue them all. Whether they like it or not.

Igor rips up the contract, maintaining eye contact with Karl the whole time.

Karl sighs. "That was a dumb move, Igor."

"No, Karl. Fucking with me was a dumb move. You think I'm this easy to manipulate? You think you can wave around some papers in front of me and I'll what? Bend over and take it like a bitch for you? Fuck you, Karl. And fuck your contract."

He stands to leave, slinging his backpack over his shoulders.

"I'm sorry to do this, Igor."

Igor looks at Karl, who is pressing buttons on his phone.

"What?"

Armed guards storm into Karl's penthouse, jackbooted and sinister. Four, five, six of them. They seize Igor as he kicks and makes things difficult for them. They drag him out the door.

"To the Week Two Pit, boys."

Igor barely hears this last comment, but it does register.

What the fuck is the Week Two Pit?

CHAPTER TWENTY-FOUR

They are outside now, moving toward a fenced-in pen that reminds Igor of a prison yard.

He stopped physically struggling against his guards, after they threatened him with their guns, but that doesn't mean he is cooperating with enthusiasm. He is walking slowly, using the time to take in his surroundings and look for clues, potential escape routes, makeshift weapon materials—anything that might help him get out of this.

"What is this? Where are you taking me?"

The guard on Igor's right is named Lenny. Igor knows this because the other guards have addressed him as such. Lenny is fat, but in a jolly way, and he doesn't seem as vicious and serious as the others. Igor is glad when he answers him.

"This is the Week Two Pen."

"Yeah, I got that. But why are you brining me here?"

One of the other guards laughs. "You're a bit of a slowpoke, huh? This is how we deal with outsiders coming to infiltrate our home. We feed 'em to our Week Two Warriors." Dickhead guard obviously takes pleasure in relaying this information to Igor, and he delivers his lines with a jocular, nudging glee, like a drunk uncle asking you to pull his finger.

Igor swallows. So this is Karl's coup de grace. He feels stupid. Had he really thought that Karl would let him out of here alive? He tries to get a better look inside the fence, but it's hard to see through the tightly woven netting.

"Should we take his backpack?"

A scoff. "Backpack won't help him in there. Screw it."

There is a loud clunk, and the gate slides open, revealing a large, dirt-covered yard. "Week Two Warriors" are tied to posts, restrained by their necks, at evenly spaced intervals. They remind Igor of mad dogs tied to telephone poles. They pull at their restraints, growling and lunging at Igor.

Igor turns to Lenny. "Lenny, don't put me in here, alright? We can talk about this. Figure something out."

Lenny looks down, away from Igor. "Sorry, man. Laws are laws."

A shove from behind forces Igor forward, and the gate closes behind him. Can he crawl over the fence? There are sinister, serrated spikes at the top, and judging from the faint buzzing sound, they are electrified. So probably he won't be climbing out today.

He counts the cannibals. Eight of them. That's a lot of hungry cannibals. He sees one chewing on something with loud, violent snaps of his teeth. He pulls it out of his mouth for a moment to examine it, and Igor sees that it is a quarter, now riddled with holes.

The dirty, metallic taste of coins must keep these guys in a heightened state of hunger, whetting their appetite for blood. The very thought makes Igor's own mouth water.

There is a loud buzz, and a clink as the neck restraints are released from the cannibals. Is he being watched? He doesn't see any cameras, though that doesn't mean there aren't any, and the guards have already gone on their way. They're big tough men when they're dragging an innocent man to his death, but they're not tough enough to stick around and watch. Igor scoffs, internally.

The Week Two Warriors have now realized that they are free. They see Igor. They smell him. And though Igor knows that their humanity is still intact, hidden deep within their broken psyches, at the moment, all he sees is starving animals, coming right for him.

He only hesitates for a moment. What he is about to do is dangerous and stupid and will probably kill him. But he has to try.

He opens his backpack and retrieves a baggie full of a blue, crystalline, powdery substance. It is innocent looking, like a small child's bag of arts and crafts glitter. But it is not innocent; it is deadly. It is the plague.

During the testing phase, in Jesse's lab, inhalation of the powder was the most efficient way to ingest the virus. Rates of infection were nearly 100%, with first symptoms appearing at less than ten minutes, on average.

Now, Igor has to get all these cannibals to inhale his powder, while somehow managing to not inhale any himself. Easy-peasy.

He pulls his shirt up over his mouth and nose. It is not perfect protection, but it is something. He reaches his hand into the baggie, bringing it out coated in blue, like he's just fisted a smurf. He wipes his hand over the eyes and nose of the first one he can. There are more coming for him, and he dips his hand again, whirling and wiping, whirling and slapping.

A Week Two Warrior has hold of his arm and is busily gnawing his way through Igor's jacket. It hurts, but it keeps the warrior still enough that Igor can slather blue onto his nose. Another guy is coming for his stomach, and Igor reaches a hand down toward his nose. He misplaces it, and the cannibal bites down on his hand, vicious and ripping.

Igor shouts in pain. Another guy is now chewing on his ankle. Igor kicks the guy's face away, and he goes sprawling. The arm-chewer is now through the cloth and is happily ripping a chunk out of Igor's arm. Igor screams and twists in the monster's grip.

He has to get away from these fuckers. They are going to rip him apart before the virus gets a chance to take hold.

Not all of the cannibals are on him. There is only so much open space on his body, and five of the unlucky warriors are crowded around the outside perimeter, waiting their turn to feast on his flesh.

Without much of a plan, he spins and flails his meaty arms. He kicks his mighty legs. The cannibals are frenzied and strong, but they've been chained up for days. He imagines that they are kept hungry, as well, to make them crazier when "outsiders" are brought in. They would still be strong enough to overtake an average person, but Igor is not an average person. Igor is a fucking He-Man.

He manages to get free of their grasp and he breaks into a run. He retrieves more powder and tosses it in the faces of each one who comes close to him. As he runs, his shirt slips off his face, and he uses his clean hand to put it back on. God, he hopes that's good enough.

He manages to keep away from them. He runs and feints and fakes them out. He is not an especially fast runner, but he's fast enough, and his brain is functioning better than the warriors'.

Just like in the lab, it takes about ten minutes for them to start feeling the effects. They slow down. Blood seeps from their noses. They cough, and cough come more, and soon the yard is a cacophony of hacking, like some terrible Victorian consumption ward. They are no longer chasing Igor. They can't. They can't catch their breath.

Now they fall to the ground, dropping to their knees, falling on their asses. Their faces turn blue, apoplectic.

Igor isn't feeling so great himself, but he's not sure if it's due to accidental powder exposure, extreme hunger, the general shittiness of this shittastic situation, or a combination of all three. He is glad he can stop running. He is covered in blood. He can see the bone in his hand where it was bitten. He can't get a good look at his arm, because it's coated in so much blood. He needs to sit.

He sits, but that quickly turns into lying on the ground. The dust is soft and silky, light and dry, like talcum powder. He thrusts his blue hand under his buttocks, trying to keep the residue from floating through the air to him. He hurts, everything hurts so goddamn much.

He closes his eyes and thinks of Helen and Elli. They are nearby somewhere. He hopes they are safe, and that he hasn't made things worse for them.

"I tried," he whispers to the silent, still air. "I tried."

Igor gasps awake, and his chest thumps like it's fueled by a misfiring pacemaker. He hears the clanging of the gate and forces himself to keep still. His face is covered by his forearm, and he is glad for the cover. He schools his breathing, making it soft and still as he can. He thinks of solid unmoving things, like stones and mountains. Fortunately, he is too exhausted and pain-ridden to move much.

"What the fuck happened?"

"How did he take out every one of these guys?"

"Shit, the boss is gonna be pissed."

He hears boots scraping the dusty ground, crunching steps and pounding feet.

"We'll have to bury them all, I guess."

"Yep. Gonna take all goddamn day to get the graves dug."

"Shit."

Someone grabs Igor's feet, and he forces himself to keep still, to play dead. It's the only way he's getting out of here alive. He cannot open his eyes, even for a second, though it would be a great relief to see who is dragging him, and to where.

He hears a thick sliding next to him, and presumes it is one of the Week Two Warriors, also being dragged out by a soldier. He wonders which one it is. The one who took a chunk out of his arm?

There is a moment of panic as he thinks of his arm wound. Is it still bleeding? Will the flow of blood give him away, let them know he's still alive? He can't look. He can't adjust his position to hide the injury. He is totally helpless.

He could jump up, force his blue powdered hand over the soldier's face. But he has no idea how many other soldiers are there, and he doesn't have his baggie anymore, either. It would be too risky. He just has to continue playing possum and hope for the best.

"Hey, Paul? All these guys have blue shit on their faces. Look at this guy."

"What?"

Igor's feet are free now, as the soldier leaves him to inspect the others.

"What is that? Is that how he killed them, you think?"

"I don't know, but it would make sense. There's no way he could have overpowered that many of them, physically. He's a big guy, but still."

"So it must be some kind of poison or something."

"I guess."

"Should we tell the boss?"

"I guess we'll have to."

"Shit."

"Yeah."

Igor's feet are back in the air, and he is calm and quiet as he is pulled out of the pen. The guy who is pulling him gets tired and has to stop frequently, and it this pleases Igor. He is glad to be an unhelpful corpse. He thinks about shitting himself, just to make things extra unpleasant for the dude, but decides against it. It would be most unpleasant for Igor himself.

There is little conversation among the guards, just grunting and occasional directions. Igor desperately wants to know where he's being taken. He is no longer on the dirt. The ground is now hard cement, and it is tearing his back up, covering his skin in a terribly slow road rash. He hopes he is not leaving a bloody trail behind him.

It is getting more difficult to keep his expression blank, to keep his muscles relaxed. The pain is excruciating. He cannot possibly hold out much longer.

And then it gets better. Not great, but better. The pavement is gone, and now he is on grass, which itches terribly, but at least it does not shred his skin. It is cool, and fragrant and blessedly soft.

"Here?"

"Yeah. We'll get the new guys to come out here and dig the graves. Our shift's over in fifteen."

"Alright."

His legs are dropped and land with a thud. He resists the urge to breathe deeply. He can't. Not yet.

He waits there, silent and patient, until all sounds of movement are gone, and all the footsteps have retreated. Then he waits some more, just to be sure.

However, he can't wait too long, because he can't be here when the gravediggers show up.

He opens his eyes. He is in a grassy field, where three tombstones poke out of the ground. Presumably this is the compound's cemetery, though it is sparsely populated and rather dull, considering those buried here must be filthy rich. Then again, if a rich guy is being buried here, there must not be a lot of fanfare surrounding the ceremony. Privacy, murder cult, and all that.

He stands up, and it's easier than he'd hoped. He'd imagined that his injuries would prevent him from moving smoothly, but it appears that shock and adrenaline are giving him a much-appreciated assist.

There is nowhere to hide, so he must move quickly. He strides out of the graveyard toward the compound, seeking shelter in the shadows of the towering mass of stone.

He finds it, near a shiny silver backdoor. There is a service ramp leading up to the door; presumably this is where the compound's supplies are delivered. There is an empty space underneath this ramp, and that is where Igor crawls now, tucking himself into the smallest ball he can. He is sure that he is visible to anyone caring to look, but it's the best he can do at the moment. Besides, nobody is outside right now.

He thinks of Helen and Elli, inside there somewhere. Has Karl spoken to them? Has he done anything to them? Are they safe?

His guts swirl and twist, and he fights back nausea. He has to keep calm, keep his wits about him. For this next part, he's going to need them.

It doesn't take long, which is good, because Igor's strength is flagging, and the adrenaline that was protecting him from the vicious pain in his arm and leg is receding.

The gravedigging crew comes out, all together. There are six of them, and he wonders if the guards always travel in sixes. He wishes he could spring up from under the ramp and hold the door open, but of course, that would be noticed. Neither can he fight six armed men at once. Still, this is something.

He lies on his back with his head poking out, just a tiny bit. The guards are not looking down; they're focused ahead, on the task at hand. He sees the door slide open, enticing. He winces, hating the damned teasing open door. He bites his lip as the guards stomp loudly over him and off into the distance.

So far, he has gathered no helpful information about how to get into the building. That is a shame, because it would have been much easier to sneak in quietly than to use the idiotic plan he's about to employ.

His backpack is gone, probably still in the Week Two Pen. The guards hadn't had the decency to bring it out with him, which sucks. Still, he is not completely without means.

When he was a little boy, he once tried to make his own syphilis vaccine, for reasons he cannot remember. The "vaccine" was taken sublingually, and consisted mostly of orange Kool-Aid, various bits of plant matter he collected from the backyard, and cough syrup. After administering this miracle medical marvel to himself liberally over the course of the evening, he had become terribly—and in retrospect, probably seriously—ill.

Vomiting and weak, he had been no match for his father's rage that night, absorbing the usual kicks and punches with unusual docility. It would have been a worse beating than usual, and Igor likely would have wound up hospitalized or dead, were it not for one thing.

A rape whistle.

Igor had found it outside his school one day, and had no idea what it was, only that it looked cool, and he liked the bright cheerful yellow of it. He'd brought it home with the intent to examine it further but hadn't had time.

But now, as his dad snarled obscenities into his ear, he saw it on the floor, within arm's reach.

He didn't know what it would do, or if it would do anything at all. But what if it was a weapon of some kind? What if had magic powers like the accoutrements so often carried by superheroes? It was worth a try.

He had grasped it in his hand and pulled on it.

The sound was screeching, deafeningly loud. It was possibly the most horrible thing that had ever assaulted his ears, and it wouldn't stop.

His dad had covered his ears and shouted. "TURN THAT FUCKING THING OFF!"

Igor had tried, but he was having trouble seeing straight, what with the badly executed vaccination and the recent head thumpings.

His father had grabbed it from Igor's hands and tried to turn it off himself, but he was extraordinarily drunk, and couldn't seem to get a handle on it either.

It wasn't long before the police came. They asked questions while Igor lay silently in his room.

"My kid's toy. Don't know how to turn it off. Sorry, officer."

The officers had explained that it was a rape whistle and showed him how to put the pin back in and turn it off. They'd all had a good laugh.

And though Igor had not been rescued from his father's home that night, he had been rescued from further beatings, as the presence of the police had been enough to scare him into submission. His dad had spent the remainder of the evening watching TV while Igor spend the evening dry heaving into his laundry hamper and trying to sleep.

Ever since that night, Igor has carried a rape whistle. People might laugh at the idea of a six-foot-six-inch man with He-Man muscles and a face tattoo carrying around such a gadget, but nobody laughs at Igor for long, or to his face, and the whistle has remained around his neck on a chain under his shirt.

He pulls the pin.

Again, the sound is excruciating to his ears, but it is necessary. He tolerates it with a grimace.

He cannot see the gravedigging crew; they are long gone, in the cemetery by now. They can hear the whistle, he's sure, but they'll assume it's coming from the compound, and they'll let someone else handle it. At least, that's what Igor hopes.

There is no one else outside that he can see.

He waits patiently under the ramp, hoping to fuck that they don't send out an entire squad of guards to investigate.

Finally, the door opens. He sticks the pin back into the whistle, silencing it immediately. There is only one guard. He looks around, frowning.

Igor does not hesitate. He rolls out from under the ramp and jumps to his feet. The guard's jaw drops, and he reaches for his gun. Igor is fast though, and he is upon the guard before the man can get it from its holster. He grabs the guard's reaching hand and pulls it behind his back. He uses his other arm to put the man in a headlock.

He waves his blue hand in front of the frightened man's face.

"Hey, you know your Week Two buddies who just died?"

The guard makes a strangled yelp.

"Well this... this is why. If I rub this shit on your nose or your mouth, you will die. Do you understand me?"

Actually, Igor doesn't think this is true. The amount of toxins left on his hand is slight. At worst, it will make the guard feel sick for a day or two. But the guard doesn't need to know that.

"So. Here's the deal. You're going to take me into this building. You will not notify anyone that I am here. You won't call for security. You will, quietly and discreetly, take me to the place where Helen and Elli are being held. Do you understand?"

The man's voice comes out in a strained whisper. "Who? Who?"

Oh, right. "I apologize. Helen is a woman in her late twenties, and Elli is a little girl who was brought in with her. Helen is Indian and adorable and wears bad shoes. Elli is eight and has messy curly hair and an infectious smile. They were brought here against their will. You know who I mean now?"

"Yes."

"Great. Let's go."

It is easier than he could have ever wished after that. The guard has no desire to die today, and he is obviously not all that committed to his job. He leads Igor into the compound, into a handprint-accessed elevator, and down deep into the earth.

Igor is displeased with how much of his time is spent underground now. He is not a fucking mole or an earthworm. When this is all over, and he's patented the cure for the virus, he is moving into the tallest skyscraper he can afford.

They arrive at a rather cozy-looking wooden door, not unlike the door to a Hobbit hole. It is incongruous with the aesthetic of the rest of the place. It doesn't look high-tech enough to present him a challenge getting in. Besides, he is sure his girls will open the door for him. Pretty sure, anyway.

He remembers Helen saying she never wanted to see him again. Elli probably hates him now too. Feminist solidarity and all that. Still. They can't hate him more than being kidnapped, and held against their will, can they?

He turns to the guard. "Thank you. You can go now."

The guard doesn't need telling twice, and he scurries away, quickly.

Igor takes a deep breath and turns to the door.

He knocks.

CHAPTER TWENTY-FIVE

At first, there is no sound, and Igor panics. Are they ok in there? Are they pretending to be gone, so he will go away?

Maybe they're restrained, tied up, or drugged.

He jerks on the door handle, inadvertently breaking it off. Shit. He's too amped up. If he doesn't get a hold of himself, he will frighten them.

"Helen? Elli? Are you in there? Are you ok?"

There is a click from inside the door, and it opens.

Of course, it's Karl. Gaping at Igor like a slack-jawed idiot, though Igor know's he's anything but. He is amused to see Karl's discomfiture, and glad that it provides him the opportunity to reach out and grab Karl by the throat.

He uses both hands, squeezing with all his might. He is not fucking around. He is not bluffing. He wants Karl dead, and he wants him dead now.

He steps forward, intending to pin the fucker to the wall and watch him die. This will be nothing like the ninja in the dark. This will be a righteous execution, carried out in the light of day, eye to eye.

Karl's face is turning a satisfying mottled color. It is beautiful to Igor. The blood is filling his cheeks and Igor can smell it, the intoxicating saltiness of it. His mouth waters. Should he? Surely it won't hurt anything, just this once. Just a taste...

"Igor!"

He keeps his grip on Karl, who is beating ineffectually at Igor's arms. Igor notices with satisfaction that his nemesis has shit himself, and a puddle of loose stool is trickling onto the floor.

"Igor!"

He looks away for a moment and gasps.

Helen and Elli are standing in the doorway, Helen's hands over Elli's eyes, shielding her from the violent display.

"Shit," Igor mumbles.

He releases Karl, who crumples to the ground, smelly and soiled, gasping in loud, slurpy gulps of air.

He strides to where his girls are standing, only now noticing that their torture cell is not exactly squalid. The doorway in which they stand leads to a thickly carpeted hallway, with trite but pleasant artworks displayed on the walls. Helen and Elli both look clean and well-fed, though both of them have red eyes and tear-streaked faces.

Helen has given Elli her sight back, and when Elli sees him, she rushes to Igor and throws her arms around his legs. "Igor! You're alive!"

"Of course I'm alive. Takes more than a few cannibals to kill me." He says it with a bravado he does not feel. It would not have taken much more to kill him. Not much at all. But he senses that this is something she might like to hear.

He reaches an arm out for Helen, inviting her into the hug. She gives a hysterical bleating chuckle and accepts the invitation. He pulls them to him, smelling their clean, fresh hair, taking in the warmth and safety of them. They are alive. They are fine. Maybe not great, not yet, but they will be. He will make sure of it.

"He said you were dead," sobs Helen.

He strokes her back. "He was wrong."

"He said —"

"Shhh, don't worry what he said. It's gonna be fine now. I'm getting you out of here."

Karl is on his feet now, and he clears his throat in a way that Igor finds especially obnoxious. Does the idiot think he's some kind of haughty headmaster, reigning in some rowdy students? Stupid pig-fucker.

Igor looks down at Helen and Elli and puts a hand on each of their shoulders. "I need to finish discussing some things with Karl. Is there a room you can go to, to give us some privacy?"

"We can go to the bedroom," says Elli, helpfully.

Helen leans toward him. "What are you doing, Igor? He has security all over this place. They're probably on their way to get you, as we speak."

He tips his chin toward the hall. "Just go on back there, and I'll come get you in a few."

"Igor—"

"Go."

He can feel her anger and her frustration, and he is sorry for that, but not sorry enough to alter his plan. They'll thank him later, when they're out of here, safe and free from this goddamned cult.

After they're gone, he turns to Karl, who is waiting patiently for him.

"You tried to kill me," says Igor. His fists are clenched at his sides. He stands tall.

"I did." Karl does not apologize.

"You tried to hurt the people I care about most in the world. With Jud, you even succeeded for a while."

"Yep." His face is like a blank canvas, waiting for Igor to paint an expression on it.

"You're an evil motherfucker, Karl, and the world is about to be a much better place." He strides to Karl, fast.

"Wait," Karl says. He moves out of the way, dodging Igor neatly. Unfortunately, Igor forgot that there is a puddle of wet diarrhea on the white tiled floor, and he slips in it, falling to the ground, coating his ass in a thin layer of feces.

"You disgusting shitbag!" Igor hollers, too grossed out to do anything else.

"It's the Crohn's!" Karl shouts back.

"Oh, you dirty piece of shit." Igor gets to his feet, angrier than ever.

Karl is on his phone now. "Yes. Down in the Welcome Center, apartment number three."

"Oh, so that's how it's gonna be? You afraid to take me on your own? Gotta call for backup?" Igor sneers and stalks him around the room. It's a spacious place, with ample furniture, which keeps things interesting. "You're a fucking coward, just like when you were a little kid."

"I'm not an idiot Igor. You've probably got a hundred pounds on me. But that doesn't mean you're gonna be the winner here today. It's about time you learned that might doesn't equal right."

"It does today, you ignorant fascist lunatic."

Igor knows that security is coming for him. He knows that Helen and Elli in the other room will very likely be traumatized by seeing Karl's dead body. He knows these things, but they don't matter to him. All that matters right now, is ridding the world of this horrible person, this pile of pestilence that is Karl.

He runs into the kitchen before Karl suspects what he is planning. He grabs a knife from the knife stand. It's a large one, a sharp butcher's knife, which seems appropriate.

It is over quickly, much more quickly than he would have thought. He supposes he has built Karl up in his mind so much, pumped him up into this super-villain with super-powers, that he imagined it would be a match of equals, pitting their respective strengths against one another.

He had forgotten that, at the end of the day, Karl is an average-sized, rather sickly man, who shits himself all the time and doesn't know how to fight.

Or should he say, Karl *was* an average-sized, rather sickly man, who shat himself and didn't know how to fight?

Karl's throat spurts an arcing geyser of blood that spreads over the kitchen floor like a terrible Jackson Pollack painting. It bleats, shortens, and finally trickles. However, Igor is not watching Karl's final moments. He is busy making a hasty plan.

He is opening cupboards, the refrigerator, the drawers, frantically looking for something, anything that might work. He can't help but notice that the appliances are all top-of-the-line, and the cupboards tastefully appointed. Fucking rich cult members and their fancy shit. Can't be eating people out of substandard kitchens, can they?

He almost sobs with relief when he sees it. It is perfect. It is exactly what he needs, and he almost can't believe his luck.

A box of blue raspberry Jell-o. He rips off the cardboard and takes the plastic baggie and puts it in his pants pocket. He cannot believe his luck.

He can't stop to celebrate though. Security will arrive in a matter of seconds. He needs to get Helen and Elli, now.

He frowns. Karl's body is looking super murdered, all covered in blood, with nasty smears of brown and red on the ground around him. He thinks of little Elli, and how this is going to frighten her. It might be the kind of thing she won't recover from; it might fuck her up for life.

He runs a hand over his head, exasperated with himself. He locates an afghan draped over a gray velvety couch and lays it across the dead body. It is not a perfect solution, but it's the best he can do, under the circumstances.

He turns to get them from their bedroom but is interrupted by the door flinging open.

Six guards storm in, all of them with serious, pissed-off faces and guns. They train their weapons on Igor.

"Get on the ground!"

Igor does not get on the ground. Instead, he reaches into his pocket.

"Gentleman. Do you know what this is?"

"I said GET DOWN!"

Igor continues. "I'm sure you've heard how your weaponized Week Two guys died today. I'm sure you already know that they had a mysterious blue substance on their faces."

The guards are looking at each other now, uncertain.

Igor holds the baggie up high. He rips open the top. "If I blow this into your faces, you'll die the same way your friends did. If you shoot me, this shit'll spill all over the place, and you'll breathe it in, and you'll die horribly. I am not fucking around."

"He's full of shit," says one guard. "If it was that deadly, he wouldn't open it up like that."

Igor shrugs. "A tiny bit in the air won't kill you. But a whole baggie of it, well. That's another story." He tips the bag on its side, nearly spilling the contents. "If you shoot me, touch me, or come any closer, I will end us all, I swear to God. I will make it my last desperate act to throw this shit in your faces."

"Look, just put that down, alright? Let's talk about this."

"I'm not gonna put it down. But I will talk. Here's the deal. You're gonna let me out of here, with two guests. You're not gonna interfere with us in any way. You let us out, and you'll never see us again."

"Where's Karl?"

Igor grins. "He's dead. So if you're worried about getting in trouble with him, you can relax."

"What the fuck do you mean, he's dead?"

The guards are obviously a little bit slow. Igor wonders how the guards are chosen, and where all the rich people are while these men take all the heat and danger and risk.

"I mean, I killed him. The body is in the kitchen." He wishes he'd thought to put some blue Jello powder on his face. It would have been a nice touch. He frowns. "After I'm gone, you can go see for yourselves. Bury him out back in that creepy-ass cemetery you got."

The guards are all looking at each other, some are waggling their eyebrows, and moving their eyes in very unsubtle signals.

"You got five minutes to get the hell out of here, with your goddamn blue shit. And if you're not out in that time, we will blast you to bits. You got it?"

Igor rolls his eyes and nods. *You've really asserted your dominance there, dude. Way to go, alpha male.*

Still, he doesn't hesitate. He walks down the hallway toward the end. "Helen! Elli! Come on out now. We gotta go."

They respond to the urgency in his voice and come out immediately. Seeing them is like a blast of oxygen to an altitude-sickened man. They are ok. Scared looking, but ok.

They follow him into the front of the apartment.

The guards are now out in the hallway, glaring at Igor and his companions.

"Ignore them, we need to hurry," he says.

They don't need telling twice, and together, they run. They run out of the building, through the back entrance. They run through the manicured lawns and into the grassy hills. They run and they run, and Igor's heart is pounding so hard he thinks he might vomit, and still they run.

"Wait!"

Igor does not wait. They aren't moving fast enough. He slows, reaches down, and scoops Elli up in his right arm, Helen in his left.

"Ooof!"

"Weee!"

His injured arm screams at him, but he ignores it. He continues to run. He will run as long as necessary, until he gets them to safety. Are the guards coming after them now? Have they alerted the others? Did he scare them badly enough that they'll leave him and his girls alone? He hopes so, but he can't be sure.

"Igor, wait. I'm serious. Stop."

Helen's voice reaches him, and he registers what she's saying. She wants him to stop.

He stops, but keeps his eyes moving, frantically scanning for signs of trouble.

"The pasture."

"What?"

"The pasture, Igor. They've got humans in there, like cattle or something. We've gotta help them."

Igor shakes his head. There is no time for that. He will have the cure soon, and then this whole place will be shut down.

"Later," he grunts. His arm is throbbing. So is his leg.

"There won't be a later, Igor. They eat fresh meat every day. That's what I'm telling you."

"Shit."

Igor cannot believe what he is about to do. He presses his lips together and frowns down at Helen. She looks up at him with big, pleading eyes.

"Goddammit." He rolls his eyes. Helen exhales.

"Do you know where this place is?"

She nods. "I can take you there. They showed it to us on day one, when they gave us their little 'tour.'"

"What about Elli?"

"There's a place she can hide."

Igor nods. He is glad that Helen was smart enough to make note of hiding places.

Elli has been watching them quietly, but now she speaks. "You're going to help the people in the cage?"

"Yes," both adults reply.

Elli grins at them. "That's good. That's really good."

No one is coming for them. The grounds are eerily silent, and it makes Igor almost as nervous as it would if there were people milling around. He is on edge as they stride through the tall grasses that cover the hill.

Elli is safely hidden in the loft of a barn, between two bales of musty, moldy hay—a remnant from the days when the barn was used for wholesome, horse-farming purposes, before Karl's little group took over. Now the barn stands empty except for some farming equipment and extremely impressive spiderwebs.

Igor doesn't like to leave her alone, but it's the only option.

They are getting closer to the pasture. It is a high-walled, barbed-wire pen, not unlike the pen where the Week Two Warriors were held. But this one is larger, and there are several "tiny houses" standing in a row along one side of the rectangular enclosure. The houses are of the basic, shipping-container variety favored by hipsters and hippies and off-grid libertarians in Oregon.

A few people sit outside their "houses" doing nothing much. One is holding her knees and rocking back and forth. Two more are sitting close together, huddled for warmth or comfort or both. They speak quietly to each other. Igor has no idea what one talks about in this situation. They are all naked. Whether this is to dehumanize them or simply to make them easier to slaughter, Igor does not know.

Though Igor and Helen say nothing, they are noticed as they come closer. The two who were talking stand up to get a closer look. They hold hands. They are a man and a woman, white and pale, with dirt smudged onto their faces and bodies. They are obviously terrified.

Igor holds up his hands in a supplicating gesture. Helen does the same.

They approach the wire fence, standing inches away from it.

"Hey! Hey!"

The naked people approach, cautious. Close-up, Igor can see that they are in their thirties.

"Hey, what are your names?" Helen is speaking softly, kindly. She is even smiling. He admires her ability to be so calm in this situation.

"Why do you want to know our names?" The woman is not feeling chatty. Igor doesn't blame her.

"Because, we're going to get you out of here, and we might

need to communicate with you. So. What are your names?"

The man and woman look at each other, barely daring to hope.

"Chad." The man points to himself. "And this is Stacy."

Igor scoffs. "Really?"

Helen elbows him. "Not the time, Igor."

Now Chad scoffs. "Igor? Really?"

"Shut up!" Stacy waves her hands in frustration. "What do you mean you're getting us out of here? How?"

"Well, we were hoping you might have some ideas," says Helen.

"If we did, we wouldn't be standing here right now," Stacy snaps.

There is a sound in the distance. Voices.

"Shit," Igor whispers.

"You guys need to hide," says Chad, helpfully.

"Yeah."

They look around. There isn't an abundance of hiding places, but there is a large oak tree on the other side of the pasture. It's not perfect, but it'll have to do.

"We'll make a distraction while you hide. Keep the focus away from you." Chad and Stacy move away from the fence and begin making out in the middle of the pen, moaning theatrically.

Helen and Igor run behind the tree and stand close together for maximum blockage.

Now Igor is holding Helen close, smelling her hair, feeling the smoothness of her skin under his fingertips. She is warm and soft and perfect. The physical danger of the situation and her close proximity and his terrible hunger are a dangerous combination.

"Helen?" He murmurs. "About that message..."

"Shh! I'm trying to listen," she whispers.

Igor shushes. She's right. There are voices, coming closer.

"And as you can see, our meats are raised humanely, in sanitary and safe conditions. All of it is sourced from local homeless shelters and prisons."

"And what sort of feed are they given?" A woman's voice now. "You see, my husband and I try very hard to avoid lectins in our diet. And you know, if the meat you eat was raised on a lectin-heavy diet, it becomes contaminated."

"You know, I don't have those nutritional facts on hand, Ma'am, but I can sure check on that for you."

"Thank you."

The voices are retreating now.

Helen is shaking.

"Those pigs," she whispers. He can tell that she is near tears, and that upsets him even more than the conversation they'd just heard.

"Assholes," he agrees. He holds her shoulders and looks down at her. "There are only two of them that I heard."

She nods with an adorably dainty sniff.

"The man was obviously some kind of tour guide. Maybe he has keys."

"Do you think?"

He shrugs. "He might."

"So, you want to what? Attack them?"

He nods.

"But what if they don't have the keys? Then we've attacked people for no reason. And they might hurt us."

"I won't let them hurt you. And even if they don't have keys, I'd say those guys deserve a punch to the head, don't you?"

She stifles a giggle, looking shocked at herself.

"Ok."

"You stay here," he says to her. He is confident that he can handle both of them by himself, and even if he wasn't, he will not risk Helen's safety.

Helen rolls her eyes. "Please."

"I mean it. Stay here."

He strides away. They are standing still, talking near the entrance to the gate, where they are pretending not to watch Chad and Stacy's increasingly graphic show, while obviously watching Chad and Stacy's increasingly graphic show. The lone naked rocker is still rocking. No one else has emerged from their tiny houses.

Sneaking up on them will be hard in this open environment. He takes a deep breath.

"AAARRRGGGHHH!" He charges.

The sight of him with his gigantic body and tattooed face shocks both the man and the woman, and they stand there motionless, gaping. The man is wearing a suit and tie, and has no weapon. He is not a guard, just a tour guide, some kind of salesperson for the compound.

Igor tackles him and pins him to the ground. The guide struggles, trying to get Igor off of him, but it's a losing proposition. He is a small man, and unprepared for fighting.

The woman is on Igor's back now, though, which complicates matters, because Igor cannot move his arm back to get a good punch, which had been his intent. He is unable to knock the man out, and unable to get off of him, because of this strange cannibal-sandwich in which he now finds himself.

Then, without warning, the woman is off his back.

"YYYAAA!"

Igor doesn't hesitate. He retracts his arm and punches the tour guide right in the temple, knocking him out cold.

He gets up off the ground and sees Helen—who obviously cannot obey orders—issuing a series of offensive kicks to the woman's abdomen. The woman, who is dressed in a long red skirt with a fancy scarf, is not fighting back with any real skill, but she is taking the kicks like a champ, refusing to topple over.

Helen screams in frustration and grabs the woman's scarf, pulling the ends of it around, yanking the woman close, choking her with her own pretty accessory.

Helen is not fucking around. She sweeps the cannibal's feet out from under her with one leg and lowers the woman to the ground, where she increases the pressure on her scarf-chokehold.

"Helen," he says.

"Goodnight, you psychotic bitch," Helen whispers.

"Helen!"

Igor grabs Helen and pulls her off the woman. The woman gasps and reaches her hands for her throat, choking in the fresh air in greedy, but probably very painful, gulps.

Igor wastes no time. He pins the woman down to the ground with his weight and uses the scarf to tie her hands. He sees with glee that her skirt has a belt on it. He unbuckles it, yanks it off, and uses it to tie her feet.

The woman is trying to scream, but it comes out quiet and raspy because of her recent throat injury. Igor has no idea how long it will take for her voice to come back, and he knows that his restraints are not going to last forever. If the woman has half a brain and an ounce of self-preservation instinct, she'll be out of there quite soon. Which means he and Helen have to move quickly.

Helen is already searching the tour guide's body, looking for keys.

And, by some miracle, she finds a set. Not a jangly, old-fashioned key ring, of course, but rather a series of key cards, not unlike the kind you get at hotels.

Together, they race to the pen's entrance, where Chad and Stacy are already huddled.

"Here's the keypad!" Chad shouts.

It is a box that looks just like the ones on hotel doors, except it's not on a door, it's on an iron-barred gate, and there are lot of naked prisoners on the other side of it. They try the keys, one after another.

The door springs open.

Stacy is already running, knocking on doors, summoning the prisoners, notifying them of their freedom.

The doors open and naked people step outside. There are a dozen of them, all different shapes and sizes. None of them look at Igor or at Helen. They barely look at Stacy. Their eyes are all on the open door.

And then they are out, running in different directions, silently fleeing as fast as they can, before their fortunes change.

Igor wants to talk to them, to help them, to make sure they get away safely, but they have other things in mind, namely, getting as far away as possible, immediately.

He looks at Helen. Wonderfully disobedient, amazingly helpful, super badass Helen. He raises his eyebrows at her. She shrugs.

They have done their duty. Now, they need to get Elli. He hopes she hasn't been too scared.

CHAPTER TWENTY-SIX

After the incident at Shadow Lake (or "The Incident" as Igor has come to think of it), Igor went through a period of mourning. The fact of the matter is, he'd killed his brother. Yes, his brother was trying to take over the world, and yes, he'd gone bad. But Karl was still his brother. They had history. There was no one else alive who had known Igor when he was a kid. That meant something.

Igor is not given to grand displays of emotion. He doesn't cry or punch holes in walls. Instead, he keeps things bottled up until eventually they disappear, disintegrating into his body like salt into water.

But this mourning is big, too big for containment. Igor is not a religious man, but he made a stop at the Island's cave-like chapel and lit a candle for Karl. He remembered attending a church service with Karl when they were small boys. A well-meaning neighbor had taken them along to Hawthorne Methodist Church and fed them donuts afterwards. Karl had eaten his donut in ten seconds flat and asked for another.

Igor knows that he had to kill Karl, that there was no way around it. He also knows that he'll feel bad about it until the day he dies. He resolves to live with it as best he can.

Helen and Elli have settled in nicely at Blackout Island. They've been given a comfortable room where they can be together and recover from their ordeal. Helen has been given a job already, doing some basic clerical work for Ms. Campbell. The two women have become friends, perhaps bonding over their unusual uninfected status. She's also been leading group fitness classes on a volunteer basis, helping the infected take control of their health with resistance training, cardio sprints, and yoga.

Elli is also adjusting well. There is technically a school in the Island, but because there are not many children living there, the format is informal, and the teacher is inclined to let the kids do mostly as they please, with occasional reading assignments, science experiments, and art projects. While this might not be great for standardized test purposes, it's ideal for a kid like Elli, who has been through a lot in her short little life, and who flourishes under the individual attention and flexibility. She is the only uninfected child there, but so far that has not presented any problems.

He is glad that they agreed to come with him to the Island. He was afraid that they would refuse, since Helen never wanted to see him again and all that. But he made a convincing case, explaining that the guards at the compound might still be looking for them, might come back for them if they returned to Helen's place.

Since arriving, he has tried to stay away from them, in order to respect Helen's wishes. He has visited Elli a few times at her school though, and the two sometimes have lunch together. He doesn't know if Helen knows about these meetings or not, but he assumes she doesn't. If she did, she would no doubt put a stop to it. He would not blame her.

He tells himself that the important thing is that they are both safe.

His work is going well and is in a very exciting phase. The serum is ready for testing. The rats are zombified and hungry.

The lab is quiet. Normally, he likes to listen to Napalm Death, Emperor or Slipknot while he works, but not today. Not on what might be a truly momentous occasion. His heart is already trotting around in his chest; he needs silence and calm and steady hands.

He selects his control-group rats and moves their cages to the other side of the room, carefully labeling them with sticky notes. Then he turns his attention to the experimental group.

He has plenty of syringes, thanks to a former junkie who kindly donated some of his supplies after arriving at the Island. He loads one up with 1.5 ml of solution, restrains the rat with his left hand, and administers an intramuscular shot to the rat's back left flank. The syringes are too big for a small animal, and Igor feels bad about that, but needs must.

He continues, administering different amounts to each of his five rats. His plan is to wait twenty-four hours before testing the rats' blood for traces of the disease, and mark which doses are most effective. He will test them again in forty-eight hours, and then again at seventy-two hours. Any rats who show clean blood test results will be given a final test—they will be put into a cage with another rat, to determine if the cannibal instinct is truly gone.

He has injected all five rats now, taking careful notes. Now there is nothing to do but observe, and wait.

At fifty hours, even the rat that was given the smallest dose of serum has negative blood panels. The rat who received the highest dose showed negative blood panels at twelve hours, but also exhibited vomiting and symptoms of respiratory distress. These side effects went away on their own after administration of fresh water, anti-nausea medication, and a few surreptitious and utterly unscientific Igor cuddles.

The troubling rat-sickness aside, he is elated at these results. The serum works. Even in small doses, it eliminates the virus from the system. Of course, it's not ready for human consumption yet. There is still more testing that needs to be done, trials and funding to be got, and lots and lots of paperwork to do.

But it works.

Infected rats, lacking human's capability for self-control, and already more disposed toward cannibalism, will immediately attack and eat each other if placed in the same cage. This will be the final test, to see if the rats are truly cured. Blood tests are one thing, behavior is another.

He has no desire to see the rats rip each other apart, and he is a bit reluctant to perform this experiment. But he knows what he has to do. There's no other way to see if they can refrain from eating each other.

He has a large fish tank that Jud got him from a garage sale. He has filled it with shredded papers and a water dish. No food. If he places food and treats and toys into the cage, it could skew the results by distracting them, or providing them with another food source.

If they are not cured, they will attack each other immediately. He is prepared with a set of tongs, to remove any cannibals at once, before things get out of hand.

Each rat has a colored string tied around its tail, so Igor knows which rat received which dose of serum.

One by one, he lowers them into the cage. He tells himself to relax, to trust the blood tests, to trust his work.

The rats are curious about their new environment. They sniff around and paw through the shredded paper. They sniff each other.

They do not attack each other. They don't even exhibit ordinary aggression. They just... hang out.

"Yes," Igor breathes, running a hand over his head, sitting down so his face is inches away from the glass. "Yes!"

He watches them closely, paranoid, worried that this peace won't last.

"You are the best fucking rats, such good little guys," he whispers to them, literally sitting on the edge of his seat. The impulse to reward them with peanut butter is strong, but he ignores it. He can't. Not yet.

He spends the next two hours watching the rats, waiting for one of them to snap. It doesn't happen.

And just like that, Igor knows that he has really, truly, discovered a cure for *Pestis Manducans.*

But of course, Igor cannot get funding for human trials. Not only is he a fugitive from the law, having gone AWOL from his Containment Center, there are a number of people who would gladly see him dead, including the entirety of Mothers Against the Cannibal Takeover, everyone affiliated with Karl's sinister ventures, and anti-cannibal zealots everywhere. Even scientists who are not facing these challenges have trouble getting funding, so Igor is feeling less than optimistic in this regard.

He no longer has any of Esteban Zappa's money, having used much of it to finance his rescue operation and having donated the remainder to Ms. Campbell to help keep Blackout Island running.

And so, Igor is left with few options for human testing. He could ask some of his fellow Islanders to volunteer but feels this would present ethical challenges. After all, these are people who are, essentially, receiving charity. He knows that many of them will feel pressure to participate in the trial, whether they want to or not.

He does not want to come across as some crusading missionary, offering food to the starving savages but only if they read this book first and pledge their souls to Jesus.

More importantly, what if it doesn't work? Or has terrible side effects?

There is one option left. If it works, he will feel more comfortable administering the cure to other people.

He fills a syringe with serum, having scaled up the dosage for a man of his size. It is an intramuscular injection, so there is no need to tie off.

He uses rubbing alcohol to sterilize a spot on his stomach. He administers the injection. It burns quite badly, and he can see why the rats squirmed so much after their shots. He sucks in air over his teeth and exhales.

After eight hours, he takes a blood sample. This is challenging for him. Injecting something into the skin is one thing, removing blood from his very own veins is another. He considers calling in Xander to ask for his assistance but shrinks from this option, knowing full well that his suitemate will strongly disapprove of Igor's DIY human-trial operation.

His blood sample shows reduced viral activity. He fist pumps in celebration.

At sixteen hours, his blood only contains trace amounts of the virus. And he feels different. Not better, exactly, since he never really felt sick. More like his old self though. His sense of smell is greatly diminished. Best of all, his appetite is reduced quite a bit. The constant gnawing in his guts has calmed.

He goes to sleep for a few hours, though it is fitful, overly excited sleep.

When he wakes, he knows that something has changed.

Something has shifted in his psyche. The urges, the constant needing is silent. He allows himself to think of human meat. Sizzling over a Bunsen burner, roasting over a bonfire, raw and dripping between his teeth.

And he feels nothing. Not a single stirring of desire.

He does a final blood test, which shows that the virus has been eradicated from his system.

There is one more test. One more thing he needs to do.

Charles. Charles lives down the hall from him and has always smelled especially good to Igor. Something about his fleshy belly and juicy, chubby cheeks. He looks as if he is dying to be bitten, as if nothing in the world would taste as good as his tender, fatty meat. As a result, Igor always avoids Charles, going so far as to look away from him when he approaches, and ignoring him when he says hello.

Igor goes to Charles' suite now and bangs on the door. Charles answers in a pair of boxers and T-shirt. He has obviously been sleeping, and the fragrance of night sweat and skin oils should be driving Igor to distraction.

But they aren't.

"Igor? Is there something wrong?"

"Shh."

Igor sniffs Charles' head. He looks him up and down, taking in all of his many chewable parts. Charles stands there, looking increasingly uncomfortable.

"Can I help you, man?"

"Shh."

Igor steps closer. He reaches out and pulls Charles into what is very obviously an unwanted hug, but Igor does not care. He has to see if he is really and truly cured.

Charles pats Igor uncomfortably on the back, his big meaty paw slapping gently on Igor's shirt.

"Did something happen, Igor? Did somebody... pass away?"

Igor searches his mind and body for any trace of hunger and feels none. Nothing at all, except... mild distaste. This guy is in serious need of a shower. Igor cannot for the life of him understand why he ever felt like eating Charles. The idea is actually really fucking gross.

He steps back, elated. The idea of eating Charles is gross.

"I don't want to eat you, Charles," he says, grinning.

Charles smiles back, with a puzzled frown. "Well, I'm glad to hear that. You know, it's hard at first, to deal with the urges, but—"

"No, you don't understand," Igor protests. "I mean, I really don't want to eat you. At all. Ever. Even if it were legal. Even if you begged me to. I just... don't want to anymore."

Charles nods. "Great, Igor. Great. If that's all, I'm gonna go back to bed, now, OK?"

Igor realizes that it is five o'clock in the morning, and he has been unpardonably rude, waking Charles like this just to ogle him in the hallway. He feels a little bad about that.

But more than anything, he is happy. Ecstatically, maniacally happy. He has cured *Pestis Manducans.* He himself, Igor Fenenko, is a non-cannibal.

All at once, the feelings he has denied himself for so long flood into his nervous system. The stress, the horror of these past months—all of that is over now. He thinks of Jud, his friend, who has been with him through all of this, who has helped him as much as he was able, who found him this place to live.

Igor is going to cure Jud.

He thinks of his neighbors back in the Containment Center, the good ones and the bad ones, the ones who grow tomatoes, and the ones who collect junk, the ones who play their music too loud, and the ones who tattle to the guards.

Igor is going to cure them too, every last one of them.

He thinks of the sleazy mayor with his hypocrisy and his hateful speeches. He thinks of Faith Gregory's son. He thinks of those Week Two guys from the video, and the ones who are in prison for visiting their kids, and the ones who think cannibals are the next evolutionary step for humankind.

Igor is going to cure each and every one of them.

He thinks of Elli. Tiny little Elli with her adorably messy hair and her scrappy nature. He can hug her now, with no fear. He can let her ride on his shoulders, while they gallop around a park. He can teach her to swim. They can share a milkshake and it won't make her sick and it won't make her a monster.

He thinks of Helen.

Before he knows where he is, he is knocking on their door. When Helen answers, cloudy-eyed, wearing a giant T-shirt that comes down to her lovely, perfect knees, he doesn't hesitate. He pulls her close to him and looks down at her.

"The serum worked," he tells her.

Her eyes widen. "Igor, that's fantastic! So wh—"

He stops her mouth with his own, kissing her with all the feeling he has kept bottled up for so long. In a flash, he understands things he never allowed himself to understand. Her nervousness at his trailer, her skittishness. All this time, he'd convinced himself that it was because she thought he was a monster, that she was afraid he would hurt her. But maybe that wasn't it at all. Maybe it was something much more ordinary, and much more charming.

Maybe she'd just liked him.

When he finally pulls back, he strokes her hair. "You never thought I was a monster," he says.

She grins up at him. "Of course not, you idiot."

And she kisses him, and it is the best kiss he has ever experienced, and probably the best he ever will.

CHAPTER TWENTY-SEVEN

The Mothers Against the Cannibal Takeover headquarters is unchanged on the outside. It is still a cozy, ordinary-looking house with a neatly trimmed yard and a few flowers here and there. There is no answer when Igor knocks, and the door is unlocked so he lets himself in.

Though the exterior is just as it was the last time he saw it, the same cannot be said of the inside, which is now empty and cold. There are no members milling about, nobody making or taking telephone calls, no activity of any kind. Some of the furniture has been removed, probably by some opportunistic unpaid interns.

Igor makes his way to Faith Gregory's office. The door is closed. He knocks.

"Yes?"

Igor is not surprised to find her here. He imagines how he would feel if his entire life's work had been destroyed with one thunderous press release. He would probably haunt his workplace for a while, too.

"Ms. Gregory? Can I come in?"

"Sure."

Faith Gregory is sitting at her desk. Her hair is flat and un-poofed. She is not wearing any makeup. There is a stack of paperwork in front of her, and a calculator. She appears to be doing the books in an old-fashioned, hand-done kind of way. This detail is oddly touching to him. He imagines that she learned to do bookkeeping back in the 1970s and never learned how to use Quickbooks or Excel. When the outbreak happened, she got to work fighting, using the only skills she had. She had done her best to protect the world from cannibalism, in the only way she knew how.

Yes, this woman tried to kill him, and no, he hasn't forgotten that. But that doesn't mean he doesn't respect her.

"Igor Fenenko." She looks up at him with a vacillating expression. One second, she looks hateful, the next, afraid, the next, amused. It is hard for Igor to keep track, so he stops trying.

"Faith Gregory. So we meet again."

He doesn't think she will try anything, not on her own. But neither is he unprepared. He has a can of bear spray with him, and his phone, of course, just in case. He does not want to hurt a woman, but neither does he want her to hurt him.

They stare at each other for a long time. Finally, Ms. Gregory breaks the silence.

"Why are you here, Mr. Fenenko?" Her face is blank now.

"We have unfinished business, Ms. Gregory."

She bleats a burst of laughter. "I suppose we do. What do you want from me? Have you come to gloat about your success? Have you come to get revenge on me for what happened with the cult?"

He shakes his head. "To be honest, I'm not sure why I came. You tried to kill me, Ms. Gregory. You had your ninjas assassinate a bunch of the infected. I guess I was wanting to know why. What was wrong with the plan we hatched together? To relocate them, get them into treatment?"

She nods at him, considering his questions. "If you have cancer, Mr. Fenenko, do you try to relocate the cancer to some other part of your body? Do you have a long conversation with your tumor and ask it nicely to stop bothering you? No, of course not. You cut that tumor out, and you dispose of it like the biohazard it is."

"Faith—I think I can call you Faith, since you tried to have me murdered — Faith, human beings aren't tumors. Those people you killed, they weren't cancer. They had hearts and souls, and they could have been saved. In fact, if you'd let them live, my cure would have saved them already. They would be back at school, back at work, getting their lives back together. But you denied them that opportunity."

She bangs her hands down on the table, so hard it must hurt her palms badly. "NO! They were kidnapping children and eating them. You said so yourself. They were dangerous, a menace. They had to be destroyed."

"And me?" Igor asks, eyebrow raised. "Did I have to be destroyed."

She sits back in her chair and exhales. "I don't know." She looks at him levelly. "I thought so at the time."

"And what do you think now?"

Her chin quivers. Her eyes water. "Now... now I thank God every day that you were spared."

Igor is so taken aback by this sudden thaw that he is speechless. He rocks on his heels. It's cold in Faith's office. He supposes she's cutting costs now that MACT has been disbanded and is receiving no funding. He crosses his arms over his chest to warm himself.

She is digging around in her purse, dabbing at her eyes. She pulls out a phone and skims through it. She holds it up, showing

Igor a picture of a smiling man, holding onto a baby.

"My son. This is the first time he's been able to hold his nephew. We would never let him, before..." she shakes her head. "You've given my son his life back. You've given all these people, all the cannibals, their lives back. You're a hero."

She clearly hates telling Igor this, and she clearly means every word of it.

Igor sits down now, in a blue padded chair, facing Faith. He sighs. "For what it's worth, I'm sorry I put you out of a job."

She chuckles. "Don't be. It's not like the eradication of the virus is a bad thing. It's what I've always wanted. It's what's best. On that, at least, we agree."

She smiles at him a little.

"Look. I don't expect you to forgive me. I tried to have you killed, and I admit that freely. If you want, I'll hand over a signed confession to the police, this afternoon. I've always been able to accept responsibility for my actions, and this is one action that deserves punishment. I get it. But I do want you to know that I am truly, genuinely sorry."

Igor thinks about that night. The night he'd been forced to stomp a man's head into the rocks. The night all those people had died. Innocent people? Evil people? Both? Neither?

Does it matter?

Faith Gregory is going to have to live with the guilt of what she has done for the rest of her life. And judging from the dark circles under her eyes, the new wrinkles, and the hunched posture as she works away in her abandoned office, he guesses that this guilt is already taking its toll.

What will be gained if Igor has her arrested? Will it bring back the dead?

But can he let her get away with it?

"I want to say one more thing," says Faith. "I want to thank you. Thank you, Igor. For saving the world."

He frowns. "I have a question for you."

"Yes?"

"After the massacre at Moonlight Run, how did you keep everything hushed up? I mean, with all those bodies, all that mayhem... how did you keep it out of the papers? How did you keep the police from getting involved?"

She shrugs. "Mothers Against the Cannibal Takeover has—had—more power than people realized. We had members in law enforcement, members in high-ranking government positions, members in pretty much any line of work you can imagine. It was all about connections, getting things handled, working toward a common good."

"Jesus." Igor rubs his face. "And when you realized I'd gotten away, why didn't you come after me?"

She bites her lip. "Well, Igor. I tried. I had no idea where you lived, or where you hung out. I had some guys look for you, but by the time they figured out where you lived, you'd skipped town."

"And you didn't send anyone to try to find me?"

She shrugs. "Honestly? It didn't seem worth the effort. I figured if you were scared enough to go into hiding, you were scared enough to leave us alone. I figured you'd learned your lesson. I knew you didn't want the police involved in any of this. So you weren't a threat."

Igor takes this in, lets it settle in his mind.

"So, what are you going to do now, Faith?"

She looks at him straight in the eyes. "Well. I guess that depends on you, doesn't it?"

Igor nods. He stands.

He looks at her solemnly. "Goodbye, Faith."

She bites her lip and stands as well. "Goodbye, Igor."

He shows himself out.

CHAPTER TWENTY-EIGHT

Igor and Helen are in the front seat of Helen's tan Honda Civic. Elli is in the back, biting her fingernails and looking out the window.

They are parked in front of a single-story ranch-style house, painted white with blue shutters. It's a nice neighborhood. Clean, family-oriented, with a park a few blocks away. He even spotted a few people having a picnic in that park, as they drove past it.

Igor loves this neighborhood.

Igor hates this neighborhood.

He wants to grab the steering wheel and force Helen to turn around, to take them back home, but of course, he doesn't. He knows that they are doing the right thing.

"Are you ready?" Helen asks brightly. She is smiling and brave, better at this than Igor.

Elli nods, pensively.

They all get out of the car.

Before they get to the house, before they even set foot on the sidewalk, a man and a woman run out. The woman is tall, with messy, crazy hair, the exact same shade as Elli's. The man is potbellied and bespectacled, with scrawny arms. He obviously doesn't lift.

But they are ecstatic, running to Elli, scooping her up in their arms. All of Elli's reticence and nervousness is gone now, and she is sobbing openly in her parents' arms as they cluster in a frantically happy group hug.

Igor and Helen stand by. Helen has tears coursing down her cheeks, moved by the spectacle. Igor frowns. He has come to think of Elli as his girl, as someone who is and will always be in his life. Now that is all thrown into uncertainty. And though he is happy that she is reunited with her parents, he is sad for himself.

He looks at the father, a man named Rick. If Elli gets kidnapped again, he does not think that Rick will be able to physically rescue her. He looks like he can barely pick up a briefcase. What does he do for a living, anyway? Oh, right. He's an accountant.

Igor rolls his eyes internally. Will he use addition to rescue his daughter? Maybe throw a calculator at someone?

Helen, sensing Igor's tension, puts an arm around his waist. He is glad for this touch. It soothes him.

Finally, the group hug ends.

The mother, whose name is Darlene, approaches Igor. "You're the one who saved her from those—from that cult."

He nods. "That's me."

She throws her arms around him in a fierce hug, the kind he supposes you get from mothers whose children you rescue.

"And you," Darlene turns to Helen, "you kept her safe all this time. You took care of her."

"It was my pleasure," beams Helen.

Darlene flings herself onto Helen now while Igor watches, smiling. It's good to see Helen acknowledged for all her hard work. She deserves this hug, and much more.

Rick shakes Igor's hand. "I really can't tell you how grateful we are to you. When we found out that Elli had run away from her aunt and uncle's we..." he shakes his head, overcome with emotion. "We were crazy, out of our minds with worry. Knowing that there are people out there like you two, well. It restores your faith in humanity, you know?"

Igor smiles at the little man.

"Well, come on in you guys, don't stand out here in the cold."

Rick, Darlene, and Elli all join hands and walk into their home together. Igor and Helen trail behind.

Helen stops Igor.

"You know this is for the best, right?"

Igor presses his lips together. "Right."

"And this doesn't mean that we'll never see her again, right?"

Igor scowls. "Right."

Helen reaches up and touches Igor's face. She pulls him toward her and plants a soft kiss on his lips.

It's enough to draw out a small smile, like sucking venom from a wound.

"Let's head on in. Gotta make sure these guys aren't psychos," Helen chuckles.

Igor's eyes widen. "Do you think—did something—"

She playfully slaps his arm. "Kidding, Igor. Kidding."

"Not funny."

Igor and Helen step inside Elli's new home. It is clean and comfortable, and Igor notes with satisfaction that it does not contain any obvious fire hazards or dangerous weapons lying around.

Best of all, Rick and Darlene seem to be decent folks. Together, they catch up on the past months, sharing their stories, filling each other in.

Three hours later, over steak and beer, the adults have made plans to meet for a "family dinner" the next Sunday. There has been some discussion of a summer trip to Lake Durian, and Rick has agreed to take strength training classes from Igor.

By the time Igor and Helen leave, hand in hand, they are not only reassured that Elli is in good hands, but they are part of a new family.

EPILOGUE

Esteban Zappa presses the throttle on his jet-ski, really allowing it to soar over the clear blue Mediterranean waters. He has optimized his jet-ski to perform at very high speeds, and that is exactly how he likes to drive it. Jesse sits behind him, holding onto his back, her hair whipping out behind them like a sail.

He flexes his fingers. He was up late the night before, playing guitar in a smoky lounge full of smoky people, and his hands are slightly stiff. It is no matter. Like most problems, it is nothing the salty sea air cannot resolve. Jesse agrees with him, and they now take jet-ski trips together daily.

After he and Jesse left the wreckage of their shared home, they traveled to Canada, where they secured a small amount of funding, and then a larger amount of funding. By the time the funding came through, and they located Igor, it was too late. Their efforts had been rendered unnecessary by Igor's intelligence, hard work, and resourcefulness.

They had never been happier to be unneeded.

They think about him now, as their limbs go numb from the buzz of the engine and the coolness of the wind ripping over their salty-wet skin. They wonder how Igor will spend the rest of his life. Perhaps he will go on to invent new cures for things. Perhaps he will become a professional bodybuilder. Perhaps he will settle down and get married, become a father. Perhaps he will do none of those things, but will go on to live a highly unconventional, unpredictable life.

Perhaps they will meet again, someday.

They certainly hope so.

CPSIA information can be obtained
at www.ICGtesting.com
Printed in the USA
BVHW091612130922
646849BV00003B/17